Con & Consequence

by

Ian Rodney Lazarus

For Inna

This novel's story and characters are fictitious. Certain long-standing institutions, public offices, and agencies are mentioned, but the characters involved are wholly imaginary.

"Everyone sees what you appear to be,
few experience what you really are."

Niccolò Machiavelli

Prologue

The laptop rested on the bottom of the bathtub in Room 209, beneath four inches of water, its power light fading from view. Outside the bathroom, a young man's body lay face down on the carpeted hotel room floor, a dark pool of blood forming around his head, slowly expanding its reach to the broken lamp that lay near him. He came to blackmail the Professor, as he had discovered the Professor's true identity after collecting an impressive cache of evidence by hacking into his email account at the university.

The student threatened to report the Professor to the authorities. He already had summoned the police to the hotel by reporting that a spy from a foreign adversary was in Room 209, so their business would have to be conducted quickly if the Professor hoped to leave the hotel without a pair of handcuffs around his wrists. He wanted money, a lot of it, and a trumped-up grade so that he could potentially graduate from the university with honors. He had thought of everything he needed to trap the Professor tonight, even though as a sophomore, he wasn't nearly as sophisticated as some of the Professor's other adversaries.

The room was dimly lit as the two sat opposite each other on simple wooden chairs, their knees practically touching. They talked about the terms of the deal, where to wire the money, and when the transcript would be updated. The Professor quickly agreed to accommodate the student's demands, failing to resist or produce any false narrative to counter the claims. After showing the laptop's content, the young man warned that a memory stick containing the same information was stored in a secret location.

As he stood up to put the laptop in his backpack, he turned away from the Professor. Seconds later, he was dead.

The Professor quietly left the hotel through the back door with the young man's phone in his pocket as eight uniformed policemen in bulletproof gear stormed through the lobby.

1

Junior Lieutenant Sergey Volkov shook the snow from his Cossack fur cap before entering the warehouse in a discreet military compound fifty kilometers outside Moscow. He welcomed the change from working security on the icy cold grounds of the Kremlin, although he understood little about the new job and recognized it was best not to ask. It was February 22, 1992, and he would be eligible for a two-week leave next month, so he was determined to keep a low profile.

To open the inside door of the weapons depot marked simply "АГЕВ 15," he pulled the badge attached to his uniform via a retractable cord and pushed it against a panel. He quickly grabbed the door and pulled it toward him, but it didn't budge. Then he remembered that this facility also required entering the soldier's ID number via keypad, a technology new to the military, as a second form of verification. He removed his right glove and tapped his identification number on a smaller panel to the immediate right of the door. The latch emitted a loud "pop" and unlocked.

Volkov was assigned to carry out the demands of the new Strategic Arms Reduction Treaty signed by President Michael Gorbachev and his counterpart in the United States, the former movie star Ronald Reagan, that sought to pare down nuclear arms and other weapons. But while START represented a historic event in the context of world affairs, most Russians, including Volkov, were still trying to process the breakup of the Soviet Union just a few months earlier. Volkov's assignment at the Kremlin followed months of being dispatched to protests across the Caucasus region, and he was relieved that for now, the tensions between Russia and the surrounding republics it had liberated would come to an end.

Volkov walked down the narrow and dark hallway to the back of the facility. Above him, exposed water pipes ran the distance of the hallway, with a naked, dim light bulb hanging between them every few meters. Condensation from the pipes dripped every so often on his head as he continued to the area where his work would begin.

In his new role, he was responsible for crating small nuclear weapons for disposal. The devices, code-named RA-115s, were about two feet long, sixteen inches tall, eight inches wide, and weighed about fifty-five pounds. Russian soldiers referred to them as bikini bombs because they were created to offer the bare minimum. These were relatively new weapons, originally designed for the Spetsnaz Special Forces to be so compact that they could be carried and detonated by one person; accordingly, no launch codes would be needed. Each device delivered a yield of one kiloton, strong enough to kill up to one hundred thousand people if detonated in a dense urban area. Now, they were to be dismantled and scrapped.

Volkov was also to catalog for purposes of verification that the necessary quantity of weapons was being properly disposed. No trace of the weapons could be left because no one wanted problems when it came time for inspections. Each crate would hold six devices loaded side by side. The crates themselves were made of cheap pine and could contain vegetables as easily as weapons of mass destruction. As the devices were to be destroyed, the Russian military could not be bothered with adhering warning labels to them. Once packed, they would be wheeled on a hydraulic forklift to the loading dock at the back of the warehouse.

Volkov made one final count of the crates that would be transported from the facility on a truck and then loaded on a train bound for the disposal facility in Gorny about 550 kilometers away. He recorded the serial numbers of each weapon on a ledger that hung from a nail on the wall. What he did not realize was that one of the crates was not going to Gorny but was addressed in care of Al Zarooni Exchange, a Dubai-based import/export broker. He noticed that officers of the Main Intelligence Directorate, or GRU, directed this crate to a separate, smaller vehicle parked nearby. Even if he had noticed the address, he had learned long ago that it was best not to ask about a break in protocol.

This crate was to leave Moscow's Kazansky Railway Station, like the others. But instead of heading to Gorny, it would travel through Kazakhstan to Turkmenistan. From there, it would be transferred to another set of rail cars designed to operate on the smaller tracks that lie ahead. Its final destination was Tehran.

It would be another five years, on September 7, 1997, when retired General Alexander Lebed, former secretary of the Russian Security Council, would tell Steve Kroft of the CBS program *60 Minutes* that he believed more than one hundred "suitcase-sized" nuclear weapons had gone missing, an announcement that immediately drew vehement rebukes and denials from the Russian government. Twenty-five years later, three of those bombs left Iran, bound for the Gaza Strip.

***

A tiny sliver of light pierced the partially drawn curtains on the twelfth floor of the Tropicana Atlantic City Hotel. As it happened, that light was shining across the face of Richard O'Brien, who did his best to ignore it. He took the most obvious line of defense and turned his face the other way, where he found a woman lying next to him, the contours of her naked body obvious under the top sheet of the bed. She lay face down, her head turned slightly to the right, facing him. Her long, dirty blond hair was distributed in equal proportions on either side of her back. Damn, she's gorgeous, he thought to himself. She was still asleep, and her breathing was soft, deep, and steady; it was clear to Richard that she would remain that way while he carefully rolled off the bed in the direction of the offending window.

As he rose, he noticed that he, too, was naked, his clothes in a pile on the floor. Her uniform and underwear were flung haphazardly not far from his. She's a flight attendant, he recalled silently, and they had met the prior afternoon on his way home from a training program in Los Angeles, where she served him in the economy cabin on the way to Newark. As only a gambler would reason, Atlantic City seemed a sensible detour on his way back to Brooklyn, and she made the trip more worthwhile by joining him for dinner and a run through the casinos. The casino had comped his room because of his gambling habit and membership in their players club, and Richard felt as comfortable there as at home.

As Richard stood naked next to the bed, he surveyed the room. A half-filled pint of whiskey on the coffee table positioned in the center of the room, two open cans of Coke, and two small bottles of rum from the hotel minifridge. Two glasses with what used to be ice. An ice bucket on the floor that had been so cold it had left a small puddle of water soaking the carpet around it, and at the edge of the table, a flat, square mirror with bits of cocaine dotting the surface.

He walked over to the door and opened it, picking up the *New York Times* that had been delivered hours before. The headline: Internet Scam Drains U.S. Accounts. Within a few seconds of picking up the paper, his phone began to vibrate. He turned back toward the room to grab it, crept into the bathroom, and gently closed the door. It was an automated notification that he had an assignment, most likely an intercepted message that needed to be deciphered, translated, and uploaded to the secure server.

Richard Anthony O'Brien was a linguist for the FBI, and occasionally on contract to the United Nations, with a specialty in Arabic and African languages. He fell upon the role accidentally, after a degree in Arabic studies that followed many years of attempted self-discovery and a summer internship in Egypt. He was fluent in Egyptian Arabic but could manage a conversation in several other Arabic dialects, which provided him an in with the New York branch of the agency on returning to the States. His job was unique and exotic enough to be a great conversation starter, particularly when you did not plan to be in a conversation for very long, as would be the case between an airline passenger and flight attendant. He reported to Elliot Pritchard, FBI director of linguistics.

Richard looked again at his phone. It was 7:30 a.m. He opened the door to the bathroom to find his date still sound asleep. As much as he wanted to slink back into bed with her, he knew it would not be wise to give the agency any reason to question his work ethic. He quietly hunted on his hands and knees for his laptop under sheets, underwear, clothes, and the hotel room service menu. He eventually found it, and after putting on his low-rise briefs, sat cross-legged on the floor at the foot of the bed, opened the laptop, and turned it on.

Most of the intercepts that Richard was assigned to translate came via Sentinel, an application developed at the National Security Agency in 2012 and now a part of the CIA's SIGINT arsenal, which includes a series of technologies to gather communications intelligence. Sentinel was created by a team that included Edward Snowden, who ironically had a change of heart and decided to leak highly classified intelligence to everyone who did not already have convenient access to it. It was designed to intercept messages over conventional channels such as those sent by email or captured in phone taps, but through repeated enhancements, its reach was expanded to include social media channels like Facebook, TikTok, and even video games where perpetrators communicate within a game itself. The system provided a warning about the January 6, 2021, attack on the U.S. Capitol, but as sometimes happens in intelligence gathering, no one noticed.

Depending on the language setting, in this case Arabic, Sentinel would detect suspicious dialogue involving discussion of subjects such as contraband, money laundering, grand larceny, or violence and flag these for evaluation. Much of Richard's job involved distilling the relevant intercepts in Arabic from those that were simple background noise and passing them up the chain of command for decision-makers to figure out if further investigation was necessary.

With over twenty million PlayStation units distributed among consumers and over two billion users of WhatsApp, Sentinel could not identify the source of messages. However, the administrator, in this case Richard, could "tag" captured messages and monitor future transmissions from the same device.

The intercepted message this time appeared to be sent from a source in Tehran to what was likely an extremist cell in the U.S. It started as a routine exchange of formalities, leading to the most chilling words Richard had ever seen during his years in this role:

Continuation of intercepted script, 1430 hrs. Origination: Tehran. Keywords:

هدم – "destroy"

هجوم – "attack"

صهيوني – "Zionist"

حماية – "security"

Fragment:

سنشرع بعد ذلك في تدمير مؤسسات المتعاونين الصهاينة.
الهجوم الأول سيكون في غضون 3 أيام في المنطقة العربية. سيكون
آخر مكان يتوقعه أي شخص. جهزوا جنودكم لتأثيره على أمن
الولايات المتحدة

From the fragment of text flagged, Richard produced the following translation:

"...we will then proceed to destroy the institutions of the Zionist collaborators. The first attack will be in three days' time, here in the middle east region. It will be the last place anyone would expect to look. Prepare your people for its effect on the security apparatus in America."

Something did not look right about the sentence structure and semantics of the message, but it was not for Richard to question its veracity. He was a relatively low-level employee and his only obligation at this point was to pass the translation back to his superior officer. He completed verification of the translation within the secure platform, uploaded it, then crawled back into bed.

He realized he had time for one more round with the flight attendant before having to head back to the city.

He didn't realize the author of the message fully intended for him to intercept it.

***

Anyone else would have worried about getting caught. Anyone else would have been too terrified to proceed. But Jelani, as everyone in his orbit knew, was unlike anyone else.

Ironically, it would take much less than the threat of being carried off and arrested to drive Jelani into fits of rage. As a child growing up in Somalia, he was considered a loner, with no friends his own age. The only person he trusted, indeed the only person he could tolerate, was Muhammed Amir Abbas, an older boy in his village who befriended and protected him from the children who taunted him for being different. Muhammed was kind and understanding of Jelani's condition without being able to give his unusual condition a name.

Jelani's world required structure, order, predictability, and routine. He could not handle surprises or loud noises. But what he could do revealed a gift that few could fully understand or appreciate: Jelani was a mathematical wizard, especially at understanding the principles of probability. Playing cards with Muhammed demonstrated just how powerful this gift could be, as he handily won every card game Muhammed could teach him. Playing cards is considered "haram," or forbidden in the Muslim faith, but that did not stop Muhammed from using games as an escape from his own painful reality, living in poverty in one of the poorest nations in the world.

At sixteen, Jelani was quite tall for his age, remarkably thin, and could easily be mistaken for being much older. He was proud of a barely visible mustache that was attempting to make its presence known above his lip. His large, alert brown eyes, dark skin, smooth complexion, and kind face could make him instantly approachable. He had no use for hair and persuaded his parents to crop it as close to his skull as possible. His teeth were crowded and never saw the benefit of a dentist, apart from one gold crown that his parents paid for after he lost his balance and fell down a flight of stairs.

The signs that Jelani was different from other young boys became more and more apparent as he reached puberty. He never demonstrated any interest in girls, and his interactions with others were so devoid of emotion that it created an awkward communication gap. Jelani was incapable of understanding the facial expressions or social cues of others, but when he spoke about a subject that interested him, information would gush from him like water from a broken fire hydrant until there was nothing left. He could as easily interrupt a conversation as abandon one that required a response, and his rigid, nervous posture conveyed a constant state of fight or flight.

Three years ago, Jelani's parents decided to move the family to Kenya, a country that by comparison to Somalia enjoyed long-term stability and relative prosperity, especially by African standards. His parents were fortunate that Kenya was so close geographically to Somalia because with nine children, transportation becomes complicated no matter where you reside. For Jelani's family, moving to Kenya took the form of long bus rides shared with farmers and their animals. They joined the predominantly Christian population and settled quietly in a village between Nairobi and the Amboseli Lodge on the border with Tanzania, running a souvenir shop and gas station on behalf of a wealthy Nairobi businessman.

The move to Kenya did indeed put Jelani on a new path, as he spent much of his time being shuffled from one doctor's appointment to another. But the meetings with physicians, the blood tests and brain scans, psychometric assessments, and seemingly infinite referrals to specialists finally yielded a name for what made Jelani different: He was autistic.

***

The Amboseli Reserve was one of the crown jewels of Kenya. It was a popular stop for American tourists bound for the landmarks such as Mount Kenya, the massive aggregation of pink flamingos at Lake Victoria, or the Great Rift Valley, which most regard as holding the secret to the origins of the human species. From Amboseli, many guests would proceed on to Treetops, the famous treehouse hotel where in 1952 a young lady named Elizabeth became queen of England the night her father, King George VI, passed away. Amboseli was also a popular side trip for adventurers planning to climb the famed Mount Kilimanjaro, just across the border.

At Amboseli, guests could mingle with baboons on the grounds of the lodge or sit on the edge of the property and observe the social behavior of antelope, zebras, elephants, and giraffes on the plains in the distance, below the small mesa on which the hotel grounds were situated. It would not be uncommon for a monkey to follow you around lobbying for handouts or sit on the armrest of your chair to intimidate you into compliance. Acacias, those majestic trees with crooked, wandering arms and a flat top, dotted the landscape for as far as you could see. If you were patient, you could see two elephants lock tusks next to a waterhole or a lion chase down a wildebeest for dinner as the sun set across the plains and projected intense red, purple, and yellow layers across the horizon. To be at Amboseli was a privilege for visitors, an escape from civilization. For Jelani, it was home.

Jelani's work as a steward for the lodge meant he had frequent contact with American guests. They seemed a very carefree people to him, at least the ones who could afford the cost of a photo safari across the plains of Kenya. Return visitors always came with suitcases full of American-style T-shirts or similar artifacts of life abroad, ready to trade for local arts and crafts. Jelani wondered why so many Americans came to Kenya and what their homes would be like.

Why should I target the Americans? he thought about the cybercrime scheme he had been running for several months now. The Americans, after all, were always quite friendly to him. He was sitting on the steps of the hotel lobby in deep thought when his concentration was broken by another steward, Daudi, approaching from one of the private guest rooms.

"*Jambo*, Jelani!" blurted Daudi as he bounced onto the lobby steps next to Jelani. "It was bitterly cold this morning, yes?"

Jelani looked at Daudi, confused. Understanding colloquial language was a constant struggle for him, as it is with many on the autism spectrum. How, for example, could the temperature have a bitter taste? What would the temperature taste like later in the day when the sun was full?

"Look, the bus is taking off," Daudi said, changing the subject and using his outstretched arm to point directly in Jelani's face, startling him.

"Yes, I see, and why is this important?" Jelani recoiled his head to create the space he needed.

Daudi shrugged. "We have our hotel back again."

Jelani wondered if he should share details of his little project with Daudi, who he considered one of his only friends in his adopted country. However, Daudi was young and not quite ready to understand the scope or motivation behind Jelani's plan. Daudi was soon off anyway, searching the hotel rooms for anything of value that the Americans may have left behind.

Why should I target the Americans? "Why not indeed?" Jelani replied out loud, forgetting for the moment that he was talking to himself.

The Americans he was targeting, after all, were not those visiting his country and sharing their wealth, but those who remained in a land so mysterious and far off that any misfortune or injury inflicted on them would pale in comparison to the difficulties of life in so poor a nation as Kenya or Somalia. This was the logic Muhammed put forth to Jelani, and he had no reason to doubt it. Muhammed was learned in the ways of the world, and Jelani trusted him completely.

Because he was considered "highly functioning" on the autism spectrum, Jelani could appear as mature and sensible as people much older than him. However, he never intended to enter the dark world of Islamic extremism. By tomorrow afternoon, there would be no turning back.

2

Myles left the graduate library about ten thirty, a full ninety minutes before closing. This made him feel only marginally guilty—it was Friday night, after all, when most of his friends were likely on their third pitcher of beer at Dooley's, the pub around the corner. He entered the chilly evening air, pitched his backpack over his shoulder, and headed back to the dormitory across campus.

In his second year at the University of Michigan, he aspired to get into law school, and if that did not work out, he might follow his brother into the FBI. He paused at the intersection of State and North University. One direction led to Dooley's and a row of bars in red-brick buildings adorned with bright neon signs and loud music leaking out from open doors. The other choice was back to the dormitory complex at the end of a winding walkway through several dark and empty campus buildings cloaked by centuries-old maple trees and evergreens.

As he headed inevitably to the dorm, his thoughts turned to his older brother. He spoke to Richard nearly every day during his first year at Michigan, where Richard had graduated several years earlier. But today was different. When they spoke by phone, Richard was so consumed by something he was working on that he could not seem to focus.

"I'm sorry, brother," he confessed, "it's not something I can talk about right now."

"Can you give me a clue?"

"I don't even know what I've got here myself," confessed Richard.

Myles drifted in thought to imagine what Richard's life might be like, as would anyone with a family member who worked for the FBI. This was made more difficult by the comparisons he could not escape: Richard was tall, with blue eyes, thick eyebrows, sculpted jaw, and generally physically fit. Myles, on the other hand, needed a haircut several weeks ago but could not be bothered by it. His wildly undisciplined hair, unshaven face, and lanky stature made him look bohemian by comparison. But alas! He got the hazel eyes from his mother, and a smile that revealed dimples could make meeting college women just a bit easier.

When he entered the dormitory, most of the other students were either at the bars, engaged in wrestling matches in the hall, or gaming on laptops in their rooms. The halls seemed to be narrower each night he returned from the library. It sucks to be working so hard that you cannot even find a girlfriend, he thought. That is, of course, if you want decent grades. He often thought of his first and only love from high school, now a freshman at UCLA. That relationship ended before it started, as Myles was as shy then as he was today, and the object of his affection never knew how he felt about her.

"Myles! Dude, don't even tell me you were studying tonight!" It was Collin from his psychology class, putting an end to his reflective mood. "Man, that test is not until Tuesday—you got until Monday night to cram."

Myles ignored this and went into his room, flung his backpack on the bed, and collapsed on it. As if psych was his only problem, he thought. He rolled back over, reached over the pillow and across the top of his desk that was wedged against his bed, creating his artificial headboard. He stretched as far as his body would allow, just barely reaching his laptop. He tapped the computer space bar to activate the desktop and the email program. Without even looking at the screen, he fell back onto the bed and rested his head on his backpack, staring at the water-stained ceiling tiles while listening to the faint sound of Pink Floyd wafting in from a room down the hall. Within a few minutes, he was asleep.

There, at the top of his mailbox, delivered just five minutes ago, was the email that would dramatically change the trajectory of his life and bring pain and suffering to his family. He did not see it for several more hours.

***

Richard woke up in his Brooklyn apartment with a hangover the size of Manhattan. He stumbled out of bed and tried to reach the efficiency kitchen at the other end of the room, nearly tripping on the coffee table that had been in the same place since he moved in, so he had little excuse for running into it. He made a cup of coffee, poured himself a bowl of cereal, and stood the box in front of him, reading the back, with just enough light from the kitchen window that he didn't need to pay for electricity. From his stool at the kitchen counter, he glanced back at the sofa against a wall with exposed red bricks and realized his apartment was not much bigger than the hotel rooms at the Tropicana in Atlantic City.

Richard's apartment in Flatbush put him within walking distance of Prospect Park, the area he aspired to be in if he could just hit a winning streak at the blackjack table. Instead, he could barely pay the rent in his below ground, one-bedroom efficiency apartment that was below a dance studio. During the day, it was impossible to concentrate with the music and dull thuds from students attempting to learn interpretive dance. By four, the apartment surrendered to the night because the sun had already set behind the buildings surrounding his tiny outpost.

It was two days since he completed the translation of a purported terrorist plot, and it weighed on his mind that there was no feedback from Director Pritchard or anyone else at the agency. *Are we going to fuck this up again?* he wondered to himself. He decided he would not wait for an update on something so important; he would push the agency for a response. But first, he had to finish his coffee and take a shower.

Once in the shower, Richard's thoughts turned to one of his favorite subjects, women, and when and with whom he would get laid next. His first instinct was to call up the flight attendant, who was based in Newark and had a place in the city. Then he remembered calling her a Karen in the casino when she became irritated because of the time it took to deliver her a complimentary margarita. It was a tease that she did not appreciate, probably because that was her *real* name and she was fed up with the label. That didn't prevent her from being great in bed later that night, but Richard could sense that their sense of humor was not in sync. Besides, he thought, while he could certainly look past a minor personality defect, she was on a short turn before heading back to LA.

He thought about the landlord he slept with as a way of getting a little forgiveness for being late on rent three months in a row. She was a divorced mother with two kids, definitely *not* his type, and he did not want to play that card again unless he was desperate. Then there was his fuckbuddy, Courtney, from the Upper East Side. He could see that Courtney was getting too close, so he did not want to increase the frequency any more than every two weeks, and he was right on the cusp of that threshold today. Courtney was the one girl with whom Richard could be himself without any pretense. On top of that, she was spontaneous, wild, and great in bed. From the moment she showed up at his apartment for a date wearing a long black coat, he was hooked because she was naked underneath it.

Courtney Adams worked as a personal trainer for a boutique gym in the city. Her clients were typically successful, middle-aged men, and it was likely that they all fantasized about what she looked like under those tight leggings. She had shoulder-length blond hair, blue eyes, and her figure was a perfect ten as far as Richard was concerned. She was always able to score the best white rock whenever they got together. The only problem with getting laid at her place was her overprotective roommate, Sandy, who was a near-constant fixture whenever he came over.

By the end of his shower, he had not resolved anything, so he tabled the subject until he could get to his phone and make some concrete plans. Before doing that, he had to call the office as he promised to do.

"O'Brien, I'm glad you called." Elliot Pritchard sounded as if he had just won the lottery. "Look, that intercept you translated has had us quite busy over here."

"Yes, sir, that's why I am checking in. Is there anything I can do to help further?"

"As a matter of fact, there is," he replied. "We are sending you to Dearborn."

"But sir," Richard objected, "I've not been trained as a field agent."

"I'm well aware of your background and capabilities, O'Brien; I conduct your performance evaluations, and I've read your file. Anyway, the Detroit office has asked for some help with encrypted messages out of Dearborn, so you are officially on loan to them."

"Dearborn, sir?"

Being from the Detroit area, Richard knew that Dearborn represented the largest single concentration of Muslim families in the United States. He had passed through Dearborn often when traveling from his home in Gross Pointe to the university in Ann Arbor.

"You'll be reporting to Agent Goodman over there. The office is investigating an email scam that they believe is originating out of East Africa, and they need help working with the local Muslim community, you know, the first-generation Arabs. There may be a connection to the intercept you translated for us, or they may be completely unrelated. Go help them figure it out."

The Dearborn connection to the case did nothing to alter Richard's suspicion about the legitimacy of the intercepted message, but perhaps he could parlay his involvement into a fact-finding mission, visit his parents, his brother, and his alma mater.

"Yes, sir. I'm on it."

In preparation for his new assignment, Richard decided to study up on the status of the email scam that was the subject of the headline he had seen a couple of days before. Within the FBI, the case was given the codename "Utapeli," which meant scam or fraud in Swahili. The codename was selected to symbolize the scheme's dependence on building trust with targets as a means of swindling them. Richard found an online audio brief available in the FBI secure portal and opened the file.

"Utapeli originated in Somalia, where the once seaborne pirates of the Indian Ocean took on more pedestrian occupations as street criminals and purveyors of mail fraud. After the 2009 incident in which the U.S. Navy shot 3 of 4 pirates holding a sea captain hostage, most pirates turned in their rifles and boats, and went ashore. The popular film 'Captain Phillips' memorialized this operation.

"Among the new crimes undertaken by the pirates is preying on gullible citizens of Western cultures, offering them riches in exchange for their bank account information. This has recently evolved into a myriad of related schemes, including promises of lottery winnings, fortunes found but not claimed, and a national program that seemingly gives away cash for free, simply for the asking. Some of the perpetrators had moved out of Somalia into neighboring countries not so much to avoid detection as to access better technology and resources with which to conduct their activities."

This is a scheme that Richard knew something about—he assisted with linguistic support as the FBI prosecuted a group in absentia a year earlier, based then in Nigeria. Of course, the U.S. prevailed in the prosecution, but it was impossible to recover any fraudulently acquired funds or capture the perpetrators. It was a victory in name only.

Richard booked his flight to Detroit for the following morning, out of Newark. He closed his laptop and walked across the room, yanking his suitcase from under the bed. He still had clothes in there from his trip to LA. He threw in his toiletry bag, a couple of white shirts, black shoes, underwear, socks, and a blue suit, the official uniform of the FBI. If he left his apartment now, he could spend the night in Atlantic City and catch a late morning flight out of Newark, perhaps rendering irrelevant the question of whether he would sleep with the flight attendant, Courtney, or someone new.

As he left his apartment, he did not notice the Ford Focus across the street with tinted windows. The driver's side was cracked open just enough to accommodate the zoom lens of a professional camera, and it was clicking away at high speed, capturing Richard as he walked toward the subway.

3

My dear friend,

I hope this message finds you well and in good health. I correspond from my war-torn country whereas general of the resistance I have been successful in capturing a good portion of the precious assets of our country before hidden from the people by a most corrupt government. I refer to the $5B in gold bullion that was previously stored in the National Bank, which now is in rebel hands. However, in that we are not yet recognized internationally as a legitimate government, I require your assistance to liquidate this gold into a monetary instrument that can feed our people.

The government accuses us of being deified by the population based on sagas we've supposedly fed them about our holy status among the people. I can assure you these are all lies.

I have found you to be a person of integrity and honesty and will level with you and reward you for your civic duty at this time. Through an intermediary in Switzerland I am able to convert this gold bullion into US dollars, for which I will provide you a transaction fee of $1.5M USD. Please be assured this transaction is perfectly legal and will result in the aforementioned funds to be deposited *into your personal accounts. Furthermore, we will act most discreetly that your assistance will not become acknowledged by those that might seek to take advantage of this situation.*

At present I must return to my forces and to the continued struggle of our country to embrace a democratic future. Please advise that you are prepared to assist us in this manner, and I will revert with further instruction.

My warmest regards,
General Abu Fayed Mohammed Okogun
National Resistance Armed Forces

In the internet café, Jelani read the draft email once more, concentrating on every word, reflecting on its meaning and legitimacy. He did not realize that his whole body was tense as he focused on the words on the screen. Meanwhile, the café was hissing with the sounds of young people whispering to each other as they engaged in gaming or whatever else had their attention on monitors in front of them—Jelani was oblivious to them. The monitors stretched across the narrow room on long, white tables, with only enough room for one person to pass behind whoever was sitting down. Outdated posters from the Nairobi Football Club's regional appearances hung precariously on the walls. A single cashier stood guard at the front of the café while those unable to get a seat would wait their turn, looking longingly inside the cavernous room, anxious to get out of the sun.

Three fans ran across the ceiling, turning slowly as if they, too, were exhausted from the heat.

Jelani tried to put himself in the shoes of an American who would be reading the message. Then, he took one deep sigh, praised Allah silently, and hit send.

Jelani was pleased with the quality of his message. He had labored over the wording for several weeks. Checking the grammar. Developing the hook. But what pleased Jelani the most was the use of so many palindromes: civic, refer, level, deified, sagas. For Jelani, the order and symmetry of these words were particularly satisfying, as they would likely be for anyone on the autism spectrum. Somewhere on the other side of the world, very soon, the message would be read. Would they believe the inquiry to be legitimate?

It was by now three in the afternoon in the village where Jelani was taking his day off, visiting first the internet café and now sitting on the steps of a non-governmental organization set up to provide job training to the region's youth and funded by the Cathedral Basilica of the Holy Family, the largest church in Kenya. It was here that Jelani was first introduced to computing and the internet and exposed to the incredible diversity in how people lived their lives. Through the church, he also learned just how different he was in his beliefs from most children around him.

In Somalia, virtually the entire population is Sunni Muslim, and Jelani's introduction to the religion was through the mosque in his hometown of Hamar (known outside Somalia as Mogadishu). A tiny minority of Christians lived in his community, and all he knew from the elders was that they were not to be trusted. This was difficult to square with the resources and benefits that the church provided around his village in Kenya. The Jews, on the other hand, were the most sinister of all peoples, and as far as Jelani knew, they would not even look like real human beings, so he was pretty sure he'd never seen one. Without the benefit of an objective mentor and role model, Jelani adopted the philosophy that he had an obligation to protect his family and, by extension, his faith and all others who were bound by it.

Jelani squinted as he watched the villagers go about their business, back and forth along the red, dusty road that ran in front of him, some balancing baskets on their heads, others pushing handmade wagons, and still others walking alongside cattle that were pulling produce carts for them. It was hot today, like most days, and the sun shined through dust that might be confused for fog anywhere else. Scooters wove in and out of the traffic as if no rules applied. The slow-moving traffic only aggravated the red and yellow dust cloud hovering in front of him. He compared this scene with the images that lingered in his mind from surfing the web. In the café, he saw cars, celebrities, massive buildings, and symbols of wealth and privilege that he believed might not exist anywhere in Kenya or all of Africa.

"Jelani!" his concentration was broken by his older sister, Kesi. "What are you doing here?" Kesi was always on the lookout for her siblings when she came to the village because she worried they could get mixed up with the wrong crowd. There were rumors of a group of teenagers trying to manage an internet scheme designed to prey on naive people. "Jelani!" she repeated. Jelani realized he had to come up with a good excuse for being there. Lying to his family did not come easily to him unless he could contrive a technically correct response based on the broadest possible interpretation of the question.

"Sister," he finally replied. "What do you think I am doing? I am here at the training center trying to better myself." This was not far from the truth; the training center taught him everything he knew about computing, including how to set up websites, how to search for people with specific backgrounds, and, unintentionally, how to set up fake email accounts and social media profiles. He even registered for and received a passport under a false name and set up a matching LinkedIn profile.

Kesi looked back at Jelani with suspicion as she walked past the training center, but she had a long list of errands and no time to quiz Jelani further.

"*Akunamata*," she replied, indicating her indifference for the moment, as she continued to the chemist for her mother's prescription. She was satisfied she would see Jelani later that evening, in time for dinner with the rest of the family.

The sun set shortly afterward, and the dusty backroads of Kenya became empty, returning control of the land to the silent civilization hiding among the trees, bushes, and tall grasslands of the savannah.

As day gave way to night, the email Jelani sent was making its way into the lives of unsuspecting families from Western Europe to the shores of California.

4

The next morning, Muhammed Amir Abbas stepped out to meet the sun in front of his modest flat in Dammam in the Eastern Province of Saudi Arabia. Already, the loudspeakers from mosques across the city began to broadcast the morning prayers in a slow, deep, pulsating voice that served as the soundtrack of everyday life there. Growing up in Hamar, his grandfather told him stories of how in ancient times, holy men would climb up the minarets of each mosque to announce the prayers to the local worshippers of Islam. Now, they have been replaced by loudspeakers that are triggered automatically five times per day.

He threw his leg over the back of his motorcycle and headed for the local coffeehouse, where computers were available for patrons willing to pay for the privilege. He could certainly use the computer system set up in his home, but the highest level of security was needed for this errand. He passed cars driving at a range of speeds, from five kilometers per hour to well over fifty. Some drove on the side of the road, others straight down the center, and still others taking two lanes. Now that women have been granted the right to drive in the Kingdom, he thought to himself, it is like the wild, wild west on the roads of Dammam. He smiled to himself that he could quote a uniquely American idiom on his way to target that very same country with a sophisticated con.

At the coffeehouse, he settled down in front of a computer as far away as possible from any potential onlookers. Today's task was simple: to confirm with his "agent" in Kenya that the con was on, and in doing so, to instruct him on the next step in this operation. As a liaison to the Al-Qaeda operatives in Iran, Muhammed's job was to coordinate a dark web marketplace for drugs and weapons of war. He modeled his business after the infamous Silk Road website with two important differences. Rather than designing the marketplace to freely accommodate any rogue actors with access to contraband, Muhammed acted as either the buyer or seller for all transactions, and Al-Qaeda was his only client. Second, he was not as cavalier as the founder of Silk Road, who put very little effort into laying low and was ultimately captured by authorities.

Muhammed did not consider himself a warrior so much as a businessman. Since Saudis were among the most active social media users in the entire Arab region, this was the perfect place for Muhammed to work without great risk of detection. He could hide in plain sight here, and it was still a step up from his home village. It was also far from the prying eyes of the FBI.

As they grew up together in Somalia, Muhammed tutored Jelani about the injustices to Muslims around the world. Even when the two boys moved in opposite directions, they kept in touch regularly on social media and Signal, the encrypted message site modeled after WhatsApp. Both were smart and creative, and they learned how to bend the internet to their will, including the creation of fake identities and social media profiles.

Recognizing Jelani's immense talent, Muhammed persuaded him to devise an email scam to redistribute wealth from the U.S. to Muslim nations like Somalia and Saudi Arabia, taking an appropriate small percentage for himself. It was Jelani who first recognized that through the email scam they could take advantage of people without requiring their banking information, and that to have them suspect that the scams *were* attempting to secure banking information could ironically work in his favor, because it would result in them letting down their guard in other ways.

It's not that Jelani was limited in how to generate income from internet schemes. He had already learned how to set up fake crowdsourcing sites for potential investors, sites that would collect donations for bogus causes, and he even learned how to set up a trojan horse virus on large mainframe computers to demand ransoms from large corporations that could easily afford to pay it. The problem with these other approaches is that they all made Jelani more vulnerable to discovery. The email con he devised was brilliant in that he operated as a ghost on the web; finding any trace of him would be virtually impossible.

For Jelani, the schemes were a way to provide for his family. For Muhammed, it was something else entirely, and soon it would be time to reveal his vision and the full scope of his mission to his young friend.

"My brother," Muhammed began in his message to Jelani, sent via Signal, "have you had your operation?" This intuitive code gave the conversation sufficient cover to be considered innocuous.

"Yes indeed," Jelani replied from the internet café in his village, "Allah has given me the strength to prevail." This was the news that Muhammed was waiting for and gave him the opening to take Jelani to the next step in his journey.

"You will have to come to the U.S. soon to visit us, in Dearborn."

***

Myles rolled out of bed Saturday morning at ten thirty to the sounds of his dormitory in full "game on" mode. Today, the Michigan Wolverines would take on Northwestern, a football game that used to be a complete rout but in recent years had become more competitive. Myles remembered Richard saying several years earlier: "The first thing we did on getting our season tickets was to rip out the Northwestern ticket and throw it out." Still, at two years in and rout or no rout, Myles enjoyed spending the afternoon in the sun, an escape from the library and the books, and an opportunity to think about something other than school while being crammed into a stadium with one hundred thousand screaming fans.

Jordan, from down the hall, burst into his dorm room, which he had left unlocked. "Dude, are you going today?" Myles thought the question was rhetorical because he came from a long line of Wolverine fans and rarely missed a game no matter that the outcome was, for the most part, predetermined.

"Yeah," he responded simply, not quite ready for the yelling, screaming, and partying that accompanied most games.

"Well, the guys are about to leave for the pancake house for breakfast, so get yourself ready or meet us there."

Myles grunted in agreement as he tried to complete the process of waking up. He looked across the room to see his roommate John still fast asleep. John was more of a party animal than Myles could ever be; he wasn't in the room when Myles returned last night, and he did not recall hearing John come in to crash. John was a pre-med student, the son of two physicians who raised two other children, also physicians. Myles and John made perfect roommates, each having respect for the other because, despite their idiosyncrasies, they were both ambitious and motivated to make a difference in the world.

Myles looked back at his desk and noticed his laptop turned sideways toward the bed, remembering that he had forgotten to plug it in the night before. When he pressed the space bar, the screen lit up to reveal a low battery warning and his emails. He had received eight new messages, mostly from the school and fellow students, as well as a message titled "To My Friend." Myles took the bait and clicked it, seeing for the first time the email sent from halfway around the world. He had seen these types of scams before, and, being the mischievous kid he always was, he would occasionally play along, thinking that if he could waste the time of these criminals he would, in some small way, contribute to law and order. He would lead them on with the appearance of being curious, one day at a time, skipping days every so often to prompt them to look harder for him. When that predictable message came asking for a bank account in which to make a deposit, he would either provide fake information or simply go radio silent.

He stared at the email for several minutes, impressed with its clarity, sentence structure, and the compelling story it told. This one was very good. Then, without further hesitation, he replied "tell me more," closed his laptop, and got dressed for the game. He took one last look at John before shutting the door quietly, satisfied that he was able to leave the room without disturbing him.

Myles didn't stop to consider he had his full name, address, Facebook link, and student ID number prepopulated as a default signature line in his email response. All the information that Jelani needed to continue his deception was on its way to him.

5

Managing the ruse he had designed was tedious. Jelani had created a program to randomly generate potential email addresses, specifically emails with a .edu extension, because unlike .com, .gov, and even .org, these accounts were least likely to have any connection to individuals who might be associated with law enforcement. Ironically, students and those working in academia were also the most naive regarding internet fraud. Unfortunately, enlightened students often laced their responses with profanity and insults, which Jelani had to endure as part of his role in the campaign.

A sophisticated program that Jelani had written would prioritize email accounts that already had significant activity, which would increase the probability that recipients would respond quickly, if only to clear their mailbox and get to the next message.

Designing the right subject line was another significant challenge in these campaigns, so Jelani did a lot of research and testing to find the best way to hook a target. Part of this was a numbers game, but Jelani believed there also was an art to crafting the best subject line. He read once that subject lines with the most impact were no more than three words. He learned from research on print media the most effective words used in any headline were sex, free, and win. He surmised that if that were true, "Win Free Sex" might be worth trying, if not for the spam filters that were now sophisticated enough to catch and kill these messages. He settled with simply "To My Friend."

Jelani had to find the time to sift through a series of "fuck you" and "eat shit and die" replies before he could ever hope to find a response that offered a genuine opportunity. What he really wanted to create next was a program to automatically detect and delete responses that contained any of the American so-called four-letter words. Until he figured that out, Jelani was determined to adopt a utilitarian attitude toward the work, not allowing himself to take the replies personally but instead focusing on identifying a new target.

Today, however, his spirits were high as he arrived at work after an exciting exchange with his friend and handler in Dammam. "You will have to visit us in Dearborn" kept creeping back into his consciousness with such force that he wanted to say it out loud, and nearly did. "Dearborn" was code for Dubai and a designation given to the place where operatives from different regions of the Middle East met to renew acquaintances, discuss strategy, and hand off funds and critical resources. The code was a simple way to throw off anyone who might be monitoring their communications. Muhammed had long ago told Jelani that a meeting in Dubai might be in the cards for him if he demonstrated his worth to the Al-Qaeda leadership. Jelani had never traveled anywhere other than between Somalia and Kenya, but he had that fake passport hidden under his mattress, waiting for its maiden voyage.

As he imagined air travel to the wonders of Dubai, he spotted Daudi approaching and returned to the reality of being a steward.

"Jelani, the kitchen just received the gazelle for tonight's buffet," he started, "and they need help to separate the parts. I told them we would come down in a few minutes."

Gazelle was a popular dish in this part of Kenya and more plentiful than just about any other protein. Cows were prized for their ability to produce milk, but gazelle roamed the plains in huge packs, and if the humans did not control their population, the lions would have to do it all by themselves. The buffets were a staple in the photo safari industry, using the bright, multicolored tapestries of the Maasai Mara tribes as the backdrop for elegant presentations under tents set up on the grounds of the Lodge, where tourists would gather after a long day of jeep rides and sightseeing.

"*Ahsante*," replied Jelani, expressing thanks for the opportunity to do something other than sweeping floors. "I'll be right there."

Maybe if there were leftovers from tonight's buffet, he mused, he could bring home some gazelle to his family. The Americans were notorious for wasting food and this was aggravating for Jelani to observe night after night. For now, thoughts about traveling to Dubai would have to wait.

***

"Leosha! Leosha! Leosha, open the fucking door!" Tamara Rosen pounded on the door of Apartment 412 with the authority of an Israeli army officer, which she was until four years ago when she joined Shin Bet, Israeli's domestic intelligence agency. It was like MI5 in the UK; in the U.S. it would be called the FBI. Her boyfriend, Leosha Simakov, was a Russian immigrant who came to Israel as a refugee five years ago and quickly fell in with the Russian Jews and Israeli Arabs seeking religious freedom and opportunity in Israel. Unfortunately for Tamara, that opportunity included living with her and staying out late with his buddies, drinking in the bars of Tel Aviv, then stumbling home after they closed. His best friend, Gali, unilaterally decided that they were done with vodka, by far the most popular spirit in Israel, and instead were adopting tequila, straight up, which Leosha does not tolerate very well at all. He lay face down on the sofa, his left arm and leg falling over the side, and a stream of drool escaping from the side of his mouth and onto the cushions.

Tamara's apartment in the swanky neighborhood of Bavli was only on the fourth floor of a twenty-five-story high-rise with no view, but it was the best she could afford in such an upscale neighborhood. She wanted to be in Bavli because it was only two kilometers from the Ramat Aviv office of the Intelligence Services, and she wanted to reward herself for years of hard work that led to becoming a special agent.

Tamara's assignments could be as mundane as monitoring activity at a border crossing to bona fide espionage work that revealed itself in a slow burn, with clues coming when they were least expected. Her caseload included suspected arms shipments to a camp in Saudi Arabia that could be moving on to the United Arab Emirates, a country where diplomatic relations had been improving. The provenance of the weapons was not known, nor was the identity of the group acquiring them. She was tempted to leverage her relationship with Leosha to see if he could help determine what Russian involvement might exist, and she may play that card if she didn't get a break soon. It was clear that the station commander was anxious for information he could pass on to the chief of intelligence at Shin Bet. For now, her focus was on getting back into her apartment, getting laid, and getting to bed in anticipation of an intelligence briefing at 0700 tomorrow. She soon realized the best she could hope for was two out of three.

6

Jelani confirmed that 150,000 Kenyan shillings were transferred into his personal account from the Al Ahli Bank of Saudi Arabia, enough for his flight from Nairobi to Dubai, as well as a hotel and other related expenses. His birthday was coming up in a few weeks, and he intended to ask his parents for permission to visit his childhood friend in Dubai. By all accounts, Jelani was a good son who turned over his paychecks to the family, and while the request to travel might seem extravagant, nobody could say that he had not earned it. If there was any doubt, it was that his parents were suspicious of Muhammed, who was six years senior to Jelani and had a sullied reputation before leaving Somalia. After discussing the topic during family dinners, his parents acquiesced to the trip so long as Jelani could afford it with his own savings.

Thoughts of air travel to a cosmopolitan city occupied Jelani's mind for much of the next few weeks. He scheduled time off for the first time since joining the staff of the Amboseli Lodge and booked a hotel at the Mall of the Emirates, just far enough from downtown that he would feel safe. Also, the mall boasted an indoor ski resort. Jelani had never seen snow before and could not imagine such a facility indoors, where outside temperatures were frequently over thirty-eight degrees Celsius. He shared all details with Muhammed, and the two agreed to meet at the top of the Dubai Frame, a 150-meter-tall structure in the shape of a golden picture frame. One side provided a view of the old city, and the other gave visitors a look at a modern, stunning metropolis that includes the largest skyscraper in the world, the Burj Khalifa. After the meeting, Jelani intended to play tourist, including a visit to the Jumeirah Mosque near the old city.

***

Tamara couldn't decide what to wear to the scheduled meeting with her source from Saudi Arabia. With her blue eyes and fair skin, she already belied the stereotype of a Jewish woman. But then, by walking into Egypt at the Taba border crossing, just south of Eilat, anything could happen. If she crossed over in civilian clothes, she would almost certainly be harassed by Egyptian soldiers. If she went over in her uniform or combat fatigues, she could unnecessarily intimidate Egyptian guards or create an unintended response. On the other hand, she would be sending a signal that essentially communicated "hands off." She decided to go with the fatigues, aviator sunglasses, and a ponytail for her shoulder-length brown hair. Underneath it all, she wore her good luck charm: The Star of David necklace that was handed down to her by her grandmother.

Tamara's background made her uniquely suited for the type of work she was about to undertake. The daughter of an affluent British family, she attended only the best schools, including for a brief time, the King David School in Birmingham, where Muslim students outnumber those from Jewish families. She grew up surrounded by Muslim families in Birmingham and London and learned to move effortlessly between them speaking English, Hebrew, and Arabic, all with a British accent. When her parents divorced, she decided to immigrate to Israel, joining the army as an interpreter.

Her Saudi source, known as Chad Kirin, meaning Unicorn, was unwilling to come to Israel, for obvious reasons. On his last visit, he attempted entry via the UK, but Israeli security embedded within El Al at Heathrow Airport detained him, nearly causing him to miss the flight, but more significantly, causing an enormous amount of stress. They insisted that "Chad" provide a telephone number for a local contact in Israel, which is standard procedure when an itinerary or passenger passport might provoke a concern. He provided Tamara's phone number, but the call went to her voice mail. Israeli security allowed him to board the flight, but phone contact between an agent and a source is strictly controlled by the intelligence community. This was a situation to be avoided to protect agents and their sources.

As much as Tamara was interested to see life inside the Kingdom of Saudi Arabia, urban legend had it that air travelers with Israeli passports might be denied entry to the KSA altogether. Still, it was decided that Egypt was the most accessible for both parties, so a meeting was set up at the Hilton hotel in Taba, just over the border with Israel.

Tamara wasn't even born when Israel withdrew from the Sinai Peninsula in 1982, the result of a peace treaty signed with Egypt three years before. The city of Taba was not returned until 1989. The Israelis would have much preferred to remain in control of this last small piece of the Sinai for its access to the Gulf of Aqaba and the high cliffs that make for a border they could more readily protect and defend, but they abided by the ruling of an arbitration commission and withdrew. Tamara wondered what the border crossing might have looked like before Egypt and Israel abandoned decades of conflict.

She took a taxi to within a quarter-mile of the border crossing. No sense communicating any privilege to those who might be watching from the cliff above the crossing. She walked the rest of the way, entering a cavernous building that appeared to have far more potential than as a border crossing. As she entered, an Egyptian soldier slept, shirtless, on a chair outside the entrance. He did not open his eyes as Tamara pulled open the door and stepped inside.

The building was dark inside, with a few lights hanging from the top of what would have been a two-story building but functioned as a warehouse with high ceilings. Offices lined the inside perimeter of the building, with more offices in the center, creating essentially a track that ran in a circle around the outer offices.

To be safe and legal, Tamara needed an entry stamp in her passport, but all the offices were empty. Then, another man approached her. He was tall, dressed in black slacks, a dark blue shirt, and a thick black belt. He did not wear a uniform, but he did have a sidearm, and his right hand rested upon it.

"Is there a problem?" he asked in Arabic, with a hint of irritation in his voice that an Israeli soldier would step on Egyptian soil.

"I need an entry stamp," Tamara replied, speaking perfect Arabic. She flashed her badge as a security officer, essentially communicating that she was not obligated to provide any additional details regarding the purpose of her visit. The man was certainly familiar with Israelis speaking his mother tongue, but that did not mean he had to appreciate the effort.

"Why are you here?" he demanded, not expecting an honest answer, but feeling like he had no choice but to be difficult.

"Classified," she said, but in the interest of being courteous, she allowed, "I'll be here only a couple hours."

The man walked past Tamara, nearly bumping her shoulder, without speaking further. He headed to an office in the middle of the building, and Tamara followed. Inside the office was a desk with a journal, and on top of it, the stamp that Tamara needed in her passport to enter the country legally. The man stepped behind the desk and held out his hand without even looking up. Tamara handed the passport to him, which he stamped and handed back, again without speaking a word. He presumed Tamara could find her way out of the building on her own, but he slowly followed her and watched with a look of disgust on his face as she left the building and entered Egypt.

As Tamara stepped outside the building, she passed another soldier sleeping in the shade on a plastic chair. Next to him was a small wooden sign, sitting about waist high, that said “Welcome to Egypt.” As she walked away from the entry gate, she understood the Egyptian border agent would alert his superiors, but Tamara would disappear before anyone could track her.

The walk to the Hilton was brief. The hotel was situated near the border with a purpose: to attract Israeli tourists who wanted to say they stepped on Egyptian soil and as a means for those visitors to access the Red Sea via the Gulf of Aqaba for some of the best scuba diving in the world. She walked up the wide avenue to the hotel lobby and stepped inside. Chad Kirin was waiting for her.

Tamara went first: “*As-Salaam-Alaikum*, my dear friend,” adopting the Arabic greeting as a sign of respect.

“*Wa-Alaikum-Salaam*” replied the Unicorn. “It is very good to see you.”

With two unique cultures coming together on foreign soil, the only matter left was to adopt a purely European practice, they embraced and kissed each other’s cheek on both sides, then walked to the docks behind the hotel and boarded a pleasure tour about to depart.

Although the Unicorn’s identity was a closely guarded secret, of course Israeli intelligence was aware of his background and qualifications to serve as an informant and asset to the Israeli government. The son of a schoolteacher, Chad was believed to be a distant cousin to Satam al-Suqami, a law student and one of the Saudi terrorists on the plane that flew into the World Trade Center's North Tower in New York. The Shin Bet dossier on the Unicorn suggested the 9/11 operation must have upset him greatly. He did not interpret the Quran in the same way as many other youths who were easy targets for ISIS or Al-Qaeda, but that did not stop the terror groups from trying to recruit him. Children of prominent families could represent sources of future funding.

The Unicorn was only twelve when 9/11 happened, but some twenty years later as a university faculty member with a young family, he feared for the future and believed Israel was in the best position to serve as a policing force in the Middle East, preventing rogue nations from acquiring or deploying nuclear weapons and stopping Arab countries from having the capability to destroy each other or other innocent people.

Tamara and the Unicorn went to the far corner of a large double-decker ship. On the bottom level were tourists who would later be jumping in the water to dive among the world-famous coral reefs and crystal blue waters that feed into the Red Sea. Others would listen as a tour guide described the historic buildings and military outposts that lined the Egyptian shore. From the back of the boat, said the guide, you could see Egypt, Israel, and Jordan, each of which claimed a share of the Gulf of Aqaba.

Tamara and the Unicorn had their backs turned to these distractions and accepted a cup of tea from one of the young boys whose job was to make every guest comfortable. A second boy who seemed to come from nowhere was now standing directly in front of them.

"Your picture, me take!" said the boy, holding the camera in the ready position. It was common practice on such tours to take professional-grade pictures that could be sold back to guests after their adventure had finished.

"No, *la shukran*, thank you," replied Tamara.

"Please, please, let me take!" The boy was taught to be persistent.

"No, no, here." Tamara took her phone from her bag, set it in camera mode, and passed it to the boy. "*Lo samaht,* please." If a picture were to be taken, Tamara would control its distribution.

The boy, demonstrating a combination of disappointment and irritation, grabbed the phone, stepped back, and took the picture. The Unicorn timed it perfectly, looking down at his own phone just as the picture was being taken. As the boy handed the phone back to Tamara, she removed three crisp U.S. dollar bills that she took from petty cash from the department cashier and handed them to the boy. He managed a smile, snapped up the bills, and disappeared into the crowd. While this was happening, the Unicorn was nonchalant, alternating between looking at the coast and whatever was on his phone.

"Something is going on in Tehran," he finally shared with Tamara. As a professor of world history at the Imam Abdulrahman Bin Faisal University, Chad Kirin was well connected to students, faculty, parents, and the broader community in Riyadh, the satellite in Dammam, and across the Arab world. He would often attend student rallies and became the confidant of students torn between pursuing a career and the immense attraction of joining the extremists. "Marginalized kids are the most vulnerable," he reminded Tamara, "and there are many of them in the outskirts of my community."

"I understand," replied Tamara, seeking to encourage the flow of information. "What is the unifying cause that brings them together?"

An alumnus of the university was organizing students in Riyadh and Tehran, Chad said, and it appeared the group was setting up a shell company to serve as the legitimate face of an enterprise that was funding Hamas. He identified the alumnus as Ahmad Salman. Chad was not entirely sure how the money was flowing, but he was relatively certain the activity was aimed at smuggling nuclear weapons into Gaza for a future attack on Israel. The group was determined to become the generation that persuaded the Israelis to leave the occupied territories and formally recognize Palestinian statehood.

Israeli intelligence had long known of Iran's nuclear ambitions and regularly conducted operations to hinder the Iranians' progress, whether deploying a computer virus to cause their uranium enrichment centrifuges to malfunction, bombing clandestine laboratories, or assassinating key figures within Iran's nuclear program, most recently in November 2020 when a remote-controlled machine gun killed the nuclear scientist known as Mohsen Fakhrizadeh. Israel's denial of such activities had become little more than a wink and a nod.

As the Unicorn spoke, Tamara watched his facial expressions to draw as much verbal and nonverbal data as possible.

At the docks, the Unicorn and Tamara made certain to disembark in separate crowds.

Tamara felt a sense of accomplishment from the day's central task, but she worried about her friend from Dammam. Although the two were raised in different worlds and prayed to a different god, they had respect for each other, and above all, wanted their people to live in peace with one another. She said a silent prayer that the Unicorn would return safely home without any lingering suspicion of any loyalty to Israel.

As Tamara entered the modern Israeli border control facility for citizens arriving from Egypt, she was met by Israeli soldiers not much younger than she. All were young women. She placed her backpack in the X-ray machine and chatted briefly with the soldiers, asking where they were from and how they liked this detail. In a few minutes, she was back on home soil and walking toward a taxi that would take her back to the Intelligence Station.

As she sat in the taxi, she experienced the delayed reaction of what the Unicorn revealed. A nuclear weapon, in Gaza, pointed at Tel Aviv. The worst-case scenario of all worst-case scenarios.

7

Sundays in Ann Arbor, especially during the fall, were for recovery. Whether you drank beer all weekend, attended football tailgate parties, the game, or all three, you needed Sunday to decompress and get yourself ready for Monday classes. You needed to make sure all homework was done. You needed to find food on your own, as the dorm cafeteria was closed on Sunday. And if you had not done so the day prior, you needed to check in with your parents.

Jerry and Jill O'Brien operated a successful construction consulting firm with an international clientele. They met at the University of Michigan School of Architecture as students and remained connected as they pursued different career paths: Jerry as an on-site supervisor for commercial projects, and Jill as an inspector for the City of Detroit Department of Public Works. Eventually, they married, and after recognizing how their talents would complement each other, they started O'Brien & Company in Gross Pointe, an affluent suburb east of Detroit. Together they built a business of which they could be proud, but not as proud as they were of Richard, Myles, and Emmalee, their three children.

"Hi Mom," Myles started out, "it's me." Jill O'Brien never had to be told who was on the line when it came to her kids.

"Myles dear, I've been waiting for your call. Have you heard the news? Richard is coming to visit!"

As much as he wanted to see Richard, Myles was disappointed he was the last to know about the visit. He checked his email to see if Richard had sent him anything, but the last conversation was on Friday and nothing since then. He noticed he had not heard from "General Okogun" either, even though it had been nearly two days since he reached out to him. That's disappointing, he thought, but perhaps he could torment him sometime soon.

"Myles," his mom continued, "is everything all right?"

"Sure, Mom."

The two continued to catch up, discussing campus life, his classes, the dorm, and how to pay for it all.

"Mom, don't forget that second semester tuition payments will be due before the Thanksgiving break. Wait, do you think Richard might come during my break?"

The two chatted a few minutes more. As he hung up with his mother, Myles decided to text Richard to get more details on his visit; it seemed harder than ever to remain close. Also, Ann Arbor and Detroit were about an hour from each other, so some coordination would be needed if there was to be a family reunion.

As he was punching up Richard's number, a text from a classmate popped on his phone:

"can u come ovr tmrw nite?"

This was the text Myles fantasized about even as he prepared for the probability that it would not happen. It was from Kristen Edwards, a petite freshman from his philosophy class. Kristen was from Southern California, with long brunette hair, blue eyes, and the sexiest smile Myles had ever seen in his personal orbit. She sat next to him recently and started up a conversation. As they walked out of the class together, and before going separate ways, she suggested it would be nice to have a "study buddy" as, in her words, "what good is a philosophy if you cannot share it?" Myles gave her his cell phone and immediately began playing out scenarios of what might happen next.

"Sure, time?"

"10? I have dance class ends at 9. Need shower after that!"

"Alright"

Ten seemed late to start a studying session, but Myles was in no mindset to negotiate. He tried his level best to appear chill in the presence of girls with whom he was smitten. He found that made him less threatening, and with Kristen the strategy was working so far. Besides, lots of things can happen after ten o'clock, he thought to himself, smiling.

Myles forgot to reach out to his brother.

***

"*Tell me more.*" Jelani stared at the reply to his email but did not overreact. Exploiting this opportunity would require a bit more work. Jelani looked down at the bottom of the email and saw the information from the signature line. There it was. More than enough information for him to advance this contact to the next stage of the campaign. The first thing Jelani did was trace the IP address that stood behind the sender: It was based in Ann Arbor, Michigan, and based on "umich.edu," so it was obvious that this email came in direct response to his outreach a few days before.

Hello Myles O'Brien, thought Jelani. A nice Irish name. *I am very pleased to meet you.*

8

Emirates Air Flight 818. Jelani looked at the boarding pass handed to him at the ticket counter at Jomo Kenyatta International Airport in Nairobi. He was happy with this flight number. The number eight, and indeed one as well, were symmetrical and conveyed a sense of order and peaceful coexistence, important qualities to someone with autism. The fact that eights were on either side of the number one was a bonus. He was relieved to have found this flight because the number alone guaranteed him a safe journey.

But boarding the plane . . . the distracting signs of airlines in the terminal, confusion about how to proceed through security, and the noise! Jelani could barely concentrate on putting one foot before the other, and if not for his raw enthusiasm for this adventure, he'd probably have found a corner somewhere to sit and rock himself.

The cramped conditions on the plane, loud utterances of passengers, and strange sounds emanating from all over the cabin added to the overstimulation Jelani was feeling. He watched from his seat as the flight attendants made their way down the aisle, observing their interaction with other passengers, listening to the conversation so that he could be prepared for when they reached his row.

"Coffee, tea, juice, water, or soda?" was what he believed they were saying. When they reached his seat, he would be prepared to say, "Coke, please." He did, conquering one more trepidation.

As the plane descended to DXB, Dubai International Airport, Jelani soaked in every morsel of sensory input that he could tolerate: the feeling of weightlessness, the humming of the engines as they slowed the cabin, and the view. Dubai was lit up, the grid pattern filling the small window next to him and offering clues to the treasures that lay below. Tall spires pierced the sky, buildings the likes of which he knew only from surfing the web. He knew Dubai was the jewel of the Arab world, and he recognized just how privileged he was to be visiting. A boy from Somalia who had done something with his life, he mused to himself.

The plane landed, and passengers began to depart. He was able to fly direct on Emirates Airlines, but the flight was full of native Kenyans and Muslims who had connected through Nairobi from neighboring countries. What if someone recognized him? But it became clear that these people were in a social class well above his. As he followed others off the plane, excitement replaced his nerves once again.

After walking behind other passengers for a half hour, Jelani was still in the enormous airport concourse, passing gate after gate on the way to passport control. He had never used the fake passport, but he had tested it in Nairobi as a form of official identification since he did not have a driver's license.

He was confident there would be no problem, but every time he walked under a sign showing the way to passport control, thoughts would poke at him. *What if they realize it's a fake?* With one hand he pulled his luggage, and with the other he caressed a few beads in his pocket, a strategy he used whenever he felt the potential for anxiety to invade his thoughts.

After a full forty-five minutes of walking, he approached an enormous escalator, collecting passengers from multiple flights, and rode it down to the ground floor where baggage claim and exits were located. First, he would have to get past the border agents. That meant he would have to do something he found extraordinarily difficult: make eye contact.

"*Marhaba,*" the agent said as he put his hand on top of Jelani's passport, slid it under the glass window, and placed it on the space next to his keyboard. "Visiting from?

"Kenya," replied Jelani, intending to keep his responses simple here, as he would anywhere. *Eye contact, eye contact!* he repeated to himself.

"Purpose of visit?"

"Visiting family," short and direct responses were one of Jelani's specialties. But eye contact was not, as he reminded himself. *Eye contact!* he screamed inside himself, struggling to bring his chin well above his chest but not so high as to appear out of step with everyone else.

The border control agent was dressed in the traditional white gown, or dishdasha, a measure of formality that Jelani had not seen since his childhood in Somalia. As Jelani scanned to his left and right, all the agents were dressed the same way. If Dubai were not so opulent, even at the airport, he would have felt at home.

The border agent began to leaf through the passport, noticing it had no stamps, a red flag for a young man traveling alone, especially in the Middle East. As Jelani waited for the next question, he began counting prime numbers in his head:

1, 3, 5, 7, 11, 13, 17 . . .

The agent held the passport down with his left hand while punching keys with his right hand on a keyboard. He drew his face closer to the monitor, squinting.

. . . 19, 23, 29, 31, 37 . . .

Reciting prime numbers, numbers that could only be divisible by themselves, is a common way for savants and those on the autism spectrum to calm themselves down. Jelani learned about this from various online forums he had consulted in the internet café.

. . . 41, 43, 47, 53, 59 . . .

"Your first trip?" he inquired.

"Yes," replied Jelani, trying his best to smile. He never felt this anxiety when speaking to people one-on-one before, so why was he in such a panic now?

. . . 61, 67, 71, 73, 79, 83, 89, 97 . . .

The border agent continued to flip back and forth through the passport, stopping every so often, then starting up again. Jelani watched the process as if it were in slow motion. The agent picked up his phone, whispered into it, then hung up. As Jelani began to perspire, he considered his options. *Should I run? Confess? Did I pick up someone else's passport by mistake? Where, on a direct flight, could that even happen?* His mind flipped through scenarios like a slot machine blasts through potential combinations. What would constitute a winning alibi?

. . . 101, 103, 107, 109, 113 . . .

Sweat formed under his clothes and ran down his body; it felt like an insect crawling on his back. Another agent, clearly the agent's superior, came over to discuss the situation. Jelani could not make out what they were saying, so he did his best to appear nonchalant. He was out of options.

Finally, while Jelani observed the airport's vast dimensions as an additional compensating strategy, he could see in the corner of his eye that the supervisor was walking away. A split second later, he heard the entry stamp pounding its way into his passport.

"Welcome to Dubai. Enjoy your stay."

***

It was Monday morning, and Jill O'Brien hated Mondays. To bring discipline to their business, Mondays involved opening mail, paying bills, and responding to inquiries from Friday afternoon, as well as anything arriving over the weekend. One of the curses of being self-employed, she thought, is that you're never truly off the clock, something can go wrong when you are sleeping, and something *always* goes wrong over the weekend.

Jill was fit and attractive at fifty-two years old, petite, five-foot-two with shoulder-length brown hair and green eyes. Like her husband, she had Irish roots and could always count on someone trying to make a clever comment about it being "a good thing" that her eyes matched her ethnicity. As she opened the door in her basement home office, she had thoughts of seeing her oldest boy in the coming weeks and wanted to clear her inbox quickly so she could make plans for the family.

Among the emails were communications from subcontractors requiring a thoughtful response; Jill would get to these after a couple more cups of coffee. A "request for proposal" from the city of Baltimore for a community center. A resumé from a promising engineering student at the University of Michigan. And below it, a bill from the same university.

As a former Michigan student herself, Jill was always happy to see the big block "M" in bright yellow within a navy-blue box. Nostalgic thoughts of her own coming of age would momentarily take her back to those days, dating Jerry, attending classes and socials, and of course, the Big Ten football games.

The bill from the university was for tuition, room and board for Myles O'Brien, in the amount of $22,500. Thank goodness we are not paying out-of-state tuition, she thought, also recognizing that the room and board costs were even higher than the tuition. She double-checked the sender's email address to ensure it was legitimate: It read "billing@umich.edu.sa" She clicked "Pay Now," completed the online form, and started to look at the other bills that arrived by mail over the weekend.

9

Agent Sarah Goodman did not fit the FBI special agent profile. At five foot four inches, she was shorter than most of her peers in the department. She had wavy black hair, pencil-thin eyebrows over blue-gray eyes, and a broad smile guaranteed to attract the attention of any man seeking the company of a woman. Growing up and during school, she made some extra money as a makeup model, but a career in law enforcement interested her the most. This would prove problematic for a woman as attractive as Sarah Goodman, so she had to learn to assert herself and her authority while keeping her male colleagues at arm's length. After sixteen years in Detroit, no one would ever come to question her qualifications for the job.

Goodman was assigned to the cybercrime division of the FBI, and when she heard that Richard O'Brien from the New York field office was coming to town "on loan," she cleared her calendar to accommodate him so that he would feel comfortable in what could feel like a hostile environment because her peers also felt the unnecessary obligation to protect her from any new blood in the office.

Richard decided it would be best to get right down to business on landing, so he headed straight downtown after renting a car at Detroit Metro

Airport. After parking in the lot next to the FBI building on Michigan Avenue, he took one last look in the rearview mirror, fixed his seldom worn tie, moved his hair out of his eyes, then made his way into the building.

While he would never admit it, Richard loved these rare field trips. No place on earth was as vibrant as New York, but traveling in an official capacity and representing the FBI was something that would boost anyone's sense of self-worth. He reveled in this brief personal celebration until interrupted by a high-pitched "ding" from his cell phone. It was a text from Courtney; it said simply, "*where are u.*" Richard silenced his phone just as the elevator doors opened on the twenty-eighth floor.

"Mr. O'Brien?" a smiling Agent Goodman inquired.

"Yes, hi, I am here to see Agent Goodman."

"That would be me," she said, extending her hand. "You can call me Sarah. Right this way. Good flight?"

"Smooth sailing after surviving the trip to Newark."

Richard immediately felt like a schoolboy in the presence of such an attractive woman who happened to be an FBI agent. *I have a guardian angel, after all,* he thought as the two walked down the corridor; at the same time, he made a mental note to turn off his "flirtatious mode."

Once in a small conference room with Goodman, Richard did a quick scan. The official FBI symbol was on one side of the wall, a screen on the other. The two remaining walls had the type of generic wall art you might find in a budget hotel. The room contained only a conference table and eight uncomfortable-looking chairs.

"So, Mr. O'Brien, or may I call you Richard?"

"Yes, of course."

"Richard, we have been trying to get a handle on this email scam, you know, codename Utapeli. I assume you've been briefed on it."

"Yes, of course." Richard recognized he was star-struck by Sarah Goodman and would have to come up with an alternative to "yes, of course." He decided to do his best to take some control over the topic. "I am happy to look over any transcripts. Do I understand you are looking for a connection between Utapeli and the intercept we picked up about the potential hostile activity?"

"Actually, what we had in mind is to bring you into the Dearborn community to see if you can see any signals we may have missed, you know, reading between the lines as only a linguist can do. We need to get our intel quickly if we will have any chance to head off the threat contained in that transcript."

"Dearborn is home to a large Arab community, but the email scams have originated in East Africa, which are largely Christian populations," Goodman said and then smiled briefly, looking for confirmation that Richard was tracking. "Now on the other hand, there has been a steady flow of Muslim immigration to some of those countries."

Richard thought this a good time to get into the technical aspects of what he needed to understand.

"Can you take me through how these email schemes work from a logistic point of view, and why a Dearborn contact would even be necessary?"

For the next forty-five minutes, Goodman took Richard on a journey into the world of money laundering and exposed the brazen risks that the actors would take, flaunting the law to grab money and conceal its provenance. She handed Richard a confidential FBI brief, a few pages including charts and graphs that added context.

"We were making good progress on interdiction with these schemes," Goodman said, "then there was the FinCEN Files report leaked by Buzzfeed." FinCEN, or the Financial Crimes Enforcement Network, is a division of the U.S. Treasury that investigates a broad range of white-collar crimes. In the leaked documents, about ninety banks were implicated in the transfer of two trillion dollars in "dirty money." These were well-known and respected institutions such as Deutsche Bank, Chase, and JP Morgan. But because the law required the banks to merely notify FinCEN when they suspected funds were of illicit origin rather than stop the money transfers, they were able to continue to operate with impunity, enriching directors and banking executives, often at the expense of marginalized communities that may have been the victims of gangs or drug-related violence.

"Now that this is all in the public domain, it's made our job harder to catch the bad guys in the act. Without containing the intelligence, they stay one step ahead of us."

Richard scanned the FBI briefing. "Which of these cases might involve funds flowing into or out of the African continent?"

Goodman reached over to pick up the report, took a quick look, and slapped it back on the table. Her forefinger poked at a name on top of a list.

"This one."

"Al Zarooni Exchange, Dubai UAE," Richard read aloud. In the same subsection of the report, he saw two organizations he recognized: Al-Qaeda and Standard Chartered Bank.

Goodman answered Richard's next question before he could ask it. "From a geopolitical and cultural standpoint, it makes the most sense. All the other actors are either Asian or Russian operatives. The Asians would never trust a partner in Africa, and the Russians, well, the Russians don't trust anybody."

A screen at the end of the room doubled as a whiteboard, and Goodman walked over to it to draw out the complex web of relationships that makes money laundering possible. She wrote "AZE" in the center of the board and drew four lines emanating outward. At the end of one spoke she wrote the name of the cooperating bank, Standard Chartered. At the end of another she wrote Al-Qaeda, and at the end of the other two, $ and weapons.

"For the past several years, under the cover of a shell company, Al-Qaeda has been accumulating cash from stolen antiquities they have sold on the black market to private collectors, or by simply taking cash from the hands of villagers where they have literally raped and pillaged everything in their path," Goodman said. She ran a path with the marker first from Al-Qaeda to the $, then to AZE, and finally to Standard Chartered. "The money is deposited by AZE into Standard Chartered, and whatever contraband is needed by Al-Qaeda, often weapons or ammunition, makes its way back to them."

"How do you know all this?" Richard asked.

Goodman's smile returned for a moment. "Well, until recently, I'd be able to say, 'that's classified.' Sarah pulled from the file a second file the latest Suspicious Activity Report, or SAR, that banks are required to complete and provide to the FBI when they discover potential fraud. She held it up for Richard to see.

"We get these reports when a bank flags large, round-number transaction,

payments between companies with no discernible business relationship or amounts and currencies that belie their origins. We could use this information to hunt down perpetrators. Then the media got their hands on them and tipped our hand."

"Hmm. Do you think there is a connection between this activity and potential suspects in Dearborn?"

"Up to the intercept you grabbed, I'd say no. We have eyes and ears all over Dearborn, in the mosques, at the community centers, and in the schools. We've been monitoring what we feel could be a sleeper cell, but it's not been doing anything in this space, it has been very quiet since 9/11, and we are very confident of that intel."

"Is Al Zarooni still operating?" Richard felt he was closing in on some information that could reveal a role for him in the investigation.

"This is the part that makes my blood boil," Goodman replied. "We really don't have a good process for bringing these perpetrators, the bankers or money-laundering operatives, to justice. The law protects the bankers so long as they file the SAR, and the money-laundering operations can simply set up shop under a different name, abandoning those companies that have been exposed. It's like trying to win at whack-a-mole, blindfolded."

The look of frustration on Sarah's face, and the subject matter, taken together, told Richard all he needed to know about how difficult it would be to up his game, contribute, and hopefully, get to know Agent Goodman. But he was determined to try.

***

Fatima arrived at work at eight on Tuesday morning, as she did every day since becoming a nuclear medicine technician at the Thermo Fisher Scientific laboratory in Rochester, New York. She did not like Tuesdays as much as Mondays and Wednesdays, when she worked in the laboratory producing drugs using robotic arms behind thick, leaded glass to protect her from the radioactive isotopes she was handling. On those days, she felt like a true pioneer in medical research. Tuesdays and Thursdays were for packing up and shipping the product produced the day before, and Fridays were for paperwork and thyroid screening to ensure her exposure to these dangerous elements did not rise above acceptable levels.

She opened the refrigerator in the packing room that was filled with lead "pigs," small containers the size of a soda can that each contained a small vial of the highly radioactive cesium chloride used by medical centers in treating cancer patients. Fatima never fully understood how the drug she produced the day prior was pipetted into the tiny vials that were subsequently placed into the lead pigs; this was a process managed by the technicians on Monday and Wednesday night. The Geiger counter would remove any doubt that the drug was sitting within the cradle of lead designed to protect it.

Fatima grabbed the clipboard hanging on the side of the refrigerator. Twenty-three shipments were scheduled from this last lot, and she counted twenty-three pigs, the first of multiple confirmations to account for all the material being produced and shipped. She made note of the signature at the bottom of the sheet from the night manager and added her own below it to confirm the count.

Fatima took the first pig from the refrigerator and carefully laid it upright on the shipping table. The pig would be wrapped over and over with napkins, the kind every cafeteria has, and taped until the total diameter was at least two times that of the pig itself. No science suggested so much paper was necessary, but this was the protocol, and Fatima was not one to take shortcuts.

Fatima placed the wrapped pig into a two-foot-by-two-foot cardboard box made specifically for the laboratory. The foam interior would suspend the lead pig and its insulation while creating a space all around it inside the box. Once this box was closed, Fatima would place it inside another box, similarly protected by foam. The result was a four-foot-by-four-foot carton with a tiny vial in the center and an international symbol on the outside designating it as containing highly radioactive material.

Before applying the shipping label, Fatima had one more step to complete. She left the shipping room and placed the box on the floor outside the door. With her Geiger counter in hand, she walked to the end of the hallway. Kneeling and pointing the sensor at the box twenty-five feet away, she turned on the device. The reading was less than one Gy, meaning Fatima was cleared to ship the box and would not need to rewrap it.

Fatima repeated this process twenty-two more times, placing the boxes in the corner of the shipping room where FedEx would collect them later that day. These shipments would make their way to medical centers and research laboratories all over the world, including to the Cleveland Clinic in Abu Dhabi, United Arab Emirates. That shipment would never reach its intended destination.

10

"You're dead to me," Tamara proclaimed as she stood and threw the dozen long-stemmed roses at him. The roses hit him in the chest and fell in his lap.

"I don't want to see you ever again," this time bringing her voice several octaves higher, while fighting back the tears.

"And get out of my apartment!"

She was screaming, of course, at Leosha Simakov, her lover and roommate of the past couple of years and someone she considered a potential long-term investment. It was now clear why the two were such a good match, so incredibly compatible that he could complete her sentences, and she could instinctively know what he needed from her, whether it be compassion, objective advice, or just a good fuck. They *were*, in fact, soulmates, except for one important detail that was left out during the full disclosure period of their initial courtship. Leosha had just confessed to Tamara over breakfast that he was an agent with the Mista'arvim, a branch of the Israeli Defense Forces focused on counterterrorism, with a similar mission to Shin Bet. The key to the success of Mista'arvim was the ability of agents to assimilate with the local Arab population by working undercover. He was so effective even Tamara was oblivious to how he spent his days.

Unlike Tamara, who came to Israel intending to join the intelligence services, Leosha was specifically recruited. Mista'arvim spotted him while he was working as a waiter in the historic Metropol Hotel in downtown Moscow. Once Gorbachev broke up the USSR in 1991, Israeli agents fanned across the region to find the most promising young people to join the agency. His rugged good looks, dark skin, and ability to speak Russian, Hebrew, and English made him an attractive candidate for the agency. He was only nineteen years old when he was discovered by agents staying at the hotel during the summer of 1994. Ever since, he had played various roles, including a recently arrived Russian and Catholic immigrant, running an import/export business, and looking for attractive women and a good party, which he played particularly well. This became more and more difficult, however, as he got closer to Tamara.

"Look, sweetheart, I wanted to tell you when we first met," he pleaded, "but they wouldn't let me."

"For fuck's sake, why not?"

"*Neshama*, c'mon, you know the two agencies aren't best buddies and don't play well together. They thought I might help them put eyes on Shin Bet, but *I swear to you*, I've not opened that door for them."

While it was not uncommon for agents from the same agency to be involved in an office romance, allowing a relationship across Shin Bet and the Mista'arvim would have required sanctioning at the highest levels. It was obvious that their relationship was not a secret to either agency, despite her efforts to preserve the privacy of her life outside the office. By now, internal affairs probably had a huge file labeled “Simakov/Rosen.”

That morning, Leosha snuck out of the apartment, bought the roses, and practiced his confession, recognizing the impact it would have on the woman he loved more than anything.

Tamara was not sure what to do. Leosha, for all his faults, was the best boyfriend, lover, and companion she ever had. He knew how to prop her up when she was feeling down, and with most of her family back in the U.K., Leosha was the closest thing to family she had in Israel.

She looked at Leosha: His shoulders collapsed into his chest like a dog that just left an unintended present on the carpet.

“I am going to Gali’s place,” he offered quietly. “Call me if you want to talk it out. I love you.”

He walked to the door and closed it gently behind him.

***

Muhammed rose early. As he stood before the mirror, his receding hairline, long face, and even longer beard portrayed a man much older than his years. His brown eyes looked sad, reflective, and tired. He stroked his beard, gently tugging it to lengthen it even farther. Muhammed was only twenty-two, but he could easily pass for a man twice that age.

He bent over the small white sink in the corner of his flat and splashed water on his face as he whispered his morning prayers. From here he would catch the morning services at the mosque in town, then stop at the internet café to check on proceeds from the various internet schemes he was running with his various agents. While at the café, he also wanted to send a wire from the National Commercial Bank to Al Mumin Trading Company, translated as "The Faithful," a name that Muhammed himself recommended to replace the now-defunct Al Zarooni. He would have a light breakfast at the café, meet with his mentor at the university, then head to the airport for his flight to Abu Dhabi where one of his operatives was holding the package originally intended for the hospital system located there. Then he would make the short trip up to Dubai to hand off the package. Following this he would meet with his beloved Jelani.

He shoved his passport and cash in his backpack, as well as some underclothes and deodorant. Wearing a thawb, or tunic as it was called in non-Arab cultures, he could afford to travel light, a wise approach when at any point he risked being detained for questioning. The only problem: He had to hike the garment up to his hips to get on his motorcycle.

***

Tamara stopped for a cup of coffee on her way into Captain Avi's office, or what was known in the department as "the Cave." She was still disturbed about the revelation from Leosha earlier in the day but not sure how extensive the knowledge was about him within the department and not in the mood to find she was the last to know. She set these emotions aside as she approached the Cave. It was time for her scheduled briefing with her commanding officer.

Captain Avi Kaplan was a veteran of the department, leader of several special operations into Lebanon and Gaza, and credited in 1985 with thwarting an assassination plot against then-Prime Minister Shimon Peres. He was a large and intimidating presence when standing before you, six-feet-two-inches tall with a fully shaven head. He was only slightly less scary sitting down. As a way of making him just a bit more approachable, the department turned to calling him "Captain Avi" rather than the more appropriate "Captain Kaplan."

The Cave was lit only by a corner lamp, desk lamp, and the ambient light behind his desk, as he did not care for the fluorescent ceiling light. One wall was covered with assorted plaques for valor and accomplishment, sandwiched in between various photographs of the captain and his unit wearing battle gear in the field and others with him wearing suits, posing with politicians and dignitaries. It spoke to a career that, had it ended a day earlier, would serve as a great tribute to a courageous soldier. The other wall told a different story: pictures and sketches of wanted terrorists, a whiteboard with diagrams trying to connect the suspects, and newspaper clippings that offered clues to the multiple plots being tracked and analyzed. Behind his desk was a window to the outside with shutters drawn. Every square inch of the desk was covered with stacks of paper, so disorganized that only the captain would know how to locate an important document. The captain reclined in his desk chair. He was wearing his standard in-office uniform: gray slacks, black shirt, and blue blazer. The light from his desk lamp illuminated the smooth skin on his head, the contours of his round face, and the wrinkles in his brow. Tamara noticed the scowl on his face as he read the *Jerusalem Post*.

"A Tolerant UAE Is Welcoming Jews into the Country"

He read the headline out loud before turning the paper in her direction and tossing it on his desk, covering two of the many stacks of memos underneath.

"It's bullshit."

Tamara glanced at the headline before making eye contact with her superior officer.

"Captain," she said, "the world is changing. Lots of countries that have ideological differences are now working together." She was painfully aware of how everything coming out of her mouth seemed to be a statement, even a validation, of her relationship with Leosha.

"It would not be a bad thing if it was the *real* thing," the captain replied. "I was there in Dubai in 2018 when the Pakistanis, Saudis, Emiratis, and the Taliban conducted a virtual love fest under the auspices of a peace deal in Afghanistan. It's disgusting. The Emirates will throw their support behind whoever is winning, which changes daily. If I wasn't undercover at the time, I would have brought them all back to teach them a lesson."

The captain's mood made Tamara unsure how the latest intelligence she collected would be received.

"We believe the operation being run out of Riyadh is planning an attack on the homeland."

"What operation?" Captain Avi could be forgiven for not knowing exactly which operation Tamara was referring to. He was always investigating at least a dozen distinct threats.

"You know, the aggregation of weapons that was reported to us by Chad Kirin." Never one hundred percent certain what could be discussed openly, even in an intelligence office, Tamara was careful not to be too specific with details.

"How reliable is the intel?"

"Chad Kirin has been a reliable asset now for over three years. His prior intel has been verified by our own people. We have no reason to believe this time would be any different."

"Fine," the captain conceded as he rose to leave his office. As he did, he launched into a directive he had given countless times before:

"See if you can track any shipments of arms, hazardous materials, and other contraband flowing into that region so we know what they may be capable of. Expect the manifests to conceal the actual material going in. Eliminate the obvious, like perishable produce in refrigerated containers. Look at the total weights and follow the money paying for it."

Then he stopped, looked up for inspiration, and added, "See if Chad Kirin can help identify the provenance of anything suspicious."

Captain Avi left his office with Tamara still sitting there. She did not have an opportunity to explain that her meetings with Chad Kirin were few and far between. More importantly, she lost the opportunity to ask what he (or anyone else) knew about her inter-agency relationship.

***

"Can we trust him?" the Professor asked.

"Unconditionally," Muhammed replied. "Jelani and I have been brothers since he was six years old, and I was twelve. I protected him and guided him on this path. He is the most capable of all my agents. He is also an expert in cybersecurity."

Of course, Muhammed was leaving out one not-so-minor detail about Jelani. But this seemed irrelevant at the time, and the Professor could become alarmed if he knew just how fragile Jelani could be if pushed out of his comfort zone.

"All right then," he replied, "tell me about your plans in Dubai."

Muhammed laid out for the Professor the movement of funds from Jelani's email scam first into the Saudi bank, then through the trading company, and finally landing in an Iranian bank account. As the Professor explained to Muhammed, the Iranians were fully on board with providing financial and logistic support for the operation.

It would be hard to say whether the Professor viewed Iranians as more of a threat than the Americans. Like Muhammed, he was born and raised in Somalia. When the United States intervened in the late 1990s, his world was turned upside down.

First it was Operation Restore Hope, a euphemism for what amounted to a hopeless military intervention into the Somali civil war. The U.S. joined with the UN in this excursion into the country but refused to be led by the UN commander and instead wrote its own rules of engagement. The operation was a public relations nightmare for the U.S., with the 24/7 news cycle demonstrating clearly that American lack of commitment was only making matters worse.

After UN peacekeepers withdrew from Somalia in 1993, the situation deteriorated further. The Battle of Mogadishu, as it later came to be known, was fought on October 3, 1993, between U.S. forces and rebel forces. To the surprise of anyone paying attention, the U.S. suffered significant losses when two Black Hawk helicopters were shot down, and a tense battle ensued to rescue the soldiers who were left behind in the rubble. When the dust settled, nineteen American soldiers were lost, but estimates of Somali casualties were up to two thousand. One of those casualties was the Professor's father, who was caught in the crossfire of a street battle on his way home from the middle school where he served as a principal. The Professor was only ten years old when he lost his father, his best friend.

The Iranians, on the other hand, represented an evil empire on a scale that could not be matched by the U.S. At least the U.S. made the pretense of intervening for humanitarian reasons. The Iranians could not be bothered with such trivial matters when imposing their Shi'ite faith on other parts of the world. It seemed wherever the Professor went, violence followed.

"My son," the Professor said, "does this boy in Kenya understand what we require of him?"

"He knows that the funds are to be transferred to the accounts we have provided him, that is all."

"Very well, and how about our brothers in the U.S.?"

"I have not activated the group in Dearborn yet. I'll do so on my return from Dubai, after I have a closer look at our target."

11

Jelani woke up in his hotel room at the Sheraton Mall of the Emirates and stepped over to the window. In the distance he could see the Burj Al Arab Jumeirah, the region's most exclusive resort, built on its own little island and reaching toward the sky in the shape of a giant sail. Looking directly below his room, he could see the deeply curved roof over what he assumed was the ski slope within the mall. A competent skateboarder would have a good time on that roof, he mused to himself. He drew his face up close to the window until his left cheek was touching the glass and strained to look right to see the rest of Dubai's skyline, including the Burj Khalifa, the world's tallest tower, but his room did not offer that perspective because he was not able to pay the premium required for a city view. That's fine, he thought, he would be underneath it soon enough.

Jelani's appointment with Muhammed was not for several hours, so he washed his feet and face, laid out his sajjada (prayer mat), and began his prayers, facing the west, in the general direction of Mecca.

The Mall of the Emirates was nowhere near the scale of the largest mall in the UAE, the Dubai Mall, but Jelani had never seen Western-style opulence on anything other than the sixteen-inch screen in the internet café of his village. While anyone else would revel in the splendor of a modern mall, for Jelani it was frightening. The crowds, the noise, the lights all served as reminders to Jelani that he was not like everyone else. As he walked in the mall, he hugged the sides, almost rubbing against the glass of each retail shop he passed. He kept his head down, as he did most times, and tried not to bump into anyone. After only twenty minutes, he had enough and turned back toward his hotel, attached to the mall via an elevator at one end. Jelani decided the best place for him would be at the mosque, where he expected a more serene and sacred environment. He had enough time to visit the mosque before his meeting with Muhammed later in the afternoon.

The metro system in Dubai was easy enough to understand. As Jelani consulted the map, it was clear you would merely take the metro directly into downtown Dubai and walk from there. He had converted a few shillings at the airport, but instead of using the vending machines in the metro station to obtain a ticket, he decided to approach the booth where a young lady in uniform was assisting tourists to ensure they made the right purchase based on their destination.

"Jumeirah Mosque," he said on reaching the booth window.

"Five AED," the attendant replied.

Jelani slid a coin into the metal chute under the booth window, and the attendant returned a small ticket.

"Around the corner, to your right," she offered while pointing to the "Downtown Dubai" sign hanging from the ceiling.

Jelani went up the escalator to the raised platform to wait for the train, bracing himself for the inevitable crowds that were likely to be meeting him once the doors opened.

As he waited, more people arrived on the platform. His gaze from left to right revealed posters for products, announcements of movie releases, and offers for apartments. All signs were in Arabic and English; the station was spotless. The people were well dressed, either in contemporary Western clothes or more traditional Arabic gowns. Virtually everyone was either staring at phones or lost in whatever sounds were coming from them, flowing through their earpieces. The young girls, he noted, were dressed in provocative outfits, something he had seen in the movies but never up close.

The train came racing into the station but slowed down as it approached the boarding zone. Jelani watched and waited for the cues from others on how best to line up for entering it. He noticed many women with children were lined up to enter a specific car near the front, while people his age were lined up for another. Following them, he stepped onto the train and grabbed one of the rubber straps hanging from above and lining the length of the train.

As the train left the station, Dubai revealed itself. To the left was the coast of the Arabian Gulf, with the domes and minarets of local mosques peeking above the landscape every five hundred meters, and beyond them, the green-gray waters of the gulf. To the right, the creative skyscrapers of Dubai, some going so high that you could not see where they might end. And there, in the distance, was the most spectacular of them all, the Burj Khalifa.

Jelani got off the train and platform only a few minutes after boarding, which was fine with him given the stress of being in such close quarters with so many people. He consulted his map for directions to the mosque, walked down the stairs from the station, and greeted the extreme temperatures of Dubai head-on.

The Jumeirah Mosque is one of Dubai's most visited tourist attractions, principally because it is so accessible and welcoming of all visitors. Opened in 1979, the mosque serves as the foundation of the region's "Open Doors/Open Minds Program" of the Sheikh Mohammed Centre for Cultural Understanding. The significance of the mosque's role in promoting religious tolerance was lost on Jelani, who saw the mosque as simply representing a part of his childhood that vanished when he left Somalia.

As he walked up to the grounds, he could see a small group of people already gathered. They formed a semicircle around a man dressed in a ceremonial gown, the mosque's imam, Jelani presumed. Within a few seconds, they disbanded and walked a few meters toward a wall lined with storage cubes for shoes and other articles the tourists may have brought with them. A couple of young priests handed out thin cloth gowns to the women who would soon join the tour inside of the mosque. Jelani caught up to the group and quietly placed his sandals inside one of the cubes.

The group followed the imam into the mosque, with Jelani trailing behind. Once inside, the imam directed everyone to sit around the perimeter of the main hall so that he could address them. He began with a welcome:

"*As-Salaam-Alaikum,*" he said with a broad smile.

The imam stood in the center of the mosque and in front of the mihrab, the center stage of the prayer hall, facing Mecca. A robe concealed most of his body, but it was clear that he was very thin. His skin was dark brown, which made for a dramatic background against his thin gray beard. His eyes were deep and dark but exuded a gentle demeanor, befitting his role. His arms were in front of him, each hand holding the other opposing wrist. He looked like a stone pillar that would not topple no matter the force.

"Welcome to the Jumeirah Mosque," he said.

The imam explained the practices of the Muslim faith to the visitors, pointing out the significant aspects of the mosque, including where the worshippers would sit, familiar prayers and expressions, and the relevance of the Quran. These were all familiar concepts to Jelani, who instead of following the lecture, spent the time examining the range of people who were part of the imam's audience.

After questions and answers, the imam invited the guests to explore the mosque on their own.

"Please," he explained next, "first join us for tea and biscuits outside the prayer hall."

Jelani realized he had not eaten anything that day but a few crackers he carried in his luggage. He followed the rest of the crowd to the table set up outside the prayer hall, content to wait his turn until he saw a safe path to the table.

He eventually saw an opening, but as he approached, a woman waiting for her companion to finish preparing her tea turned around to face him. It was a development Jelani had not considered in the range of possible alternative scenarios.

"And where are you from?"

Jelani came face to face with the woman. He realized he could not escape.

"Kenya," he answered instinctively.

"Oh, I hear that Kenya is beautiful! My name is Barbara, what's yours?"

"Jelani," he replied, forgetting for the moment that he was traveling under an assumed name. *Barbara*, he thought. *Bar* combined with *Bara* was as poetic a name as he had ever heard; the repetitive syllables conveyed a form of symmetry and naturally appealed to Jelani's need for order.

Barbara continued to speak to Jelani about her limited knowledge of Jelani's adopted homeland, but he did not hear any of it. Instead, his eyes were focused on what he recognized around her neck as the Star of David. Jelani understood this was a symbol of the Jewish faith and the defining characteristic of the Israeli flag. His eyeballs grew in proportion to the shock he felt, coming face to face with a Jew for the first time in his life.

"You are Jewish," Jelani interrupted her, stating his observation as a fact, not a question.

"Well, yes," she replied with a slightly startled expression, not entirely clear if Jelani's claim was a threat or an innocent observation. "We are visiting from London. We came to see the opening of B'nai Moshe, the new synagogue in Dubai."

Jelani took a tiny step back to observe Barbara further. She was dressed very modestly, in a bright blue dress, his favorite color. The dress fit tight around her waist and ran down below her knees, and she had open-toed sandals on her feet. She had smooth, shoulder-length brown hair, a soft, pale complexion, bright blue eyes embraced by thick eyelashes, and thin eyebrows. She was wearing lipstick but no other makeup, and she clearly did not need it. She was probably no more than thirty years old, traveling with a female companion. To Jelani, she was one of the most beautiful women he had ever seen. And yet, she was Jewish.

Jelani was speechless and without a plan. As difficult as it was for him, he looked the woman in the eye and said with a forced smile, "Okay, thank you," which did not fit the conversation at all but allowed him an opportunity to escape without appearing rude.

"Nice to meet you!" she yelled back, waiting for him to turn around one last time. Jelani didn't notice that Barbara took a picture of him as he turned back to acknowledge her and again as he walked away.

Jelani wandered the grounds, as far from the crowd as he could get. His worldview was changing at breakneck speed, and it was hard to handle. *Jewish people look just like us!* he thought. He had been exposed to stereotypes casting Jews as controlling business and banking, but he never imagined that they could be so warm, friendly, and even beautiful.

For the next fifteen minutes, Jelani walked in circles around the grounds of the mosque. He would meet Muhammed in another hour, but he wanted first to speak privately with the imam. This was his chance to clear up in his mind what seemed a contradiction. *Are we that different from the Jews?* he wondered.

Jelani returned to the prayer hall to seek out the imam. He was nowhere to be found. A young priest told him the imam had left the grounds but would return later that afternoon. A private talk would have to wait.

***

The Dubai Frame was a short taxi ride from the Jumeirah Mosque. Completed in 2018 and standing 150 meters high, it was one more expression of Emirate superlatives. The UAE already boasted the largest mall, tallest building, largest man-made island, so why not the largest gold-plated picture frame?

The Frame had an elevator on one side, and at the top, visitors could walk along and see far into the distance on either side. A glass floor allowed you to look straight down. Foreigners were known to make fun of the Frame, but it did have a symbolic purpose. From one side the view was predominantly that of the old city—deteriorating and drab low-lying structures representing how the region has looked for centuries. Domiciles made from mud and wood. The old market, a labyrinth of small stalls under the protection of a long, brown, decaying tarp. From the other side, spectacular skyscrapers, the metro, the highways, the beaches, and the glamour that represented "The Riviera of the Arab World." The Frame gave a view to Dubai's past and future, and indeed all of the UAE, depending on where a person looked.

By the time Jelani stepped off the elevator at the top of the Frame, Muhammed was already waiting near the center. Jelani walked along the top of the Frame, past a group of British tourists focused on the view. Only one person on the floor, about midway down the long hall, was turned with the view of the city to his back. Jelani instantly recognized his friend and walked quickly toward him. The two hugged. They did not notice one of the tourists in the crowd taking a picture of their embrace.

"My little brother," Muhammed started, "praise Allah that we are together again. Was your journey here at all difficult?"

"I'm fine. We are together. Nothing else matters," Jelani replied, content to forget the stress and anxiety of the past couple of days.

"Do you think you may have been followed?"

Jelani had not considered the possibility but instinctively shook his head in the negative.

Muhammed kept his arm around Jelani as the two turned back toward the view. They both felt most comfortable looking out on the old city.

"My little brother," Muhammed continued, "we don't have much time."

Jelani realized that while they had an important mission, nothing so important should ever be rushed.

"What do you require of me?" he returned.

"The money that you've collected for the Muslim brothers, we need you to send it to a new depository, in Iran."

"But Iran is our enemy."

"My little brother, you may have heard: 'The enemy of my enemy is my friend.' We are all in a struggle to redistribute wealth to our Muslim brothers. We require assistance from the Iranians to do so. Do you understand?"

"I do." He didn't.

Muhammed continued: "We have three enemies: The Iranians, the Zionist Jews, and the Americans. In the coming days, we will exact revenge on all three of these demons. We will make a statement for the world that our brothers will not be subjected to religious persecution by the Iranians, and we will prove to the Americans that we alone will determine our destiny as a people. The conflict will start and end on our terms. This will be an attack that will fundamentally alter the world order of things."

Jelani listened to Muhammed but struggled to connect the pieces. All he could derive from Muhammed's lecture was that the email scam he conceived, originally focused, harmlessly enough, on the redistribution of wealth for the benefit of his Muslim brothers, was being sucked into a larger, more nefarious plan that would somehow become violent. Muhammed realized he needed to reframe the story he was sharing with his fragile friend.

"My brother, please do not concern yourself with the details of all this activity, for I am being supported by many others that have joined us in this struggle. For now, I simply need you to direct funds to this account." He gently took Jelani's right hand and placed inside it a folded piece of paper. "All the instructions are there."

Jelani placed the piece of paper in his pocket.

The two walked slowly along the top of the Frame, Muhammed continuing to keep his arm on the shoulder of his younger friend. They did not speak. The dynamic between them had been changed, perhaps forever. They both knew it.

Once outside the Frame and about halfway to the street, they embraced again.

"My little brother, I must now go to further our preparations. I will be in touch with you soon. Be careful but know that you are loved. By Allah, by your wonderful family, and by me. Enjoy your time in Dubai."

With this, Muhammed turned and stepped toward a black Mercedes waiting outside the Frame. Just before getting into the back seat, he paused, turned again, and walked back to Jelani, who had not moved.

"One more thing, my brother," Muhammed said, "from now on, you must assume that someone is always watching your movements." With this, he returned to the car and was whisked away.

Jelani watched the Mercedes leave the circular drive where taxis were waiting for tourists leaving the Frame. He felt that he needed the guidance of the imam more than ever and took the next available taxi back to the mosque.

***

"How may I help you, my son?" the imam asked. Jelani found him hunched over his desk in the corner of the Jumeriah Mosque.

"My imam," Jelani started, "I have many questions."

"Well, I may not be qualified to answer all of them but go ahead."

"Tell me," Jelani continued, "what is the difference between the Quran and other biblical texts?"

What the imam said next hit Jelani like a brick against his head.

"They are all the *same* stories, with the *same* characters."

"But the Jews are the enemy of the Muslims, aren't they?" Jelani objected.

"My son, the Jewish story is our story. We have the same struggles. Our Allah is the same."

Jelani just stared at the imam, confused.

"Look," the imam said, "our Allah, or our *God* as the English call it, is derived from 'al-ilah,' which is the Hebrew word for God. We are all part of what we call the Abrahamic religions. Abraham is the founder of the principle of one Allah, one God. The Jews, Christians, and Muslims all want to think of Abraham as being the founder of *their* faith. Honestly, it doesn't matter. It's all the same story as told in the Quran, the Bible, and even the Torah, and that is what matters most."

"My son, what other questions do you have?"

Jelani stood still, staring at the imam. Once more, his view of the world was being reshaped. His head was spinning out of control. He was dizzy. He had not eaten anything for over ten hours.

12

"Your turn!" Kristen egged on Myles to take another whiskey shot. Instead of studying as they had planned to do, the two ended up at Dooley's along with Kristen's roommate, Kelli, and her boyfriend, Greg. Myles felt oddly connected to Kristen merely because of the other couple, as it seemed to imply his status was not far from where Kelli and Greg were right now, making out in the corner of the bar. The bar was packed with students, loud rock music, beer flowing freely, and an atmosphere that was intoxicating even if you *weren't* drinking.

Kristen was wearing a tight red T-shirt and jeans, both showing off her athletic figure, with slightly damp hair from a shower taken about an hour before. She went straight from her dance class to the shower and suggested the detour to the bar when Myles came to pick her up. It was her roommate's birthday, which served as a good enough reason to put off studying one more night.

"I'm done," he confessed, "I'm toast." As much as Myles wanted to impress Kristen with his tolerance for alcohol, he had the presence of mind to realize that if he got drunk tonight, she would not likely respect him much tomorrow. Besides, she looked so incredibly awesome tonight that Myles enjoyed fantasizing they were a couple, and this was a goal that required a plan that alcohol could easily derail.

Kristen made the first move. "Can we go back to your place? Kelli and Greg are going to want some privacy for at least the next few hours."

Myles did not need time to consider the calculus of how his roommate might work into this scenario. "Sure."

"Wait right here." Kristen walked over to her roommate, whispered something into her ear, and came back toward Myles with a smile that said, "I'm yours for tonight," or at least this is what Myles hoped was the intended message. She looped her right arm around his left. The two walked out into the cold and headed for his dorm.

Making out in a dorm, let alone anything more intense, is a complicated matter. For one thing, there is the nonstop partying in the hallway, the intense attention whenever a new face, particularly a girl's face, comes on an all-male floor, and then there is the roommate. For Myles, the roommate issue was easily handled because John was almost certainly going to be MIA until the early hours of the morning. He had another advantage: His dorm room was one of the closest to the outside exit.

The couple quickly made their way into Myles's room, undetected by the other students socializing about midway down the hall. Closing the door, the two were alone. Again, Kristen made the first move, pulling Myles close to her and closing her eyes, inviting him to kiss her. She had just enough alcohol in her to be a tad promiscuous. "Mmmm," she cooed, "you're a good kisser." Myles guided Kristen to his bed where the two collapsed, wrapped in each other's arms with no light between them.

Myles woke up the next morning, Kristen by his side. He turned his head slowly to the other side of the room, where John slept. He must have come in after they fell asleep. Myles could not have asked for a better roommate.

Turning his head back toward Kristen caused her to wake up. She smiled, and Myles was dazzled by how gorgeous she was, even at this hour. He pointed to John so Kristen would realize they were not alone. She slithered out of the bed, grabbed one of Myles's shirts, and left the room, seeking out the women's bathroom down the hall. If it weren't so early, she would have caused a stir by walking around in nothing but a man's shirt.

By the time she returned, Myles had made a small pot of coffee, one of the few things he could prepare in his room. The two talked quietly about school, classes, and professors they liked and disliked. Kristen asked Myles to check on the next philosophy assignment as maybe they could work on it together before she had to head back to her dorm.

Myles opened his laptop while Kristen looked over his shoulder. The assignment was sent by email and rested just a few lines above an email titled, "My dear friend."

"Who is your dear friend?" Kristen inquired with a touch of sarcasm.

"It's one of those email scams, you know, he has a couple billion dollars of my money."

"I've heard about a new one going around."

Myles explained his philosophy to Kristen about these schemes, toying with some of the bad guys as a form of entertainment.

"Let me borrow your computer for a sec."

Myles got up from his desk, and Kristen slid into his chair. He sat on the bed and watched as Kristen logged him out of his email and logged into her own. Before doing so, she copied the sender's email address, then opened a new email from her own account.

"We know who you are. Your cover is blown. We are coming for you. It's over." She smirked, clicked send, then closed the laptop.

***

We have a problem, Jelani thought as he read the email on a new laptop that Muhammed had suggested he purchase in advance of his trip. It was late, and he was in his room marveling at the lights of Dubai and preparing for his return trip home the following day.

Jelani searched his databases over and over and had no record of a Kristen.Edwards2523@gmail.com. This account was never targeted and therefore should have no knowledge of his operation. Because it was a Gmail account, he had no way of determining whether the person sending it was connected to law enforcement or other agencies he wanted to avoid. His current email campaign was targeting American and British campuses from USC in California to the London School of Economics, and there was no Kristen Edwards in any of his lists. Because of the volume of emails in his campaign, he did not recognize any connection between Kristen Edwards and Myles O'Brien.

He did, however, have a signature line. Like many other university students that would otherwise rely mostly on text to communicate, Kristen was in a similar business communications class as Myles which emphasized the importance of establishing a formal signature line for the purpose of communicating with companies offering a summer internship.

Jelani took a piece of hotel stationery out of the desk drawer in his hotel room and began to write down everything he could find about Kristen.Edwards2523@gmail.com.

1. According to the servers that handled the email, it originated from Washtenaw County, Michigan. Major cities in Washtenaw County include Dexter, Ypsilanti, and Ann Arbor.
2. The signature line showed Ms. Edward's address as 200 Observatory Street, Ann Arbor.
3. Observatory Street contains three dormitories; the address would correspond with the dormitory called "Mosher Jordan."
4. Social media accounts corroborate that Kristen is a university student at Mosher Jordan and there are several pictures of her to aid in identification.

Jelani could not ignore something else: If someone intended to expose the operation that he and Muhammed put in place, would they broadcast this to him in advance? Jelani knew this much: He could never really understand nor anticipate the actions or motivations of others.

Jelani took his carefully prepared notes and sought out the hotel's business center, which was still open. He considered putting all the information into an email, but he doubted the hotel's internet was fully secure, and he worried about an email being traceable or reproducible. Instead, he requested a DHL label and, using his fake credentials, prepared the label for sending to Muhammed's home in Dammam. He dropped the notes in the envelope and placed the envelope in the pile of outgoing mail. One piece of paper going out to his controller was the safest strategy, and one match could make it go away once Muhammed was done with it.

***

Rabbi Levi stood in the middle of his new office at B'nai Moshe in downtown Dubai. He admired the beautiful rosewood panels that surrounded the room, a testament to the workmanship and sacred nature of the place of worship that was now under his direction. The built-in bookshelves with arabesques were still largely bare but would soon contain the many scriptures, biblical texts, and rabbinical commentaries he had dutifully guarded for so many years. The walls would also soon proudly display the milestones in the rabbi's personal journey to lead a full congregation. He had come a long way from the days of hosting prayer with just a few families in the unmarked communal villa in Umm Suqeim, an upscale residential area in Dubai. Finally, the Jewish community of Dubai had a synagogue it could call its own.

He stepped behind his new desk and settled into the executive chair, one he selected for its ergonomic features that would be kind to the fragile, bent, and twisted seventy-two-year-old spine that he carried around with him. He leaned backward, and the chair supported him as if he were being held in someone's arms. He closed his eyes in meditation and prayer, the first opportunity he had to reflect on his good fortune before he would step into the congregation and lead the prayer for the Sabbath. It was late Friday afternoon, and the sun would soon set, signaling the beginning of the holiest day of the week. After a few minutes, he opened his eyes, slowly stood up from the chair, and left his chambers for the main congregation. In the vestibule between his office and the main hall, he stopped to look in the mirror and adjust his yarmulke and tallit.

Before stepping up to the stage, or bima, to open the service, the rabbi mingled among worshippers who had arrived early. Various leaders within the Jewish community were on hand to congratulate the rabbi and to say *mazel tov* on the opening of the synagogue. He posed for pictures, something not necessarily condoned in a conservative synagogue, but the occasion was deemed an exception. Tonight was about as joyous an occasion as there ever was for the Jewish community in Dubai.

***

The explosive devices were set in three parts of the main congregation by a janitorial team made up of Pakistani expats: under seats in the middle section and on either side. They detonated almost in unison at 5:25 p.m. local time, just before the service and before most worshippers would be sitting down and potentially discovering them.

Those shredded by shrapnel were killed instantly. The explosion blew several holes in the synagogue ceiling, which caused the enormous gold dome to crash down on others. It was the last thing those gathered under it ever saw. Others lived briefly under the rubble but were asphyxiated by the smoke from the fire that followed.

It was the biggest explosion in the forty-year history of the UAE. The blood, the screams, and the chaos that emerged from the blast would follow the few survivors for the rest of their lives.

By the time of the explosion, Muhammed was already flying over the Arabian Gulf on his way home. It was a clear day and, if he was not so far along on his route, he could have looked down to see the horrifying cloud of black and brown smoke emanating from the grounds of the synagogue. The plume was visible for a hundred kilometers in all directions.

All of Dubai was on edge. Everywhere were the sounds of ambulances, fire trucks, police cars, and other emergency vehicles rushing to the scene of the explosion. The Dubai police flew helicopters and drones at low altitudes around the perimeter of the blast area. The cacophony was so loud that people on the street were unable to communicate with each other and to answer the simple question, "What just happened?"

Black smoke moved across the city streets as if shot from a cannon. Dust, dirt, trash, and soot floated everywhere. The columns of the synagogue were lying on top of each other in a pile of rubble, on top of the gold dome that for a brief period had proudly served as the roof of the building. The pristine neighborhood in which the synagogue stood was unnerved.

Then there were the bodies. Strewn everywhere, all ages, bruised, bloodied, and torn apart by the power of the explosion. Parents lying next to their children, elders still wearing their silk tallits. Severed limbs every few meters. A few people groaning and searching for their last breath; a few more walking slowly and aimlessly, stumbling to find some support from others.

A war zone would not look much different, except that these were all innocent people who had come to Friday evening prayers. Now, about fifty of them lay dead, dying, or critically wounded. And among them, beneath a wooden platform that was once the *bima,* the center stage of the synagogue, lay a woman in a bright blue dress, traveling with a fake UK passport in the name of Barbara Klein. In reality, she was an Israeli agent by the name of Tamara Rosen.

***

Captain Avi's elbows rested firmly on his desk. His hands held his head. His eyes were closed. Losing an agent was always difficult; he considered each a member of his family, a part of his flock.

How old was she? he thought. *I didn't hardly know her.* The anguish he felt was palpable and all too familiar.

What was she doing in Dubai? He then remembered the brief discussion with Agent Rosen a few days earlier. She was pursuing intelligence on the acquisition of weapons in Saudi Arabia. She had found what looked like a listing for remote detonators on a manifest for a shipment en route to a warehouse in Dubai. They had talked about the political situation there. He told her to follow the money. She was doing her job.

A large manila envelope sat on Avi's desk, including Tamara's personal effects: a necklace, friendship ring, tube of lipstick, plane tickets, and her phone. In front of his desk was another officer.

"Captain," he asked gently. "How do you want to handle it? Her parents live in Birmingham, in the UK."

Avi lifted his head, wiping the tears in his eyes. He slowly stood up from his desk and walked over to the window, rested his arm on the windowsill, and stared out at the horizon.

"I'll contact the parents," he replied, his back to the agent. "Get the cellphone into forensics and get inside her apartment. Find out what she knew.

"And bring me Leosha."

13

The 24/7 news cycle wasted no time in prioritizing coverage of the attack. BBC, CNN, and Al Jazeera all had correspondents in either Dubai or Abu Dhabi already, and each set up shop near the site of the destroyed synagogue. By Monday morning, when weekend news summaries are consolidated with the stock market's opening, nobody had claimed responsibility. That left correspondents, anchors, pundits, and analysts to start floating theories of their own.

The B'nai Moshe synagogue was a collaboration between the crown prince of Dubai and the local Jewish community that had remained in the shadows of the Arab nation until very recently. It was estimated that only two hundred to three hundred Jews lived in all of the UAE, but the anticipation of a new synagogue brought many of them out to celebrate. Ironically, many Jewish families were attracted to the UAE not only because of careers in banking, technology, healthcare, and the arts but as a way of escaping the constant fear of terrorist attacks from Hamas and other Palestinian militant groups determined to kill Israelis. The name jointly selected for the synagogue was intentional; Moses, or Musa in

Arabic and Moshe in Hebrew, is named 135 times in the Quran, more often than any other biblical character.

***

Somewhere in the basement of a heavily fortified government building, a young Israeli analyst sat at his desk in a dark cavernous room in which at least five other staff members worked. It was ten thirty, and he would not have noticed even if other people were working this late. The faint light from his computer monitor revealed the contours of his face. He was focused on the cell phone laid upon the table and connected by cable to his computer. As he imported the photos from the phone, he documented each picture, starting with the most recent:

Saturday, 12 November:

1: Agent Rosen pictured with Rabbi Joseph Levi (deceased) from B'nai Moshe, appears to be before services. Corroborated subject with file photo.

2: Agent Rosen pictured with local worshipper (deceased) at B'nai Moshe, possible friend or local associate. No file photos to corroborate.

3: Group picture of several worshippers (all confirmed deceased, pending further identification), likely taken by Agent Rosen at B'nai Moshe.

Friday, 11 November

1: Two men of potentially Arabic origin, speaking privately, at the Dubai Frame, a popular tourist attraction. No file photo to collaborate.

2: Young man, potentially of Arabic or more likely African origin due to complexion, at the Jumeriah Mosque, Dubai. Subject was also seen at the Dubai Frame in preceding picture.

Tuesday, 2 November

Agent Rosen with Israeli asset Chad Kirin (a.k.a. Unicorn), taken on cruise ship in Gulf of Aqaba. Subject confirmed via file photo.

The analyst continued to catalog the photos. When he finished, he would compare photos Tamara Rosen had taken with those stored on the Interpol database, which had a computer application that would present the best matches for comparison. He paused to refresh his coffee at the mini-kitchen at the back of the office. It was going to be a long night.

***

Muhammed parked his motorcycle on the side of his flat and came around to the front entrance as the sun was about to set in Dammam. A large white envelope sat on his doormat. He did not appreciate that one of his contacts might use an express mail service that was traceable and sent a clear message to neighbors that he likely had contacts outside the Kingdom. He scooped up the package and held it to his chest, then examined his door frame carefully. The tiny wood chip he had jammed between the bottom of the door and the frame was barely visible and remained undisturbed, confirming that nobody entered his flat while he was away. Once inside, he tossed his backpack on his bed, sat next to it, and opened the package.

The package was sent from the Sheraton Mall of the Emirates Hotel in Dubai. Muhammed instantly recalled this as where Jelani had stayed, and he was relieved that at least Jelani had taken the minimum measure to prevent traceability, both in location and sender's identity.

He studied the handwritten notes carefully. Jelani could be prone to exaggeration as a somewhat naive agent. The revelation that someone may know about their activities, with a potential tie to the FBI, was not something Muhammed felt he could ignore. He would discuss the matter with the Professor at their meeting the following morning.

After his evening prayers, he opened CNN.com on his laptop to see the continuing coverage of the synagogue bombing in Dubai. Images from the blast site, still smoldering, blanketed the screen with the caption

DUBAI SYNAGOGUE BOMBING – 52 CONFIRMED DEAD

running across the bottom. Still, no terrorist organization had claimed responsibility, leaving the anchors to speculate on every possible motive:

"Why would an extremist group target an Arab country?"

"Was Dubai simply an easier target than Israel? Or is this a warning to the UAE that their

progressive views are not welcome in the Arab world?

"How will the UAE and Israel respond?"

"Why has no group claimed responsibility? Could this be the beginning of a new extremist playbook?"

Muhammed watched the coverage with rapt attention, sitting on his bed. He did not betray his feelings by showing any emotion. The job was not finished. On the contrary, the UAE was only one of a handful of Arab countries that had normalized relations with Israel, joined by Sudan, Bahrain, and Morocco, and in time, all had to be punished for it. He pulled his legs onto the bed, shut off the light, and closed his laptop. It had been a long day, and he fell quickly asleep.

***

"My friends, more blood has been spilled in the name of 'religion' than for any other cause," the Professor proclaimed to his class at the Bin Faisal University. "From the crusades at the beginning of the first millennium to contemporary times in Northern Ireland, where the Catholics and Protestants continue to massacre one another, this is the one constant in the history of our world." The Professor, if anything, was known for his provocative views on campus, and this was one reason his classrooms were almost always at capacity. The students were mesmerized by the Professor's lectures, which often were laced with outrageous proclamations and predictions. In the back of the room stood

Muhammed, who listened closely as the Professor continued to deliver his personal manifesto.

"And so I say to you, my children, you must recognize that the perpetual tensions between tribes, whether they be feral or civilized, in the West or here in what they call 'the Middle East,' is a necessary condition not only for survival but for advancement of our species. In this regard, the Western anthropologist Darwin got it right, but he did not go near far enough."

With that, the classroom bell rang, and the students vacated the auditorium. Only Muhammed remained, and he walked silently with the Professor through the side door to the courtyard outside the lecture hall.

"I want to talk to you about loyalty," the Professor broke the silence as students passed by in both directions. Behind them, the classroom building that included the lecture hall stood ten stories high, with orange bricks surrounding a mural containing the likeness of his holiness Ibn Saud, the first monarch of Saudi Arabia and recognized as the country's founder. Tall queen palm trees lined the perimeter of the building and stood every twenty meters along the walkway between the lecture hall and other campus facilities. Kiosks along the way posted announcements of campus activities, offers for babysitting and guitar lessons, and invitations to join various prayer groups. It was well-known that many of the so-called prayer groups were focused on pro-democracy activism. It was less known that others were a cover for extremist activities, including the one that Muhammed was coordinating.

Muhammed was wearing a T-shirt and jeans today, an effort to mix in better with the more progressive student body, few of whom wore traditional gowns. The pant legs of his jeans were turned up, and he wore sneakers but no socks. The T-shirt he had picked up the day before celebrated the 2021 World Expo in Dubai. On campus, he could be mistaken for an older graduate student. In reality, he had just coordinated the deadliest attack on innocent civilians in the Arab world.

The Professor wore a dark brown suit, yellow shirt, and matching brown tie. While most in his academic circle wore either traditional gowns or collarless shirts, the Professor preferred the Western form of dress.

"Our little demonstration in Dubai was a success," he said quietly. "The next stage in our campaign will require the utmost secrecy, and you must report to me any contact you have outside our existing network. Do not keep any information from me, no matter how trivial."

Muhammed told the Professor about the message received from Jelani. He shared that there was no proof that the woman known as Kristen Edwards was aware of the true nature of their activities, despite the loose connection to the FBI. However, the inability to trace her identity to any existing email campaigns was cause for concern, and the name was very common, so it could be difficult to find her. Jelani had not connected Kristen to the same Myles O'Brien that was in his existing email scam. Had he done so, the manhunt for Kristen might have been rendered unnecessary.

***

Myles was in the middle of a challenging calculus assignment when he heard a faint knock on his door. Kristen had just left, so he presumed she had forgotten something. He was excited to be able to tease her, hold her, kiss her, and perhaps persuade her to stay longer. Just a day after having her sleep over, he was smitten and excited at what might be the first girlfriend of his college years. He took the four steps necessary to get from his desk to his dorm room door.

His brother Richard, a much larger presence than the petite Kristen, stood there, a six-pack hanging from his left arm.

"Richard!" Myles lunged forward to hug his brother, drawing attention from his dormmates. "Mom told me you might be coming!"

Myles pulled Richard into the room and shut the door. Inside, Richard looked even larger than Myles remembered him, due mostly to the fact that the dorm room itself was so small that whenever there were two people in it, conditions felt a bit intimate. And the fact Richard was wearing a suit contributed to his larger-than-life image at this moment.

"It's good to see you, bro," he replied. "Here, this is for later."

Myles grabbed the beer and tossed it inside his mini-fridge that was wedged between his bed and John's. Good timing, he realized, as the six-pack that had been in there just a couple of days before was gone.

"What are you doing here?" Myles was already planning to tell Richard about Kristen but felt that to blurt it out now would demonstrate just how immature he was. No, he'd save this news for later.

"Checking out a lead on some bad actors, potentially in Dearborn. That's all I can say right now. It's great to be back on campus again. I'd rather be here than ask you to come to mom and dad's place. How often do I get to throw back some beers with my little brother? Especially since you're barely old enough to drink!"

"Can you stay until this evening? There is someone I'd like you to meet."

A campus house party was the best option of all on a Saturday night in Ann Arbor. No other environment felt quite as carefree and casual, and the beer was free. If you weren't with someone, chances were good that you would leave with someone. And as the evening wore on, everybody's standards fell just as the object of their affection grew more and more attractive.

Myles texted Kristen to meet him at the planned party on Catherine Street, about three blocks from the graduate library near central campus. The house already had the reputation of being the "animal house" of the university. The Wolverines were playing in South Bend, against Notre Dame, and highly favored. The vibe would be off the charts with students releasing the pent-up energy of studying for finals while celebrating a signature win against a national rival. Kristen acknowledged she would meet Myles at the party around ten. Richard promised to meet there as well after running an errand related to work.

Meanwhile, in Dearborn, a man posing as a university student was receiving coded instructions from his handler regarding a critical assignment. As Richard took his rental car on I-94 East to visit Dearborn, the man was preparing to travel in the other direction, on I-94 West, to track the whereabouts and movements of Kristen Edwards.

14

"Synagogue Bombing Leaves Israel, UAE at Crossroads"

Agent Goodman stared at the newspaper headline in disbelief as television monitors in Detroit's FBI field office streamed the coverage. Detroit had a large Jewish community, Goodman among them, and the news coming from the Middle East was just one more injury following centuries of similar senseless tragedies. She reclined in her chair, closed her eyes, and recited the familiar prayer for the dead.

Goodman slowly opened her eyes as she brought her chair upright. She stood up, grabbed her purse, and headed out the door. She had an appointment with Richard O'Brien and a community leader in Dearborn.

***

Avi walked with purpose into the conference room where his team was assembled and slammed the door behind him with such force that the blinds on the door window popped out and back again. The room was sparsely furnished; a long conference table with chairs, a framed picture of the prime minister on one wall and David Ben-Gurion on the other. A clock that one would have last seen as a student in middle school hung on the third wall, and a whiteboard filled the fourth. The ceiling had one long fluorescent fixture and the floor was tacky linoleum because luxuries had no place in the critical work of the agency.

Senior agents from across the department were seated, and the chair at the head of the table was vacant until the captain claimed it. The badges hanging from the necks of those in the room communicated the relationship they had with one another as employees of Shin Bet. However, one badge did not belong and attracted the attention of everyone else. It was around the neck of Leosha Simakov.

"I've asked Agent Simakov to join the meeting," the captain barked. He did not have to explain why; these were intelligence agents.

"We will dispense with the formalities," he continued. "We've lost one of our own. I know this will be hard for those of you that have grown accustomed to our success in the field, but this should serve as a reminder that we are not invincible."

Avi looked first to his left, expecting each agent to sound off with what they could contribute. "What do we know about the perpetrators of the bombing?"

"They were definitely not Emiratis," the first agent said. "There is too much evidence to the contrary, we know of explosives coming in from outside, and this is a huge embarrassment for the royal family."

Avi was not impressed and looked to the next agent for something useful.

"Security footage provided by the SIA shows a crew on-site that arrived after completion of the synagogue, never seen before, without a known purpose. The images don't appear to show suspects of Emirate origin, but we know that most native Emiratis would not be in any construction-related industries anyway, those jobs are held by Pakistanis and Indians."

The SIA, the intelligence agency of the United Arab Emirates, had established a formal collaboration with the Israeli intelligence apparatus. The event presented an opportunity for the SIA to learn from one of the most respected intelligence operations in the world.

"Did the crew have to complete any paperwork for the work they were supposedly doing?" Avi pressed further.

"I'm sure they did, but any paperwork would have been destroyed in the bombing, anyway. The SIA have not come forward with anything like that."

Avi remained unimpressed and was now looking across the long table to the next agent.

"Captain, we think there may be a connection between this bombing and a money-laundering operation that Agent Rosen was looking into. Her purchasing request for tickets to Dubai indicates this is what she was working on. You approved the travel." Avi did not like being reminded of what he should have known already, but this was the first nugget of information he regarded as a lead.

Finally, he turned to Leosha.

"Did she mention any of this to you?"

Leosha was still feeling the pain of his loss, compounded by the angry eyes on him at this moment, as if he were somehow responsible for what happened to Tamara Rosen.

"No, Captain, I am sorry, she did not. She never spoke about her work to me. That was the arrangement, and I honored it."

Then Leosha got to the hard part.

"You may know this by now. She discovered I was with the Mista'arvim just a few days ago and threw me out of her apartment. She left for Dubai after I was effectively kicked out of her life."

The captain decided not to pursue how his cover was blown but to use all the leverage he now had to enlist Leosha's help to find the terrorists.

"So that's it?" The captain's head panned the room, looking each agent in the eye. "Is there anything else?"

For what seemed like an eternity, the room was as quiet as if it were empty. Then, a technician assigned to the team, seated outside the chairs organized around the table, tentatively raised his voice.

"Sir, I was part of the team permitted on-site at the blast site in Dubai. I am trained in explosives and in anticipating their after-effects."

"Yes, and so?"

"Sir, there were detectable traces of radioactive cesium chloride at the blast site."

"And?" Avi's patience was not unlimited.

"Sir, in small amounts such as what we detected in Dubai, it's relatively harmless, but depending on dispersion of larger quantities, it could create casualties on a much larger scale than what we saw in Dubai. If it were the source material in a dirty bomb . . ."

Avi's face spoke volumes.

"Get the fuck out of my conference room, GET out! All of you! Find out who is responsible for this, or you won't be with this department much longer because you will have proven yourself useless to the agency and especially useless to me."

Chairs began to jettison backward as agents got the message, just as the captain made one last demand.

"Simakov, sit down. You're not going anywhere."

***

On the way to his car, Richard googled "how many mosques are in Dearborn?" and his phone returned the following:

***Dearborn** Michigan can boast two thriving business districts, ten **mosques**, two Islamic schools, and an impressive range of village clubs, advocacy groups, business associations, and human service agencies.*

His appointment, set up by Agent Goodman, was at the Islamic Center of America, the largest mosque in the United States, on Ford Road in

Dearborn. As he pulled into the parking lot, he faced the enormous gold dome flanked by minarets, and for a moment, could easily forget that he was on American soil. The structure was quite impressive, even to a man that grew up in the shadows of the Roman Catholic Church.

Richard wandered around the grounds a bit. He arrived early to do as much reconnaissance as possible before the meeting. As he was reading a poster in Arabic, he received another text from Courtney. "*Call me, I need to talk to you.*" Richard made a mental note to call Courtney later in the day, but what he really wanted was for her to stop pinging him. As he approached the Office of Community Affairs, he saw Goodman waiting for him outside the entrance.

"Richard," Goodman said to him softly so as not to be overheard. "Allow me to lead the questioning, but feel free to join in if you sense an opportunity to gain additional intel."

"Sounds good," Richard replied, careful not to repeat the line he overused when they had first met. The two entered the oversized lobby of the office. The cavernous room was dimly lit and lightly furnished.

"Good afternoon," said a slight man, no more than five feet tall, who approached them with outstretched arms. The man was likely in his mid-seventies, graying, with a salt-and-pepper beard. He wore a pair of spectacles that sat a bit crooked on his tired face and a noticeably old, pinstriped blue suit that was much too big for him. He offered a cautious smile as he held both of Richard's hands in his own, then repeated the exercise with Goodman. "I am Doctor Basheer Aktar. I am the director of community affairs. We've been expecting you."

Aktar guided them into the center. It was opulent by Muslim standards, with red curtains lining the walls; they displayed rhythmic linear patterns of scrolling and interlacing foliage, typical arabesques. A long counter was the focal point of the center. It was here that residents of the community would register for programs and activities. Because the sun had set and afternoon prayers had ended, the center was essentially deserted. The three sat in a corner where three oversized, heavily padded chairs were arranged around a small coffee table.

Aktar went first. "My friends, we are honored by your visit. How may I help you?"

"Thank you for seeing us, we really appreciate it," Goodman replied, watching carefully to assess the baseline behavior of her subject. "As you know, we are with the local branch of the FBI, but investigating a crime that ignores all borders."

"And what might this crime involve?" Aktar was not a novice. He was skilled at navigating these inquiries while simply appearing naive.

"You know how kids can get themselves into trouble these days." Goodman decided to take the theoretical route rather than jumping to anything that might appear accusatory or threatening. "Using the internet to persuade vulnerable people to give up their security, you know, their savings."

Aktar was indeed familiar with these schemes and relieved that his guests were not suggesting his community was behind the incident in Dubai, as this was the more typical conversation he would be having with certain people from local law enforcement.

"Tell me," Goodman continued, "do you feel any of the youth in the community might be attracted to this type of activity?"

"Ms. Goodman," Aktar replied, "here at the center we are focused on providing a positive environment for our children, an opportunity for them to grow and explore new horizons."

"To grow and explore new horizons?" Goodman replied. Richard did not think the statement required further clarification but dared not to interrupt the conversation.

"Yes, of course," Aktar continued. "We offer a range of programs to provide a sense of worth and belonging. We have a variety of them: social programs, prayer groups, and some limited vocational training."

"Vocational training?" Goodman repeated. By now, Richard realized he was witnessing a form of covert interrogation. Sarah was giving Aktar the illusion of control, but he was trapped into revealing more than he had intended.

"Yes, Ms. Goodman, vocational training. Do you see a problem with our center assisting our youth to find an opportunity to fit into society?"

"To fit in?" she asked.

Aktar was getting increasingly agitated by the agent's line of questioning.

"Ms. Goodman, our youth grow up in a society where they feel marginalized, unappreciated, and unaccepted because they don't fit the Judeo-

Christian mold that defines the American family. You can't honestly blame them for feeling they are not welcome here in the U.S."

"It sounds like you believe the conditions might exist for some of the youth here to get involved in a plot to harm Americans."

Aktar recognized he had allowed himself to be led exactly where he did not want to go.

"All I can say is, we at the center do all we can to engage our youth in creating a positive atmosphere in which to learn and grow. I don't think I can help you any more than to stress this fact, which is part of our mission." Goodman could sense that Aktar's body language had transformed from someone feeling in control to someone feeling threatened and intimidated.

Goodman had heard all she needed to confirm the potential for the Muslim youth in Dearborn to be involved in the email scam, or potentially worse. She turned to Richard to allow him to join the conversation.

"How has the community reacted to the bombing of the synagogue in Dubai?" Richard felt the time was right to move the conversation in the direction of current events.

"This is a tragedy, an insult to humanity in the eyes of Allah. My friends, the Quran and indeed our entire community respect the sanctity of life, even among our Jewish neighbors. We condemn this *masa* in the strongest possible terms."

"Dr. Aktar," Goodman said, "if there are members of your community that are involved with this email scam to steal from other vulnerable people, then they are doing so without regard to religion, politics, race, or any other criteria. It is a cowardly act that is creating real harm, potentially robbing seniors of their life savings. If you hear anything that you believe might help us put a stop to it, can I ask that you please contact me?" She handed him a business card.

"Of course, my friends. We in the Muslim community want to live in peace with our neighbors," Aktar replied, offering a line that he often used several times a day.

With that, the three stood, shook hands, and Aktar walked them to the double doors of the center. Richard could not wait to initiate the debriefing, although he could sense that Aktar was watching them from behind the glass, with even more suspicion than when they met.

"That was fantastic," he nearly blurted out. "His answers weren't very revealing but his body language sure was."

"It's FBI interrogation 101," Goodman replied. "A combination of mirroring and labeling. First you repeat back the last few words of every sentence, then you pivot to a provocative conclusion. Human nature is that people love to be heard, and they often won't realize they are giving you valuable intel in the process."

Richard was in awe of Sarah Goodman, and for a moment, thought about asking her to join him on his trip back to Ann Arbor and the house party he planned to attend with his brother. He stopped short of doing so, realizing that it was far too early to consider upgrading their relationship and that had to remain a fantasy—for now.

As the two were leaving the parking lot, they could not help but notice a group of young men loitering in the back of the building. One of them had just left the center and was heading west, in the general direction of Ann Arbor.

And Basheer Aktar retreated to his office to send an urgent encrypted message.

15

Hassan Isa Saliba was born on the fourth of July, 1998, one of five children to a second-generation Iraqi-American family living in Livonia, near Dearborn. He was already significantly overweight at a young age and unemployed. Rather than engaging in sports or girls, as other kids his age did, he became self-conscious and introverted. He found safety and acceptance in the online chat rooms frequented by marginalized Muslim youth seeking an outlet for their frustrations in finding opportunity within the U.S. It is here that Muhammed found him, three years earlier, and recruited him as a potential asset.

Hassan was one of three young men dispatched by Muhammed to seek out and silence one "Kristen Edwards," a threat suspected to be living in the area. The men met in the rear parking lot of the Dearborn Islamic Center to compare information they had received and to fan out to Detroit, Grosse Pointe, or Ann Arbor. Hassan was pulling his 2009 Toyota Corolla into a dormitory parking lot in Ann Arbor just after eight. His notes indicated that Ms. Edwards was a resident at Mosher Jordan dormitory on Observatory Street. Hassan had taped her profile picture to the dashboard of his car just in case he should see her walking in or out of the dorm as he waited.

Hassan positioned himself so that if his target left the dormitory, she would have to walk past the front of his car. He opened a bag of chips and settled in.

***

Leosha opened the door to the glass-lined, soundproof room at the Shin Bet station in Tel Aviv and slid into an office chair in front of two computer screens: one with a permanent link to Interpol and other outside agencies, the other connected to a PC tower and containing files that would never leave the State of Israel without the highest-level authorization. The room was only large enough for two people to sit side by side in front of the computer screens, and it was visible to anyone from the outside so activity inside could be monitored. He was prepared with a thermos of hot coffee, which he placed next to the phone in what little space remained on the desk in front of him.

Before turning on the computer, he noticed his face in the still dark monitor. He lost a woman he loved and saw as a permanent part of his future. Now, she was gone, and he could not help feeling responsible for what might have been poor judgment on her part in the hours following their separation. *Jewish guilt knows no bounds*, he thought. As he stared at the blank screen, Captain Avi walked past the room. Their eyes met briefly, snapping Leosha out of this stream-of-consciousness moment. He leaned over the back of the screen, flipped the switch, and brought it to life.

***

About nine thirty, students began filing out of the dorm, no doubt on their way to either the library, bars, or private parties. Hassan continued to snack on one chip at a time. It would be important to appear natural, he thought to himself. This was his first real assignment for Muhammed and indeed his first foray into the world of espionage, and he was determined not to fuck it up. He practiced the art of simultaneously sourcing a potato chip from a bag on the passenger seat with his right hand while examining each pedestrian carefully, comparing them to the picture taped to his dashboard, and his left arm perched nonchalantly on the steering wheel. He was not expecting what happened next.

"Hey, buddy!" the booming voice came out of nowhere it seemed. Hassan's heart skipped a beat. The large body owning the loud voice was standing next to his door, shining an intensely bright flashlight into the car. It was a campus security guard, who tapped the flashlight on the car window for extra effect. "You can't park here unless you have a pass. You'll have to move. Like right now."

Hassan took a deep breath and nodded compulsively to the security guard while simultaneously cranking the engine to get out of the permit-only parking lot as quickly as possible. He backed up the Toyota, slowly edged the car off the lot and onto the street and turned the corner in search of a spot where he could park and leave the car unattended. One thing he knew for sure: He did not want his car to get a parking ticket.

***

The comparison of photos from Agent Rosen's phones did not yield a direct match against the automated face-recognition application that Interpol developed, so Captain Avi ordered Leosha to undertake a manual review. Leosha put up no resistance. He admired Avi, but he wanted to solve this case for his own reasons.

Comparing Interpol photos with those obtained by Agent Rosen would be tedious, but at least there were some limited selection criteria to focus the scope of the search on Interpol's site. Leosha viewed the filters and made his selections:

Gender: Male

Ethnicity: Arabic

Age: 20-30

Location: Asia

He hit "Submit," and the system conducted its search of profile matches. The hourglass icon made three turns before returning the following message:

1,638 matches found

With images of the two men Tamara had photographed on the right side of the computer screen, Leosha began the comparison search, hitting the return key for every mismatched pair of photos.

***

Hassan found a parking spot about four blocks from the dormitory, downhill from the cross-street where the dorm was located. By the time he parked, he realized that Kristen, if she was even in the dormitory at dinnertime, might be on the other side of campus by now. It was a chilly and humid night, and Hassan could see his breath as he locked his car on the side of the road, under a streetlamp. He hustled as best he could up the asphalt street to get back to the dormitory entrance, but he was not in the best physical condition. By the time he reached the dormitory steps, he was doubled over in pain and breathing heavily.

"Oh God, are you okay?" a voice from above him was speaking.

"I'm fine," he managed. "Thanks. Just went out for a run."

If Hassan's clothes were suitable for a run, he needed a fashion consultant or physical trainer, maybe both. He managed to stand up partially, still panting, hands on his knees, and found himself looking up at three young women staring directly at him, one of them fitting the description of Kristen Edwards and the photo he had in his pocket.

"Seriously, are you okay? You don't look so good," it was Kristen speaking, or maybe the girl next to her, Hassan was not sure, and he was still feeling a bit dizzy. Already, he believed he was failing in his mission.

"Thanks . . . I'm okay," he responded and hobbled away from the girls so that he could reboot his mission. The girls giggled and whispered, then moved in the opposite direction.

***

Close to three hours into his assignment, Leosha needed a break. Staring at the same screen and flipping through pictures of suspected terrorists was beginning to take its toll. The screen read 429/1638 when he surrendered. He stepped out of the glass office and decided to go for a walk. He hoped he would not run into Captain Avi. He stepped outside and took out a cigarette.

"How is it going?" asked Avi, coming from around the corner and extending his lighter to Leosha. Leosha accommodated the light as Avi produced the flame.

"I'm about one-quarter of the way through the matches, based on Arabic men aged twenty to thirty."

"See me in the morning. We need to make a move whether you find something or not."

Ten minutes later, Leosha was in front of the computer again. He had the presence of mind to go back about twenty-five pictures, recognizing that he had fallen into being "unconsciously incompetent" before he took the break. Then, at 414/1638, he saw it. He compared the photos. Then compared them again. He looked at the suspect's profile in a window under the picture:

414/1638: Muhammed Amir Abbas

Aliases: Akeem Abdulla, Ibrahim Kahlili, Farham Gazi Emami

Last known whereabouts: Somalia, Saudi Arabia

Wanted for: extortion, cybercrime, possible terrorist ringleader

Last updated: 25.3.19

"I've got you, you motherfucker," Leosha said quietly, contemplating the gravity of this discovery. He realized the match did not necessarily implicate Abbas in the synagogue bombing, but Tamara would not have snapped the photo if she did not suspect him of something. He picked up the phone to call Captain Avi when he saw in the corner of the screen "Photo 1/6." Without looking where the phone was located, he put down the receiver, and clicked "Next."

More pictures of Muhammed Amir Abbas followed. A driver's license photo, a couple of shots of him apparently unaware a picture was being taken, and a class picture with other students, and what was likely the class professor off to the side, next to the back row. Leosha studied each image of Muhammed carefully, reconfirming the fit. Then he returned to the class photo, hoping to find the other young man from Tamara's photo at the Jumeriah Mosque and Dubai Frame. He scanned the faces, ending up at the back row and the professor standing next to his class. He'd seen that man before.

Leosha turned back to the screen with Tamara's photos. He backed up through them, one at a time, slowly. A picture with the rabbi. A picture with Jewish worshippers, pictures of a young man at a mosque, a picture of Muhammed with the same young man. He clicked to the first photo of the series, an image of Tamara with a man looking down at his phone, confirmed in the notes as the asset "Chad Kirin." Leosha turned back to the class photo, his eyes trained on the class professor. He was looking at the same man.

***

Hassan was familiar enough with the university campus from previous visits to know that his target would likely be headed toward State and Liberty streets, where the bars and libraries were concentrated, so he set out to find her again on the main footpath that students use to head into the campus. He figured that if he could manage to walk at a decent clip that he'd catch up to the three young women who were likely chatting away on their way to whatever function lay ahead. He was right.

Waiting at the crosswalk ahead of him were the three women. Hassan approached slowly, but by the time he was within twenty yards of them, the light had not changed, they were still in the same spot and noticed him approaching.

"Oh, hey, are you feeling better?" one of the girls shouted. Hassan did not answer, he just stood there, making his presence more noteworthy than if he had continued walking toward them. He was officially being a creep now, and the women decided he was to be avoided from that point on. They continued to Catherine Street where they went separate ways, Kristen's friends to a sorority party, while Kristen headed to the house party where Myles was waiting for her.

The residential neighborhood was not as well-lit as the university campus. Streetlights illuminated the path ahead of her, but she was more concerned about what was behind her. She recognized the plump figure following her from about the same distance as before. She had not been to the house where the party was located, but based on the address, she suspected she had about five blocks to go.

Catherine Street had some beautiful homes, many more than a century old, and most converted into multiple dwellings for student rentals. The architecture was grand colonial style, and even if they were rented out, they were well preserved and gave the university an important part of its character. Kristen tried to distract herself from the guy behind her, so she did her best to admire the homes even as she increased her pace toward the party.

Before long, she could hear "Louie, Louie" in the distance, a musical staple at university parties. She looked back to see if the guy was gaining on her, but now she felt confident she would be with Myles by the time he could catch up with her. She was nearing the entrance of the home when she saw Myles on the steps with a red Solo party cup in his hand.

"You're going to have to get me one of those," she said, "but first you're going to have to give me a kiss."

Myles was happy to accommodate her requests and could not be prouder of the fact that he was at a house party with a person he could introduce as his girlfriend. He bent down to put his beer on the step, grabbed her arms, pulled her toward him, and tightly wrapped his arms around her as their lips came together. Kristen forgot all about the man following her, and the two went inside to get warm.

Once inside, it became difficult for Myles and Kristen to stick together. Students were packed in tight, with many dancing in the living room and others lounging around the kitchen. The music was so loud that the house was pulsating with the bass. Half-open bottles of whiskey and gin were on the kitchen table; the keg was in the backyard.

"Let me get you a beer," Myles shouted to her. "Wait here."

"I need to use the restroom," Kristen shot back. "I'll meet you back at this spot." Myles smiled in agreement, and the two fought their way to their respective destinations.

Kristen looked around for the bathroom, eventually finding it at the top of the stairs. Once inside, she settled down, looked in the mirror, and took out a tube of lipstick she had in her front pocket. She felt secure with Myles and happy to be in a relationship with a guy who seemed to be somewhat normal. She looked forward to what the evening might offer the two of them, their first night out together as a couple. The music continued to reverberate as she opened the door and took a step out.

She found herself face to face with the guy who had trailed her.

Hassan pushed her back into the bathroom with both hands, followed her in, and locked the door.

16

By the time Richard turned the corner onto Catherine Street, the alternating red and blue lights made it impossible for him to see the address he was looking for. However, with three police cars and an ambulance, he wagered correctly that the party was close by, or it had been. He parked his car as close as he was able and moved quickly toward the commotion.

When he arrived at the house, two paramedics were rolling a young woman on a stretcher and just about to lift her into the ambulance, a bloody bandage across her forehead, her eyes looking up at the stars above her, seemingly unaware of what was going on. Myles was standing by the doors of the ambulance, looking distraught. A pudgy man sat in the back of a squad car. Students were standing around on the lawn of the house, hands in their front pockets, others making their way back to their dorms and apartments. The music was no longer playing; all house lights were now on. The faint streetlamps shrouded the block in dim light and fog.

"Myles, what happened?" Richard asked when he found his brother.

"She was attacked. They say she is going to be okay. Her name is Kristen. She's my girlfriend." Myles collapsed into his brother's arms, sobbing. "I don't get it; I just don't get it."

Richard held his brother close, trying to assess the situation. A house party that devolved into an altercation? No guys with black eyes? He walked Myles back to his car, arm around him, and put him in the passenger seat.

"Wait here, we will go to the hospital to make sure she's okay, but I want to see what I can find out from the officers first."

Richard gently closed the passenger door and returned to the scene. Canvassing the area with his eyes, he saw several officers taking notes, talking with students, and collecting evidence. He saw a police officer leaning against the car that held the man Richard assumed was a suspect.

"Officer," Richard started out, "can you tell me what's going on here?"

"Who wants to know?"

"FBI," he said tentatively, choosing not to specify which branch or department he represented and hoping this would be enough to elicit some cooperation. If necessary, he'd have to reveal his very limited scope of authority as he did not even carry a badge. Would the fact he was still wearing a business suit and overcoat be enough?

"That young man assaulted the young lady over there," he offered back, pointing toward the ambulance. "If you want to know any more, you'll have to visit the precinct after we book him."

"Thanks. What hospital is she being taken to?"

"I believe she is going to St. Joseph's. We'll need to take a statement from her once she is up to it."

Richard thanked the officer again and returned to his car, where Myles was still in shock.

"Buddy, let's go to a coffee shop, settle down a bit, then head to the hospital to check on her. What's her name again?"

"Kristen."

"Right, Kristen, she's cute. I am sure she'll be fine. She looked alert on the stretcher. In any case, we'll see her at the hospital. First, I want you to tell me what happened."

Richard took Myles to the closest twenty-four-hour coffee shop. Like most university neighborhoods, it wasn't far from the campus. As they settled into a booth, Myles began:

"We met at the party, and I went to get her a beer. She went to the bathroom upstairs, and I guess this guy forced his way in. I've never seen him before, and who knows if he's a student here. Anyway, it's a good thing that so many people wanted to use the bathroom because a bunch of people heard her screaming in there, broke the door down, and tackled this guy. But he had hit her pretty hard already. I don't know, maybe he wanted to kill her. But why? I just don't get it."

"Slow down, brother," Richard cautioned. "If you and Kristen just met, you really don't know what was going on in her life before. Could it be a jealous ex?"

"I don't think so, he did not look like her type. I think he was from India or something. He had dark skin. Not that I'm racist or anything, I'm just saying." Myles put his head in his hands. He was exhausted, but more than anything, worried about Kristen and what was expected of him at this moment.

"Okay, finish up your coffee and let's go see how she is doing."

"Don't you have to go back to New York tomorrow?"

"Brother, I am not going anywhere."

***

Hassan sat on a metal chair at a table in a room with gray cinder block walls. There was nothing on the walls, save for a large rectangle of glass on one side that looked like a mirror but which he correctly presumed was used for observation. It seemed cold in the room, and Hassan was tired, hungry, and scared. It was 1:30 a.m., about forty-five minutes since he was led into the room, when he was visited by Todd Hermann, a detective in the Ann Arbor police department. Hermann walked casually into the room and nodded to Hassan while carrying a folder in one hand and a cup of coffee in the other. He pulled a chair from the opposite side of the table, settled in, opened the folder, and started the interrogation.

"Your name?"

"Hassan."

"Full name?"

"Sorry, Hassan Isa Saliba."

Hermann used his pen to touch the spot on the paper within the folder corresponding with the questions he asked and answers he sought to confirm that his suspect was being honest.

"Where do you live, Hassan?"

"Livonia." Hermann moved his pen down the page.

"What were you doing in Ann Arbor, Hassan?"

"I was invited to a party."

"Are you a student at U of M?"

"No, sir."

"So, who invited you?"

"A friend of mine."

"Who's your friend? Was he at the party with you?"

Hassan could see the ruse was not sustainable. He was out of his league and knew it. His head fell into his hands, his elbows on the table.

"No, sir. He was not with me. Actually, sir, he doesn't live here. I am not sure where he lives. He told me to bring harm to Kristen Edwards." With this, Hassan lost all control and began sobbing. "Please forgive me! I am sorry, I have sinned. I only wanted to be admired for supporting our struggle. I wanted to belong."

Hermann's next question came to him after recent training on recognition of emerging terrorist threats.

"Hassan, when you say the man who gave you instructions to harm Ms. Edwards does not live here, does he live in the U.S.?"

"No, I don't think so."

"Okay, Hassan," Hermann said gently. "I'll be right back."

***

Agent Goodman arrived at the police department in Ann Arbor on Sunday morning, around ten thirty. The call came in the night before about a suspect in custody that may have been operating on behalf of a foreign adversary. The suspect was spending the night in the precinct and being kept as comfortable as possible. Todd Hermann was off duty, but his notes were provided to Goodman.

Richard arrived at the station at eleven fifteen. The past twelve hours were not what he had expected from his visit to Ann Arbor. After finding Myles at the party, the two headed for St. Joseph Hospital to check on Kristen. She was in stable condition and sleeping from the sedatives she was given after tests and X-rays were completed. Myles insisted on staying the night with her in her private room, so Richard went back to his hotel to get some rest and a much-needed shower.

He wanted to know more about the man who assaulted Kristen. He had seen his silhouette in the back of the squad car, and Myles had provided some limited details. If Myles was serious about this woman, he felt he should use whatever influence he had to find out if she had any history that needed to be fully exposed. And this started with Hassan. Richard felt he was probably a jealous ex-boyfriend that Myles was too star-struck to consider even existed.

"He's in interrogation," said the officer at the front desk.

Once more, Richard decided to stretch the truth just a little to gain the access he needed.

"I am with the FBI, New York division. Your suspect is a person of interest in an investigation we are leading. Mind if I observe the interrogation?"

The officer made a call, and soon a police lieutenant came out to greet Richard. After a couple of brief introductions, handshakes, and exchanged business cards, she led him through a metal detector, then to the glass door affording entry to the station's back offices. She placed her badge on the magnetic reader, the door buzzed, and the two were inside. Richard followed her down the hall to an office. From there, he could see through the observation glass that Hassan Isa Saliba was not speaking to a police officer as he expected, but to Agent Goodman.

Richard had to wait twenty minutes until Goodman was ready to take a break from her questioning. During that time, Richard tried to make a mental list of questions. What was Goodman doing here, and was Kristen mixed up with some extremist group? Was Goodman working on something else that she might be involved in? Otherwise, why would she be here?

"Sarah, can I speak to you?" Richard blurted out as Goodman left the interview room.

"Richard, good to see you. What are you doing here?"

The two slipped back into the office adjoining the interrogation room, speaking directly in front of the one-way mirror with Hassan sitting patiently on the other side.

"My younger brother was with the woman that was assaulted by this man. I was with them last night just after it happened. What can you tell me about this guy?"

"He's just confessed to being involved in an Islamic extremist group, but it looks like he's just a pawn. Didn't realize what he was getting involved in and desperate for attention. At this point, he's giving us everything he's got. It's not much, but we may be able to gain access to the decision-makers using his credentials on the web."

"Why would the girl be involved?"

"It seems she knew something that represented a threat to their operation. We need to speak to her, of course. As soon as possible."

"That makes two of us."

***

Sarah Goodman and Richard O'Brien arrived at the hospital in separate cars. In the hospital lobby, Goodman took Richard's arm to emphasize the significance of what she was about to say.

"Richard, until we can clear Ms. Edwards, I am going to have to ask you to respect my authority here and allow me to direct the questioning. That goes for your brother as well."

"Do you think he needs a lawyer?"

"Let's hope not. I'll let you make that call if it comes to it."

Richard texted Myles to alert them to their arrival, indicating only that "an officer" had some questions for Kristen. Myles replied that she was still sleeping but that he'd come down to speak to them as a starting point.

Moments later, the elevator opened, several people emerged, and Myles was among them.

"Myles, how are you doing, buddy?" Richard prioritized his brother's welfare above all else.

"I'm fine." It was clear that he wasn't.

"This is Agent Goodman. She's with the FBI. Let's go over to the cafeteria and talk."

Myles could barely register the significance of the FBI joining Richard versus a garden-variety police officer. He simply extended his hand to Goodman, they shook, and all three silently walked toward the hospital cafeteria.

"Myles," Goodman started after they were seated at a table, "Thanks for agreeing to meet with me. First off, what is the relationship between you and Kristen Edwards?"

"She's my girlfriend." He looked down at the table as he answered.

"Do you know Hassan Isa Saliba, the young man accused of assaulting her?"

Myles shook his head.

"Do you know why anybody would want to hurt Kristen?"

Myles shook his head again.

"According to the confession of Mr. Saliba, Kristen was in possession of some information that would threaten to foil a plot of an Islamic extremist group. Are you aware of any information she might have had?"

Once again, Myles shook his head.

Goodman decided to take a different tack. "Myles, why don't you tell me more about how you met Kristen, what things you have been doing together, especially in the past five days." Goodman realized that if Kristen was a target for elimination, it was because of something she did or something she learned very recently.

Myles recounted the last several days with Kirsten, leaving out the details of their most intimate moments. He and Richard were beginning to sense the futility in the line of questioning at this point.

". . . then she sent a threatening email the other day to some dude running one of those email scams. She was just having fun with him."

Agent Goodman looked up from her notes. Richard's eyes practically doubled in size.

17

One of the things Goodman found most rewarding about her work with the FBI was that, because of its broad reach, leads often came from the least expected source. She was fully expecting to pick up some chatter from patrons of the Islamic Center following the synagogue bombing, but they had some unwritten rule to exercise radio silence after an attack that could implicate the Arab community. But for a potential assassin to show up over an email scam was even more suspicious. Goodman deduced that either Kirsten had information about the synagogue bombing before it occurred, was aware of the perpetrators' next move, or there was simply no connection between the email scam, Kirsten's prank, and the bombing.

After nearly an hour with Myles in the hospital cafeteria, Goodman asked if it might be possible to speak with Kirsten. She was sitting up in her bed on the fifth floor, having a light breakfast. When she saw Myles coming in first, she smiled broadly.

"Hey, how are you feeling?"

"Like I had one too many beers last night. Did I?" She was kidding, and Myles knew it.

"Look, these guys want to ask you a few questions. Oh, wait, this is my brother!" Myles was a bit overwhelmed by everything.

"Hi Kristen, I'm Richard, Myles's brother. Nice to meet you—sorry it's under these circumstances."

"Hi! Myles has told me so much about you. Yeah, sorry I am not looking my best right now."

"And I'm Sarah Goodman, Kristen, FBI." Goodman decided the party could resume after she finished her business.

In the next thirty minutes, Kristen recounted the same details already provided by Myles. The independent corroboration made it easier for Goodman to dismiss any direct concern over the potential culpability of either Myles or Kristen; eye contact he made with Richard seconds earlier confirmed the same. These were two college kids caught up in another of the many email scams that infiltrated the U.S. over the past decade. Richard was as relieved as anyone that his brother's new love interest was just a naive and innocent kid. Goodman thanked everyone for their cooperation and made a move for the door.

"Agent Goodman, may I have a word with you?" Richard was not quite ready to end the conversation. The two walked into the hallway, leaving Myles with Kristen.

"Sarah," Richard began, "what do you make of this? Is this email scam really a threat when even in this case Myles didn't fall for the ruse?"

"Well, right now my concern is with the assault on Ms. Edwards and how it might be connected to violence on a potentially larger scale. I am less concerned with the economic damage from the email scam right now."

Richard was embarrassed not to see the logic of Goodman's argument before he had opened his mouth.

As she walked out of the hospital, Goodman began working scenarios in her head where an email scam could precipitate a bombing that killed over fifty innocent civilians.

Richard turned back and was about to re-enter Kristen's room at the hospital. As he reached for the handle, he could see through the door window that Myles was standing next to her bed, bent over, holding her hand, and whispering to her. He could see the smile on her face and realized that it would be best not to interrupt. He left the hospital.

Back at his hotel, Richard called his parents. He suspected with everything that had happened the past twenty-four hours, they would worry about Myles because he did not call over the weekend as he would normally do.

"Richard, you won't believe it!"

"What, Mom?"

"We've been the victim of identity theft, or internet fraud, or some such thing. Richard, it's awful. I paid the university thinking it was tuition, room, and board for Myles. They are telling me that they never received the payment. I'm in a panic right now, I'm shaking, I don't know what to do, what if they get into our bank accounts and . . . "

"Mom, slow down, slow down, Mom," Richard interrupted. "Take a breath. I need to hear the details."

Jill O'Brien told her son as much as she knew about the fraud. She paid a bill online, thinking it was from the University of Michigan because it resembled every other email she had received from the university business office. It was not until she received a second bill for the same term that she contacted the business office and put the pieces together. The funds had already been transferred, but to whom was unknown. In going back through the emails, she found the bogus one, which was sent from "billing@umich.edu.sa." When she compared this to the emails she received previously from the university, the sending address was identical except for the ".sa" at the end. It was a domain extension for entities operating in Saudi Arabia. Anyone could have missed it; thousands did.

"Mom, I want you to forward that email to me as soon as possible. Start changing your passwords, run a credit report, and let me know if you see any changes to your rating." Richard knew his mom was vigilant in monitoring the use of her credit cards and did not need to remind her to do that again.

"Okay," she replied. "I already checked all credit card statements, and there is nothing else out of the ordinary."

"Right, Mom, I gotta go right now. I'll call you later, everything's going to be fine. Oh, by the way, I am with Myles, and he's doing great." Richard decided now was not the best time to tell his mom about Myles and his new girlfriend.

Within seconds of hanging up, Richard's phone rang. It was Courtney. Uncharacteristically, he answered the call without first thinking to check who it was.

"Hey, baby, are you in the city?"

"No, I'm in Detroit. The agency sent me here. I'm coming back tomorrow."

"Detroit? Wow, what are you doing there?"

"I can't talk about it," Richard replied, a hint of irritation in his voice. The adrenaline running through his veins was not ready to accommodate the interruption.

"Will you come over tomorrow night? I really need to see you."

"Sure, okay. I'll see you tomorrow night."

"Okay, baby, I can't wait to see you. I miss you."

"You too. Later, Courtney."

Richard was reasonably sure he would not be seeing Courtney for some time.

***

"Sarah, it's Richard. Are you back in your office?"

"Hi, Richard, yeah, what's up?"

"I think I have something here. It seems my little brother somehow opened the door for that email scam to rob my parents. They paid over twenty K to someone thinking it was going toward their university account." Richard realized he had some leverage to negotiate a continuing role in an FBI investigation and remain involved with Goodman. The email his mother provided was the smoking gun the FBI would need to take the investigation to the next step. And he knew exactly how to begin putting the pieces together.

"Let's take this to the Cyber Forensics Unit in New York." Richard said. "Those guys are the most qualified to tackle this."

In 2013, the Cyber Forensics Unit within the FBI's New York branch famously brought down the dark web enterprise known as Silk Road. The founder of Silk Road, Ross Ulbricht, was so confident he was invincible that he granted an interview to Forbes magazine on the success of his internet creation, which was estimated to have created a marketplace where over $200 million in fake IDs, drugs, and weapons were openly exchanged, at least among those who knew how to navigate their way to the site. The Cyber Unit infiltrated the encrypted site, located the person running it, and captured him while he sat unsuspectingly in a San Francisco library.

Good idea, Goodman thought. With the cooperation of Hassan and help from the cyber guys, Goodman figured they could pose as Hassan, establish a connection to the perpetrators, and unequivocally identify them. And they could help figure out if there is a connection between the email scam that targeted Myles O'Brien and the synagogue bombing. She also knew that if she referred the inquiry to New York, she would likely be denied any role in the collar. She wanted in, but there was one problem: She knew a guy over there as well. They broke up for good about a year ago after an intense, three-year on-and-off-again relationship.

"Okay, Richard, sounds good," Goodman finally replied. "How about you forward that email to me as well, I'd like to have a look. Then before you head back to New York let's talk again about how best to organize ourselves."

Organizing meant figuring out how to collaborate with the New York Cyber Forensics Unit with a minimum of interpersonal drama.

***

When the synagogue bombing occurred, Jelani was still in Dubai. He watched the coverage on the television in his hotel room. It was difficult to follow it all in Arabic as his language skills had deteriorated since his move to Kenya. He kept hearing the phrase that "no group has claimed responsibility" and wondered who would be proud to announce they had committed such a heinous crime.

He could not see the smoke from his hotel room window, but it was visible from the rooftop bar. From there, about two miles to the southwest, a thick plume of smoke rose slowly to the heavens, a swirl of death and destruction. Jelani felt the weight of the moment and wondered if the pretty lady in the blue dress might be among the casualties.

Of course, the thought also crossed his mind that Muhammed had something to do with the bombing. As much as he wanted to deny it, Muhammed had provided so many clues over the past couple of weeks that his presence in Dubai was probably not a coincidence. While he wanted to reach out to Muhammed to find out if he was indeed involved, he worried that his communications in

Dubai could be intercepted and decided to wait until he returned home. He wanted to leave for Kenya immediately, but he felt that would attract unnecessary attention to himself. No, he would remain in Dubai until Sunday night, as originally planned, and remain in his room until then.

***

Leosha and Captain Avi sat in the glass booth looking at the pictures of the Unicorn and of the professor who appeared in the class picture with Muhammad Abbas. It was likely not an accident that the Israeli asset was looking down at his phone when the picture was taken a couple of weeks before—the fewer photographs in which he is identifiable, the safer he'd remain. His carefully crafted identity was in question now that he was seen in a picture with a suspected terrorist in the Interpol database, someone Agent Rosen felt was worth capturing secretly in a photo just a few days ago.

"What do you think?" Leosha spoke first.

"I think this son of a bitch played us," Avi replied. "Rosen's notes suggest they were planning an attack on the homeland, organized in Tehran. We now know that's not true—this guy is from Dammam, not Riyadh, and the attack was in Dubai, not here. He threatened us with a nuclear bomb, but Dubai was a dirty bomb. I wonder what else he's told us that is bullshit."

Leosha continued the thread. "He may very well know who was behind the bombing and what they are planning next if anything. Maybe…"

Then, an inspiration. “Look, he probably doesn’t know that Tamara died in the explosion, so perhaps . . . ” Leosha mused aloud.

Avi was on the same wavelength. “We reach out to him posing as her, and bring him in.”

“Exactly.”

18

Muhammed and the Professor met at Al Qarah Mountain, a popular tourist attraction about 140 kilometers southwest of Dammam, a slight diversion from the highway to Riyadh. The Professor had a meeting in the capital later that evening, and Muhammed welcomed the opportunity to ride out of town for a change of scenery and the opportunity to escape the heat.

After the meeting with his student at the Lavona Hotel in Dammam, the Professor decided it was no longer safe for him to meet with Muhammed in the city. He continued to regret the outcome of that meeting and the fact a student was able to hack into his email; it was the first time he had to kill someone so young and innocent. Having to smash his skull with the marble base of a table lamp was particularly gruesome, even to the Professor. No, he would be taking extra precautions from now on, especially given the depths he had now reached in the current operation. It was his idea to meet at Al Qarah.

Al Qarah Mountain features tall, red, sedimentary columns reaching seventy meters high, creating a cool microclimate for escaping the desert heat. Walking between the dark, tight passages of the columns provided a sense of serenity and isolation that was the perfect environment for the two men to speak without fear of being overheard. Nevertheless, they whispered as they slowly made their way deep into the mountain passages.

"Have you heard from your people in America regarding the girl?" the Professor started out.

"I sent three men out in search of her. Two have returned without success in locating her. I have not heard from the third."

"Do we have cause to worry?"

"No, I don't think so. He's probably making progress and is waiting for a successful outcome to report back."

Once again, the Professor felt regret for harming a young woman whose only crime was to stick her nose where it did not belong.

"And what of the young man from Kenya?" The Professor decided to move on to a subject that carried less disturbing imagery.

"He is back home by now. He understands very little about the scope of our operation. He is focused on generating the cash to fund our needs in the name of Allah."

The two men had reached a dead-end in the passage they selected. They turned around and backtracked until a new passage revealed itself. Then they continued down it.

"You have done well," said the Professor. "We've proven we can obtain highly radioactive materials. We've proven we can detonate a dirty bomb. But getting these into the UAE was much easier than the next phase of the operation."

"Yes, I know."

"Before long, the world will know we have a nuclear bomb trained on Tel Aviv."

***

Richard had hoped he could find an opening to suggest that Sarah Goodman fly back to New York with him. Unfortunately, the logistics of checking on his brother and making an appearance at his parents' home made it all too complicated to figure out. Besides, once Goodman was on his turf, he imagined he would be more comfortable and confident about getting closer to her. For now, imagining was as good as it would get.

Sarah, meanwhile, didn't have a choice about what was coming. The special agent in charge of the Detroit field office would inevitably order her to contact John Swanson, her ex, to provide the resources necessary to carry out the investigation. As she saw it, it would be more advantageous for her to maintain the upper hand in what would ultimately be an uncomfortable situation, no matter how it came together.

Her phone interrupted her planning. "Richard?"

"Hi Sarah, have you got your tickets squared away? Anything I can do to help?" Richard silently hoped Goodman might suggest they take the same flight.

"No, but I'll take care of it. I'd just like to ask that you set up a meeting this week with the team over there so we can share intel and get set up as soon as possible. I think the guy you'll want to coordinate with is John Swanson."

"Yeah, that's the guy I know. Have you worked with him before?"

"We know each other," was all Goodman said.

"Okay, text me your flight info so I know when we can expect you. I'll set up the meeting."

"Thanks, talk to you soon, and see you in New York."

Well, that's that, Richard mused. There would be no traveling with Agent Goodman on this particular trip. He tossed his phone on the bed and opened his suitcase, intent on getting out of the hotel quickly so he could see Myles and then get to his parents' house for dinner. As it landed on the bed, it vibrated again. This time, it was a notification that another intercept required translation. *Fuck*, he thought, as he pulled his laptop out from under his packed toiletry bag.

Richard gently placed the laptop on the hotel room desk, opened the lid, and initiated the log-on process as he had done hundreds of times. The intercept was in its usual place, so Richard got straight to work on the translation. The message from an operative in Riyadh to his counterpart in Dearborn demonstrated just how quickly he needed to get back to New York:

"Praise Allah that the attack this week on the Zionists was a great triumph and test of our capability. Our struggle on behalf of the Palestinians will achieve the goal of statehood for our brothers. We are finalizing preparations for the next operation, and you will receive instructions before Al-Jumu'ah."

The week had been such a blur that Richard had to look at his phone again to find out what day it was. It was Monday, and "Al-Jumu'ah" refers to the holy day Friday, the day that all commerce in the Muslim world is suspended in favor of prayer. If the FBI was to determine the true nature of the threat and be successful in interdiction, the pace needed to be significantly accelerated.

Richard stared at the intercept before sending it through to the agency. Just like the last one, something did not look right about the message. The level of formality, the ambiguous syntax, the nearly arrogant attitude was unlike other chatter, email messages, or other translations he had made. He could not put his concerns in words just yet, but he would speak to Director Pritchard about it on his return to New York. The revelation of the group's support of the Palestinians was the first important clue to their motives so far.

***

Apart from the headquarters in Washington, the New York field office was the FBI's busiest, occupying the twenty-third floor of 26 Federal Plaza, otherwise known as the Jacob K. Javits Federal Building, in downtown Manhattan. With 41 stories, the Javits Building is the largest federal building in the United States. Compared to the impressive architecture of nearby structures, however, the State Courthouse, Church of St. Andrew, and City Hall, it was also the most generic and unassuming.

Before 9/11, Richard enjoyed commuting to the building by taking the A train from his apartment in Brooklyn. That routine ended during the COVID-19 pandemic when all nonessential personnel were sent home to work remotely. Ironically, he was once again on the A train having landed at JFK an hour before, but now bypassing his apartment to get into the office as soon as possible. Ninety minutes after getting on the train, he was at Pritchard's office, perspiring heavily, his luggage in tow. Pritchard was on the phone.

"Yes, sir," he said, eyeing Richard standing in the doorway to his office, which instantly produced additional lines on his forehead. "I understand, sir. No, sir, we can handle it. Yes, sir, you'll hear from me by the end of the day. Sir?"

Pritchard set down his phone and looked at Richard, the space between his eyebrows narrowing.

"It seems you have a relative that got himself involved in our operation. And he has a girlfriend that may have jettisoned any chance we had to catch the suspects. What the fuck, O'Brien."

Richard had forgotten the probability that his supervisor would have heard about his brother's unintended involvement before he could explain the matter.

"All due respect, sir, but my brother was targeted by this email scam, and it's merely a coincidence. He and my family are the victims, sir." Richard may have been a low-level employee within the FBI, but he would not allow himself or his family to be insulted.

"Well, that's not the way they see it within IA," he barked back. "IA" was internal affairs, and Pritchard now had to answer to them, as well as the assistant special agent in charge of the New York field office, who had just hung up on him. "We will have some clean-up to do when this is all over, O'Brien, and you will be pushing the broom."

"Sir, did you see the intercept I sent over?"

"I did. You and your guest from Detroit are expected in the east conference room at 1600 hours. That's in forty minutes, O'Brien, and you look like shit. Clean up and get your ass in there."

Richard realized that the trip back to Ann Arbor to check on Myles followed by the visit to his parents last night had put a significant strain on his schedule, but if he had left himself too much time on the ground since getting back to New York, he might have been tempted to go in the wrong direction from the airport, that is, to Atlantic City. Besides, he felt good. He was in the middle of this case, he was contributing, and he was working with a beautiful and intelligent partner. It's what he wanted from the day he joined the agency.

"O'Brien!" Pritchard barked one final time as Richard was turning to walk away.

"Sir?"

"How's the girl?" For a second, Richard presumed his boss was referring to Sarah Goodman, which would have made the question somewhat inappropriate. Then, he remembered.

"She's fine, sir. A little banged up initially, but she was released from the hospital today. She'll be under local protection for now, until things settle down."

"Tell your brother to keep his head down as well."

"Yes, sir."

Richard turned around and slowly dragged his bag toward the showers, trying to get dialed in so he could rise to the demands. He forgot to share with Pritchard his concerns about the veracity of the intercepts.

***

Richard was grateful for the showers on the twenty-fourth floor of the Javits building, part of the exercise facility made available to agents. After cleaning up, he put on a slightly crumpled but fresh white shirt that he would partially hide under his blue suit. He shoved the suitcase and contents into a locker. As he was looking in the mirror to wrestle his hair into compliance, he got a text.

"I'm in the lobby." It was Goodman.

She had been to the New York branch several times and certainly did not need an escort to the meeting. However, she also did not want to allow John Swanson the opportunity to be alone with her, and Richard served as a perfect solution.

"Be right there." Richard was excited to see Sarah and returned to the mirror for one last look before heading out to greet her.

The east conference room provided magnificent views of the city and the "BMW," the locals' name for the Brooklyn, Manhattan, and Williamsburg bridges, leading to Brooklyn. However, this afternoon, all attention would be on the agent leading the meeting, John Swanson. People began filing into the conference room for the briefing that would start promptly at four. As they did, two former lovers came face to face outside the entrance to the room.

"Sarah?" Swanson was apparently the last to know Goodman was attending the meeting. "I wasn't expecting to see you here. Wow, you look great."

And what about my competency, you narcissistic, abusive goon, Goodman thought. *Can you get past the packaging?*

"Hello, John," Goodman replied. "I think you know Richard O'Brien from Linguistics." As an FBI linguist, Richard had not earned the title of "agent," although he would often be referred to in this way. He was merely an employee of the FBI. But what bothered him more than not sharing the same title as virtually everyone else in the meeting was that he sensed something was going on between Goodman and Swanson.

Swanson opened the meeting after several minutes of people finding their peer of choice and deciding where they would sit. About fifteen agents sat at conference tables organized in a giant square, Swanson at the front of the room, a large white board behind him. With his wide shoulders, blond hair, blue eyes, and commanding presence, he looked more like a superhero or male model than a public servant.

"Okay everyone, look it's late in the day and we have a lot to cover. I think you all know Agent Goodman from the Detroit field office."

Not only did everyone know Sarah Goodman, but they also knew about "GoodSwan," the pet name the office gossips had given the couple during their extended affair. Eyes were focused on Swanson to see if he would give away how he felt about having Goodman in the meeting. They would be disappointed.

"What we have here are potentially intersecting tangents or completely unrelated investigations. We can't take the chance they are not connected. So, we will be looking at both tonight. Richard, let's have you start with the recent intercepts first."

Richard and John Swanson did not interact very frequently, but the two shared a sort of unspoken machismo respect. Both were well-built, handsome, and successful with the opposite sex. They had never competed for the same woman, so neither had been a threat to the other. Until, perhaps, tonight.

Richard described the two recent intercepts, the one from before the synagogue bombing in Dubai and the other received just yesterday, revealing the ultimate motive of the perpetrators: to force the Israelis to support statehood for the Palestinians. Although bombing a synagogue in the UAE was an unexpected way to pursue this agenda, it was perhaps intended to attract a broader set of actors into the conflict than the Israelis alone. How far this strategy could go was the question on everyone's mind.

As the first intercept was so predictive of the bombing that followed, Richard chose not to talk about his suspicions about the source that was sending them. He did share the fact that the first message originated in Iran and the second in Riyadh.

"And the intercept from yesterday implies another attack is imminent. Based on the text, it suggests that instructions will be provided before Friday, with an attack following afterwards."

"Thank you, Richard. Now we have in custody an extremist operative in Dearborn that has provided us the credentials to potentially engage with the enemy, while posing as him. Is that right, Agent Goodman?"

"That is correct," Goodman replied.

"Thank you," Swanson continued. "Now let's briefly discuss the email scam with the codename Utapeli. I know we've been working on this in the cyber division for some time, and I am not convinced there is a connection. But the actors may be related in some way because of the timing and geopolitical relationships involved. Who has something current on this?"

The room went silent. Richard looked around the room, hoping that someone would speak up with fresh findings. Nobody spoke.

"Umm, I may have something." It was Richard again.

19

"Do you have plans for dinner?" Richard and Sarah stood outside the Federal Building on Broadway, watching the traffic pass by as day gave way to night. It was seven thirty, and they were expected back at the office later that evening to initiate a transmission, posing as Hassan. After her breakup with John Swanson, Goodman swore off intra-agency relationships, but she could not deny being attracted to Richard O'Brien and besides, she was hungry.

"No, did you have something in mind?"

"I know this great little Chinese restaurant just outside Chinatown. They make their own hand-pulled noodles and XLB."

"XLB?"

"Xiao long bao. Seriously, are you telling me you never had it before?"

Goodman was beginning to feel a bit vulnerable in the presence of her host, but under the circumstances, she did not see a reason to resist.

"No, is that a secret code?" Only an FBI agent would suspect this.

"It's a soup dumpling, you know, like a pot sticker, but the soup is *in* the dumpling. You absolutely have to try it!" Richard then demonstrated a skill that he had honed over years spent in the city; he stepped into the street and hailed the next taxi coming down Broadway. Richard held the door open for Goodman, and the two went off on an unofficial date.

***

The joint meeting of Mossad and Shin Bet agents was a rare occurrence within Israeli intelligence, but on orders from the minister of defense, the rival agencies were working together whether they liked it or not. They gathered in a small conference room in the center of Mossad headquarters in Tel Aviv. The topic was Muhammed Amir Abbas, and how best to observe, capture, or kill him. Shin Bet agents wanted him in custody for the Dubai bombing. Mossad, on the other hand, wanted to subject him to surveillance as a means of determining and preventing his next act of terror. Several agents would not admit out loud their desire to see his execution.

"We've triangulated his position in the Dammam region," said the young Shin Bet agent assigned to the case, the first to take and run with the photo identification Leosha Simakov had provided. Within twenty-four hours of receiving an identification, and with the help of telephone forensics, the most capable intelligence agency in the world can find just about anyone.

"Why don't we know his precise location?" came the first question, from Leosha.

"This perp is very clever, he never uses his phone in the same place twice in any week, and according to our surveillance, he disposes of his phone every Thursday, so we lose track of him."

"We know," said a Mossad agent. "We've been monitoring him for over a year."

Nothing like an in-your-face comment from a Mossad agent to rile a Shin Bet counterpart, but the agents remained professional and focused.

"Look," interrupted David Barnea, the Mossad director. "We need to be smarter than this. I've asked Daniel Katz here to present a plan that I believe is bold but within our capabilities."

Katz was one of the brightest minds in the Mossad, having conceived of the agency's most audacious schemes, including the computer virus that disrupted the operation of centrifuges in Iran's nuclear program in 2021 and the distribution of a clandestine iPhone hack enabling the agency to spy on their adversaries shortly after that. Whatever Katz had in mind would most certainly reflect innovative thinking.

"Good morning," he started. "So, we have looked at the Dammam region carefully and we know it pretty well. We also know that with the right passport, we can easily get into and out of the Kingdom, as our agents have been doing this for some time."

Both agencies knew the Kingdom of Saudi Arabia would prevent Israelis from entering the country, or even those whose passports from other countries contained an Israeli stamp. But the country had just implemented an online visa request portal that was glitchy and easily hacked. That, combined with Mossad's ability to produce high-quality fake passports made for a porous border.

"Furthermore, we know that there are three small shops selling prepaid phones within the area we've triangulated. These are the types of stores the perp would likely be using, rather than a large retailer that would likely keep better records."

"What we propose is this: We send an agent into the country that will visit these stores. He will propose to the proprietor that he is introducing a new, cheaper, but more advanced phone. The phone takes advantage of new technology and represents the future of the industry. He'll propose to purchase all the existing prepaid phones and leave a limited number of the new phones at no cost, then propose to return the following week for, quote, 'feedback on sales.' He'll add a few extra riyals for the man's trouble, just enough that he'll not want to turn away from the offer.

"Of course, we'll monitor every one of those new phones, and when the target comes for a replacement, we'll find him as soon as he uses it. We'll be able to track his movements for as long as he carries it. We'll maintain the stock of the new phones if necessary, keeping the price well below what the shop was paying before. Getting them into and out of KSA is easy as we'll ship them to our agents in-country if we have trouble getting them through passport control."

Daniel paused to allow the team to digest the plan. In the past, his schemes sometimes drew responses like "you've got to be kidding" or "are you out of your fucking mind?" Several seconds passed as Daniel continued to stand before the two teams.

Leosha was the first to speak, "I love it."

***

Richard and Agent Goodman returned to the FBI office at nine thirty. The meeting had been moved to the FBI command center on the twenty-third floor, with an entirely new team of about eight agents. But as before, Swanson was in charge.

The command center was an impressive testament to the capability of advanced technology, similar in look to NASA's Mission Control Center in Houston, with two important differences: This room had no windows to the outside world. Without ambient light coming in and with no overhead lighting either, the only light was from monitors. Also, this center was not overseeing a single launch pad but the activities of agents and their targets around the globe. One massive screen was surrounded by about twenty smaller screens, each monitoring a different region or activity. Some were relaying a drone's solitary surveillance, some were watching dormant missile launch sites within foreign adversaries, and still others were playing the news stations like CNN that, rarely but potentially, got the news before the FBI did. Seats were arranged around a huge semicircular table, the arc providing a perfect view of all monitors from any position. The chairs were on rollers to allow staff to move quickly from one control panel to another, enabling them to change the view on any monitor as often as necessary.

"Okay," Swanson started out, standing in front of the large screen and in the center of the circle, "so we have these credentials for accessing the suspect's TOR, is that right Smiley?"

Agent Smiley was a graduate of MIT, and many of his Cyber Forensics Team colleagues joked that he must have invented the internet on a kindergarten lunch break. He was central to solving the most complex schemes in cybercrime, including the infamous Silk Road. He also had a passion for explaining technology to his colleagues even when they weren't interested to hear it. This would be one of those times.

"Well, we are about to find out," Smiley replied.

"For those of you that may be unfamiliar," Smiley explained yet again, "'TOR' stands for 'the Onion Router,' an open-source software application for enabling anonymous communication over the internet. It can mask a user's location and correspondence from anyone that might be conducting network surveillance, like us at the FBI."

The "onion" refers to some seven thousand relays designed to serve as layers of encrypted code to conceal the provenance and substance of activity flowing through it. Ironically, TOR was developed in the mid-1990s by the United States Naval Research Laboratory to protect U.S. intelligence communications online. It remained a legal, technical instrument of the web, abused increasingly by tech-savvy criminals.

Deciphering messages directly off TOR was something Richard was already doing on his laptop with the application that Smiley installed there, but while they could intercept many messages, the effectiveness of this work was a function of how much effort the sender invested in protecting them. Also, while the application he used could capture messages, Richard could not actually send them.

There was an additional benefit that would be afforded the team if Hassan's credentials were proven authentic: Once inside the perpetrator's private site, Smiley could track any communications with other devices using the same encrypted pathway, thus extending the FBI's reach within the extremist's cell, no matter where the "bad guys" happened to be operating.

"Richard," Swanson spoke next, his commanding voice filling the room, "we will want you to construct a message, posing as Hassan, to his handler. We want his handler to believe that his mission was accomplished, you know, that he eliminated the threat. Are you comfortable doing that in a convincing manner?"

"Sure, I can do that," Richard replied. "That's it?"

"No." Swanson was not done. "We want you to ask how you can help further. We want to see if we can get involved in the next attack without them suspecting that we know about it. We want the what, when, and where of their next move."

A tall order, and the long silence that followed punctuated the ask. Persuading the target to give away details of an attack when his operative was not already involved would almost certainly make him suspicious. Plus, it was necessary to catch the individual when he was online and willing to engage in real-time conversation, creating a dynamic where he would more likely let down his guard and the maximum amount of intel could be gathered. Adding to these challenges was the fact that the perpetrators would likely be communicating in Arabic, meaning that Richard would have to do the same, at a pace that increased the chance of saying something improper, something that might tip off the person on the other end. Richard began to wonder if he was out of his depth in this assignment.

It was now 10:00 p.m. in New York, meaning it would be six in the morning in most parts of the Arab world. The best opportunity to catch the perpetrator in a live chat would be in two hours, after their morning prayer. It would be a long night.

***

Leosha walked into the Cave. Another agent from Shin Bet was already seated in the chair opposite Avi's desk.

"Good morning," the agent said, standing and turning toward Leosha, "here is Agent Rosen's phone. It's unlocked and ready to go. You'll find Chad Kirin's contact information in there. Rosen used the Signal app to reach out to him, and generally adhered to our agent codebook for communication with intelligence assets." The agent handed the phone to Leosha.

"Here also is a document showing you their most recent exchanges, so you can get a feel for how they communicated with one another. They are in reverse chronological order." With that, the agent left the room. Leosha looked at Avi, who was sitting behind his desk, observing.

"So, are we going to do this?" Leosha asked the captain.

"Let's get on with it. I've had my team construct a series of possible outreach messages. I've selected this one. Look."

Avi tossed another document across his desk to the Mista'arvim agent who was beginning to feel more like Avi's new partner. Leosha studied the paper.

"It's good. I like it. Short and to the point, not giving anything away that might drive suspicion."

"Send it."

Leosha opened the Signal app and located the contact information for the Unicorn. He cross-referenced the last message exchanged with the document the other agent had given him to make sure the right recipient would receive the message. Then he typed it into the phone:

"I need to see you. Have new information we need to verify. Can we meet in Petra, Thursday at 1930. Same meetup spot as before."

The message was vague enough to make the Professor curious. The location was one they had used before for clandestine meetings at the Petra tourist attraction in Jordan. The meeting was proposed for one of the few nights during the week when it was possible to walk the grounds up to the Treasury, the famous structure built into the side of a mountain.

Leosha took one long look at the message he had just typed, then hit the send key.

"Okay," he said, "it's done."

"Take the phone," Avi said. "Don't keep me waiting if you get a response."

***

With two hours to kill before attempting to engage with Hassan's handler, Sarah Goodman was faced with a choice: sit around and wait for John Swanson to approach her, go back to her hotel, or take a walk outside. She really could use a nap, after all, her day started in Detroit. But she wanted to stay sharp for what lay ahead. That was when she noticed John Swanson staring at her from across the room.

"Hey, wanna take a walk?" Richard came to the rescue again. "I can show you a couple things that you'll never see on your garden-variety walking tour of New York."

Goodman smiled back her approval, and two walked out of the command center on their way to Broadway.

It was a chilly evening in Manhattan, and even with the microclimate that tended to raise the temperatures slightly above the other boroughs, Richard could see his breath as he spoke.

"So, are you from Detroit originally?" he started out.

"Yeah, you?"

"Same! University of Michigan, you?"

"Michigan State. I assumed you were probably from Michigan when I saw you and your brother at the hospital. What made you leave, not that I can blame you?"

"I guess you could say I was following opportunity, then the agency found me."

The two walked silently for a short while, admiring the lights of Broadway, when Richard could not wait any longer to say what was really on his mind.

"You and John Swanson. You're the 'Good' in 'GoodSwan,' I assume." Richard had heard the term before but was too far removed from office politics to know much more, and he could not have cared much less until tonight. He did not want the question to land too hard or to sound too accusatory, but he absolutely felt the need to know.

"Yeah, John and I were together for a time, but that's over. And I'd prefer not to talk about it."

Richard didn't care that the details were off-limits. He was just glad that Sarah was, as far as he could tell, available. As the two continued to walk, Richard's phone went off. Richard could tell it was from within the agency.

"O'Brien."

"Mr. O'Brien, you've got to come back to the command center right away," the agent said excitedly. "We've intercepted a message here related to the current operation. We need you to interpret and certify the translation as soon as possible."

20

Muhammed woke and initiated the routine he followed nearly every day that involved splashing water on his face and kneeling in prayer in the direction of Mecca. The Professor wanted to see him later that morning, as he had to head out of town unexpectedly later in the day. He would want to know of any news from America so, rather than proceeding to the coffee shop as he would typically do for the sake of protecting his identity, he decided to check his laptop while still in his flat.

"Are you available to chat?" came the message in Arabic from within his secure site. Muhammed looked at the message carefully. It originated from an ISP in the U.S., but the specific location was not revealed. *If the message came through to me, I can at least take the time to verify the sender,* he thought.

"Who is this?" he replied, not wanting to presume anything until the sender provided verifiable identification.

"It is Hassan, from Dearborn." This was the message that Muhammed was waiting for, and the timing could not have been better. He had started to worry about his young and unproven agent. He was painfully aware of the fact that Basheer Aktar was not capable of sourcing the best talent for these operations.

"How is the weather in Dearborn?" Muhammed replied, using the pre-arranged code to verify the agent's identity.

"It is cloudy with a 30 percent chance of rain."

Muhammed was delighted to hear from Hassan, with hopefully good news about his efforts in America to find and silence the threat to their operation.

"Was your operation a success?"

"Yes, praise Allah, the operation was a success. However, I have a question."

Muhammed was not sure he liked the response from Hassan. Young operatives are not supposed to question their superiors in this culture and certainly not in the militant-style organization that he created. He stared at the monitor to consider if he would even respond when the next message from Hassan appeared on his screen.

"How else can I contribute to our struggle for freedom from oppression and from this godless America?"

Muhammed could not help but smile at the ambition of his young agent. He was clueless about the big picture, but nevertheless he demonstrated moxie and commitment. After the next attack, he could use Hassan to spread conspiracy theories across social media sites from within the U.S. as a means of further intimidating western democracies.

"Meet me here in four days' time, at 2000 AST, and I will have another assignment for you," he returned. "You've done well, and Allah will be pleased." AST was Arab Standard Time, and 2000 equated to noon eastern standard time.

Back in the command center, Richard and the rest of the team exchanged high fives going around the room. The predator took the bait.

***

Agents filed again into the conference room in the Javits Federal Building. A few of the faces were new. Dragging themselves in toward the end of the line were Richard and Agent Goodman who had worked through the night.

"Okay, listen up," John Swanson's voice boomed across the room. "We've got some heavy action here from last night we need to assess and act upon. Special Agent Hunter will take over from here. And just to make sure we are clear, everyone: This is *not* a drill."

The assignment of David Hunter signaled the scope of the investigation was going beyond the purview of the Cybercrimes division. This operation would now leverage all the assets of the agency. Agent Hunter came to the FBI from the Army branch of military intelligence, which would be apparent to anyone working under his direction. He was fifty-nine years old with a large frame that was as firm and rigid as the walls around him.

"Good morning, everyone," Hunter said. "First of all, I'd like to thank Richard O'Brien from Linguistics for some good work in getting us to this point. We've learned a lot in the past forty-eight hours." Richard beamed. This was a nice way to start the day, and the first time he was ever publicly acknowledged for his work.

"Now, here is what we know: We have a suspect in Dammam, Saudi Arabia, whose position was triangulated last night during an exchange with our team, posing as his agent in Dearborn, Michigan. He may be involved in the recent bombing in Dubai and/or planning another attack at this very moment.

"We have used our access to the perp's laptop and the Onion Router they operate to identify another contact in his sphere, and this operative indicates he will be traveling to Petra in Jordan in the next twenty-four hours for a meeting, ostensibly to contribute to the planning for this attack and/or to pass along some form of material assistance.

"We have an activity operating in parallel that is scamming people, students mostly, to pay into an Iranian account through a Saudi intermediary. The students or their parents believe they are paying for tuition. This has been monitored for some time, and we've traced not only the laundering of money through these exchanges but the acquisition of explosive materials through them. Because of the incident in Ann Arbor, Michigan, this week, which we believe was triggered by an email falling into the wrong hands, we are operating as if there is a connection between these activities."

The scope of the activity laid out by Agent Hunter was breathtaking, and it was clear from the sense of growing tension in the room that Richard was not the only person feeling it.

"O'Brien, I want you to continue to engage with this individual in Dammam," Hunter continued.

"See if you can get a name out of him, which may be an alias at best. See if he is willing to give you an assignment that will get us closer to the action."

"Yes, sir," Richard replied.

"Agent Goodman," Hunter continued, "I'd like you to work with our Cairo team and the attaché to the International Ops Division in that office. We are clearing the operation with the Jordan Ministry of Foreign Affairs as we speak. We will be sending two agents to Petra. Give them the necessary background about what we are dealing with, what to look for, and make sure we get good physical descriptions of the suspect or suspects. We will have drones in the area. Hopefully, we will get eyes on the meeting.

"Sir, shouldn't we advise the Israelis that we will be operating in the area?" Goodman asked.

"We definitely want to share whatever intel we collect or suspects we detain," Hunter replied, "but we don't have the time to coordinate with them on the front end of the operation. We also haven't established if Israel is the target of the next hit."

"Okay people," Hunter continued, "We have a purported serious threat on our hands. Support the leaders in your department with getting the intel we need as quickly as possible. Respect the chain of command, don't make careless assumptions, and stick to your protocols for engagement with the enemy. We'll meet here again three times per day until further notice. You'll be advised of the schedule. Meeting adjourned."

The audience scattered. Richard and Goodman looked at each other.

"Well," Goodman went first, "nobody ever said working for the agency would be boring."

Richard needed a break from the exhilarating work of the past few hours, a far cry from the monotony of his typical routine, waiting for intercepts to interpret and return, a process that most computers could already capably do without him. If not for the sensitive nature of the work and the lack of tolerance for ambiguity, his position probably would have been eliminated by now. He ducked out of the conference room and went to the men's locker room. Since he had not returned to his apartment yet, his toiletries were within reach. He grabbed his toothbrush and toothpaste and went to the sinks.

While in front of the sink with a mouth full of foam, he heard the locker room door swing open and saw Swanson walk to the urinals. There were at least two other restrooms between the conference room and locker room, so Richard was not expecting to see anyone from the meeting, least of all Swanson. A few moments later, Swanson walked up to the sink next to Richard and began washing his hands.

"You fucking her?"

Richard nearly choked on his own spit.

"Excuse me?" he managed.

"You heard me, *are you fucking her*?"

"John, if you are referring to Sarah, no, we are keeping it professional."

"So, you want to fuck her."

Richard could see where this was going, and it was the last thing he needed. "Look, I understand you guys had a thing, and I am trying to do my job. That's all there is to it."

"Well, buddy," Swanson said, "it seems you've managed to expand your job description to include chasing after my woman." Swanson turned off the water and squared his body directly toward Richard. "Back off, or you'll regret it." With that, Swanson left the locker room.

Richard noticed in the mirror that toothpaste was now drooling down the side of his mouth, dripping onto his belt.

***

"Simakov, you don't need to do this. I've a team of capable agents."

Avi and Leosha sat opposite each other in the Cave, the captain with his elbows on his desk, his hands pushed toward Leosha and trying to frame the situation as being no bigger than a breadbox. "We don't need you."

"All due respect, Captain, I *do* need to do this. Tamara would have been my bride. I need to bring her murderer to Israel to face trial." Both understood the complications of trying the murderer of a covert agent who was operating in a foreign country, but Avi decided that conversation could wait.

"Look, Captain," Leosha continued, "my station chief already knows I am essentially on loan to your department. If we can simply keep this off the books of my department, it will greatly reduce the paperwork necessary."

Avi respected how Leosha pivoted from the emotional topic of who would go into battle and perhaps not return, to the trivial matter of filing the paperwork involved. He made up his mind but sat in pensive silence just long enough to give his decision the maximum amount of legitimacy.

"Okay, you're in. Report to the conference room at 0930 for the briefing. The team leaves for Jordan at 1600 hours."

***

At the FBI office in New York, Goodman was running a conference call with the team in Cairo that was heading for Petra. She was not in the best position to instill confidence in meeting the goal of the operation.

"So, we don't have a good physical ID on the perpetrators. I know this is going to make it difficult for you guys to do your job."

A voice from the other line responded, "What are we actually looking for?"

"The meeting is at a popular tourist attraction, so we can expect these guys might stick out. It will be after dark when only a small fraction of the daily totals show up," Goodman said. "I'd expect two men of Arabic origin…"

"You've got to be kidding. You've just described like everyone here," came another voice. Goodman expected this.

"Right, I understand. I wish I could give you more. Obviously, the meeting will involve suspects that are dressed or acting like tourists and not focused on the exhibit. There may be an exchange of information or material. We are working on getting more intel that we will radio to you, so be sure you remain connected to the command center once you are in position. And we will have eyes in the sky so we can potentially ID vehicles traveling in from outside the tourist hub."

Silence on the other line indicated the team was either processing the information or stunned by the lack of it.

"One more thing," Goodman added, "we are operating under the presumption of this as being a prelude to an attack on U.S. soil, so you are authorized to initiate ER if necessary to detain and interrogate a confirmed suspect."

ER was an extraordinary rendition, a globally criticized practice as it allowed the agency to operate outside most legal jurisdictions that might otherwise demand due process for the accused. That was a luxury that Agent Hunter did not feel was necessary or appropriate if the goal was to protect innocent civilians from a violent attack.

***

In the main conference room in Shin Bet's Tel Aviv station, a half-dozen agents in fatigues sat waiting for Captain Avi to arrive. Leosha sat among them, keeping to himself. He understood that the Shin Bet agents did not trust the Mista'arvim, and he could not blame them given the history of how the two organizations have functioned and often failed to cooperate. He hoped that could be set aside in the interest of finding and bringing to Israel the lowlife degenerates that blew up a synagogue and murdered a fellow agent, the woman he loved.

Avi came into the meeting room, fired up a projector, and turned to face the screen when an image appeared. The agents in the room straightened their backs and leaned forward. The image was a photo of Muhammed Amir Abbas and his handler, a man known by many aliases, including the Unicorn

"These are your two suspects," Avi said. "We know this man, alias Chad Kirin, is attending the meetup and expecting to talk to Agent Tamara Rosen. The other suspect is Muhammed Amir Abbas, an associate with significant ties to Al-Qaeda. We don't know if he will be present, observing from afar or somewhere else, but you should be on the lookout for him. You'll receive everything we have on him shortly.

"The meeting is tonight in Petra, near the Treasury. You will set up a perimeter around the area. We want a distraction to draw attention away from them, then we want both taken into custody and brought to Tel Aviv for questioning. Let me be clear: I want BOTH men if they are present, not just one of them."

Avi waited a moment to allow the details of the mission to sink in. The team members all had experience in crossing the border into Jordan for similar missions to capture suspected bad guys, and in this case, the mission seemed straightforward.

"What is he here for?" one of the agents asked, looking in Leosha's direction.

Avi had no choice but to respect the question, but he was not in the mood for papering over any differences between the two agencies.

"I will tell you what he is here for. He is a member of this team, and I expect you to treat him with respect as you would any Shin Bet agent. He has done the research to ID these two perps, he will be traveling with you to Petra, and he will be on the ground and responsible for apprehending them with your support. Any questions?"

The agents understood that last statement to be as rhetorical as it gets.

After a few seconds of silence, Avi motioned to his assistant to pass a folder to each agent. She walked behind each agent and placed a folder in front of each one of them.

"Schalit here is your commanding officer. Hila, we will be outfitting you to resemble Agent Rosen. Your packet has a copy of the last picture that Tamara had taken with the suspect.

"Each of you is also being given hard copies of the photos. You'll see we've prepped your passports for entry into Jordan and entry tickets to the grounds at Petra. A map is in your folder showing the region; we've highlighted the roads and passages and color-coded the ones we feel represent the best way in and out, but once on the ground, you guys call the shots. Study the information. You won't be taking it with you." Avi paused once more to look at what amounted to his family. He was good at tough love, but he also had faith in his team.

"I'll leave you now to plan the mission. We will be monitoring the activity from here. Remember, I want both suspects ALIVE and back here by tomorrow morning. And don't bring any Jordanian police back with you."

21

The FBI team landed at the Muwaffaq Salti Air Base in north central Jordan. The U.S./Jordanian military cooperation is extensive due to the country's commitment to support NATO and the war against terror, and the U.S. Air Force operates at the base independent of Jordanian supervision. It was unnecessary to explain why six men and two women, dressed as tourists, got off a plane and into two minivans outfitted with state-of-the-art mobile communications technology.

Harry and Peter Robinson, brothers who had both wrestled for Penn State, would pose as two gay men and remain near the visitor center so they could monitor people coming in and prevent any suspects from running out. Two of the men, Agents Brown and Steele, would pair with the women, Agents Kroll and Levi, and blend with whatever crowds they encountered at Petra. Each agent wore a well-concealed earpiece to connect with the command center in New York. The remaining two men would stay in their vehicles, prepared to hustle team members back to the air base, along with whatever live souvenirs they might acquire.

The distance from the Petra visitor center to the Treasury was about two kilometers and could be covered in about twenty minutes. Each agent pair, Kroll and Brown, Steele and Levi, was assigned a specific walking route to and from the Treasury, as tourists were not permitted past the Treasury after dark. During the evening program, a hundred or more lights illuminate the area, music is played, and tourists can sit on mats to take in the surreal atmosphere in the presence of structures that date to the fifth century BC. The agents reviewed what little information they had to identify their target: Male, Middle East origin, appearing not as a tourist but looking to meet and exchange information with a contact of similar characteristics. With most of the tourists sitting on mats outside the Treasury, the agents felt reasonably confident that if something were going to happen apart from the tourist's experience, they would see it. The two minivans approached the Petra visitor center, stopped just short of the taxis, and dropped the agents.

"Agents Kroll, Brown, I want you to stroll on the eastern side of the path, and Steele and Levi, you work the opposite side," Goodman directed from the command center in Manhattan. "Kroll, Brown, I want you to hang back until Steele and Levi have reached the far side and start heading back toward the exit. I want maximum distance between you and optimal coverage of the area." Through individual GPS trackers Goodman could get a general idea of where each agent stood on a monitor in the command center. The agents also wore concealed body cams, but these were of limited value as the sun was starting to set.

"Copy that," one of the agents replied on behalf of the team.

"Robinson," she continued, speaking to the brothers as a unit, "I want you to hang around the exit. If you see anyone coming in that fits the description of the suspect, you will have first eyes on him, and report anything suspicious immediately. Also, take pictures of each other with the suspect in the background if the opportunity presents itself."

"Yes, ma'am," Henry replied.

"Okay, team," Goodman concluded, "radio silence until we have something to report."

***

The Israeli agents crossed into Petra via the King Hussein Allenby Bridge. Although they carried valid passports and visas for travel into Jordan, they drove three compact vehicles across the border and exchanged them for a full-size van on the other side. The intent was to avoid alerting the Jordanian police or military.

Agents Schalit, Hila, and Leosha were accompanied by four other agents. Two of them, Cohen and Lefkowitz, would nonchalantly stand guard at each of the emergency exits within the grounds. Mills would remain in the vehicle, and Friedman would shadow Leosha and Hila to assist with the takedown of any suspects until Cohen and Lefkowitz could come to provide additional muscle.

Leosha and Hila, now disguised as Rosen, planned to enter the visitor center together. Schalit would stand outside the visitor center, smoking and posing as a driver waiting for his customers to finish their tour. Through a comm device hidden in his collar, he could communicate with the Shin Bet command center in Tel Aviv. Once the agents were in position, Schalit verified their comms device was operational.

"Okay, fellas, sound off. Hila and Leosha?"

"Check, making our way to the Treasury."

"Friedman."

"Check, watching Hila and Leosha, trailing by about eight meters."

"Mills."

"Check, vehicle is parked about fifty meters from the entrance."

"Lefkowitz."

"Check, standing by, west emergency exit."

"Cohen."

"Check Schalit, at the east exit."

"Okay, boys and girls, settle in. When the Unicorn arrives, you will hear it here first."

***

The Professor arrived at the King Hussein International Airport and took a private car to Petra, arriving at the visitor center at eight, after the night program had started. He wore a tan suit with no tie. He was concerned that his meeting with Agent Rosen might reveal that the Israelis were closing in on him, but overall, he was confident the meeting was just her effort to confirm some details, parts of the puzzle that they had gathered since the synagogue bombing in Dubai, data points he could twist into another blind alley of intelligence gathering. Nevertheless, the Professor immediately began to practice his own form of surveillance of the immediate environment, looking at the tourists to confirm that there would be no agents other than Rosen within the Petra attraction.

As he paid his entry fee and made his way beyond the visitor center, he observed two very large men holding hands and reading an informational plaque outside the center. He looked ahead to see many couples and young families still making their way to the Treasury, and he increased his pace to come within a few yards of them, attempting to blend in. He expected to see Rosen sitting on the outside perimeter of the area by the Treasury, the spot where they met before.

"Attention, team, the Unicorn is in the den, wearing a tan suit," Schalit whispered into his collar. "Ground team, he is heading toward you."

"Copy that," Leosha replied.

Leosha resisted the temptation to turn around and look. He was about halfway to the Treasury in his back-and-forth routine, and he needed a natural obstacle that would force him to change his orientation without appearing suspicious.

By now, the FBI and Shin Bet teams were gathered outside the Treasury, standing to either side of the thirty or so tourists who were seated in a semicircle in awe of the structure before them. If the agents from the two countries were not so focused on identifying a man of Middle Eastern origin, traveling alone, and looking for his contact, they probably would have noticed each other; it would have been hard not to.

As the Professor approached the gathering, he slowed his pace, hoping to notice Rosen among the crowd on the outside perimeter. Nobody immediately stood out. He decided to casually stroll outside the seated tourists to the far end, presuming Rosen would reveal herself in time. There was no reason to suspect any other scenario, until now.

At the far end of the crowd was a large rock structure that, combined with the side of the mountain in which the Treasury was carved, created a narrow, natural passage that led to the many other monuments within the attraction. The passage was blocked off tonight but turning in front of it were a man and woman who strolled toward the Professor. It was unclear if the couple was together, but the Professor could see the woman looked vaguely like Agent Rosen. This woman was a bit taller than the Professor recalled Rosen to be, and as she walked in his direction, he could see that her feet were turned out just a bit more than Rosen's would be. It was not Rosen. This person was either trying to look like her or merely another tourist.

One thing the Professor had mastered after nearly a decade of training as a spy was the ability to size up people instantly. While it was too early to presume the woman in the distance was attempting to impersonate Rosen, it triggered a rapid response from the Professor to scan the area for other potential risks. First, there was the man walking behind her, a man of pale complexion who bore all the physical characteristics of a Russian national. To the side of him and behind him, he noticed several couples that did not appear to be the slightest bit interested in the attraction for which they would have come to see, but instead their eyes were darting around. Then he noticed someone hanging around the emergency exit, looking in his direction.

As a precaution, the Professor turned around and began walking back toward the visitor center. Rosen's request to meet was not important enough to the Professor that he would risk his life over it; he could afford to wait outside for things to clear out. And the more he realized this, the faster he began to walk toward the main exit.

"We may have been exposed," Hila whispered into her collar. "The Unicorn is heading to the exit."

The FBI team also picked up on the fact that a man was walking rather quickly to the exit, but since this man had not contacted anyone, Goodman told them to hang back and observe further.

"Do you think he's on to you?" Goodman asked Kroll, who realized the person of interest was making his way toward the exit.

"I don't think so," Kroll replied. "He's not really laid eyes on us. Something else has spooked him."

Leosha was the first to make a significant move, realizing that the opportunity to take down the Professor would be lost if he did not act. He did not trust that Schalit, who was outside the visitor center, could detain the suspect on his own. Leosha started to move very quickly toward the exit, the back of the Professor in his sights, about five hundred meters away.

"The Unicorn is attempting to leave, Schalit, stop him at the exit."

Schalit had not expected the operation to diverge from the plan so quickly. He entered the visitor center, waiting for the Professor and hoping for backup. Meanwhile, Harry and Peter Robinson could see a man in the distance, running toward them.

The Professor slowed his pace just in time to walk casually past the Robinsons and into the center, only to see Schalit blocking his path to the street, his gaze making clear that the Professor was not going anywhere. He smiled at Schalit and extended one hand in the air, pretending he's just recognized someone.

"My son!" he cried, embracing Schalit before the agent could grab his weapon. As the two embraced, the Professor drove a blade deep into Schalit's body just under his rib cage. Schalit fell slowly into the arms of the Professor, who called out for help.

"Please, call an ambulance, this man has collapsed!"

As a security guard rushed to provide aid, the Professor gently lowered Schalit to the floor and backed away. Blood from his side started to slowly gather in a puddle on the linoleum floor of the facility. The Professor turned around and left the center through the double doors in front, hopped into his waiting car, and disappeared.

"Suspect approaching rapidly, appears to be preparing for a confrontation," Peter Robinson advised Goodman over the radio. "He appears to be alone."

"Detain him," replied Goodman. "Use deadly force if necessary."

With that unambiguous order, FBI agents Harry and Peter Robinson tackled Agent Leosha

Simakov. Harry lunged for his legs as if he were back on a wrestling mat, and Peter grabbed him at his midsection. Within seconds the two men had Leosha struggling face down on the pavement. He was swiftly handcuffed, hands behind his back, dragged out the front door, and put in the minivan that Goodman had directed to park outside. In the final of all insults, a black felt bag dragged over his head from behind. The other FBI agents, monitoring the transmission, were seconds behind and jumped into the back rows of the van. And then they were gone.

22

"What the fuck just happened?"

Captain Avi watched a monitor intensely as Leosha's pocket transponder showed him leaving Petra at high speed. On another monitor was drone footage, obscure because it was evening, showing an ambulance and police car arriving and general chaos at the scene.

"Is he pursuing the suspect or is someone pursuing him?" another voice chimed in from within the command center in Tel Aviv. Avi ignored the question, his eyes fixed on the monitors.

"Captain, it's Hila," her voice coming in forcefully over the speakerphone in the room. "Schalit is down, knife wound, it's critical. He's getting attention now. Agent Simakov was assaulted and taken away in a van. We don't have a good ID on the enemy—they looked to be American or European."

Avi's response was instinctive. "Get your team out of there, NOW."

***

Leosha spoke Russian, Hebrew, and English fluently, and he employed all three to prove his identity to the team that had abducted him moments earlier. The more he screamed at them or tried to reason with them, the more convinced they were that Leosha was the person they were sent to capture.

"Look, I am an Israeli agent," he pleaded, "you've made a big mistake." His argument may have been more believable without his Russian accent, which tended to attract attention from FBI agents. Nobody in the van spoke to or acknowledged Leosha for the duration of the trip back to the base at Muwaffaq Salti, a typical practice. They wouldn't decide Leosha's guilt or innocence anyway. A plane was waiting to take him to the location where he would be interrogated.

"We have a man in custody," Agent Goodman reported to the team at the command center, "but we know very little about him at this point. The interrogation has not been initiated yet." Goodman was giving her update to the team during one of the rotating meetings that Hunter had ordered.

"How do we know he is connected?" Smiley complained. "The last thing we need right now is another Richard Jewell."

"We will just have to wait until we can get him out of Jordan and in an area where we have the jurisdiction to operate freely," Hunter interrupted. "In the meantime, we still have an active threat and so the investigation continues as before."

Leosha wouldn't get a chance to plead his case for several hours.

***

Avi's first call was to his counterpart at the Mossad, Moshe Peretz, who pleaded ignorance to the operation. The Mossad's mission was focused on intelligence gathering, and the meeting in Petra was not on their radar.

"Avi, we agreed to have Simakov work with your team, and you allowed him to be captured? How am I to explain this to the PM? This is a total clusterfuck, Avi. A real career-limiting event for both of us."

"You think for a second that I don't recognize that?" Avi snapped back.

A captured Israeli intelligence agent would be worth an exchange of hundreds if not thousands of detained Hamas soldiers.

"Who was the target in the first place?" Peretz asked.

Avi explained the intercept from their agent, codename Chad Kirin, and rising suspicions that they may have a double agent in the agency. He briefed Peretz on the Unicorn's background as revealed in the Shin Bet dossier. This, for the moment, deflected the attention from Leosha.

"Look, we believe the Americans may have taken Simakov," he continued. "None of the agents we laid eyes on were of Arabic origin. I'll be calling the minister next. I felt I owed you the heads up first."

The guilt outweighed the embarrassment that Avi would suffer for losing Leosha, a man he had grown to respect for his courage and determination to seek justice for Tamara and the other innocent Jews murdered in Dubai. He realized he needed help to guarantee Leosha's safety. He called the minister of defense to make his report and to discuss the agency's response. Meanwhile, Peretz picked up the phone in his office and opened a secure line to his agent working in Saudi Arabia.

"Aloo?" came the answer from the other end.

Peretz wasted no time in getting to the point. "We have a problem."

***

By the time the Professor reached the Saudi border, he had considered over a dozen potential scenarios of what he had witnessed earlier that evening. It was enough to convince him that attempting to board a plane to return to the Kingdom was a risk; the Jordanian police would have alerted the security forces. And the people who looked like foreign agents did not seem to be Israelis, particularly the two large men guarding the rear entrance to the visitor center.

Did Israeli intelligence connect the dots to reveal his true identity? he wondered.

The Professor's thoughts turned to Muhammed, the one person who knew the most about his movements and contacts. If he didn't need Muhammed to coordinate the next phase of the mission, he would cut him off now to avoid further exposure. Before crossing the border at Aqaba, the Professor instructed his driver to stop at a gas station where he discarded his knife in a trash receptacle.

***

“The subject captured at Petra is an Israeli agent with Shin Bet,” proclaimed Special Agent Hunter, who had received an angry call from the FBI director himself. The director had earlier fielded a call from Israel’s very agitated defense minister. Everyone in the FBI conference room looked down at their notes.

Jordan was one of the few countries that cooperated with the United States to host extreme rendition tactics such as torture and carry out the interrogations themselves. This meant that there was no immediate need to fly him out of the country. But more importantly, it meant Jordanian security forces were required to be present during questioning, and it was evident to them once Leosha was seated and his hood removed that he was likely *not* working for any Islamist or extremist cause. The Jordanian agents had a good laugh once they realized the Americans had likely captured an Israeli intelligence officer.

“The bad news is that obviously we don’t come out of this operation looking competent or effective, and I take responsibility for the fact we did not alert the Israelis that we were operating there.” Hunter said to his team. “If there is any good news, it is that the Israelis were on the same trajectory as us, and now our interests are aligned.” Hunter could not possibly load any more sugarcoating on the catastrophe at Petra, but he didn’t want to demoralize his team. The weight of what would become known as “the fuck up” would be permanently attached to his name, and his focus now was on redemption.

“The Israelis suffered one casualty. They blame us for the botched operation. Agent Goodman,

I want you to continue to quote policy and protocol the next time I am persuaded to take any short cuts. Thank you, everyone. That will be all."

With that, the harsh sound of 12 office chairs backing up from the table reverberated like thunder. Goodman and Richard sat next to each other in an empty conference room.

"Well, we really did fuck that up," Richard said, realizing only as the words left his mouth that Sarah was managing most of the operation. To pivot away from the self-inflicted wound, he quickly added, "What is our next move?"

"We need to leverage Hassan further," she replied. "He's the most direct link we have to the intelligence. I also think Aktar may be hiding something. And we need to know what intelligence the Israelis have. What we really need now is a black swan."

That magical term, which the intelligence community used to describe a turning point leading to investigative success, seemed to be flying nowhere near them. The Petra operation could have offered that opportunity, but it had been squandered. Hassan remained in custody but had already surrendered whatever information he could offer.

"Right now, I can't think straight," Goodman confessed, "I'm too hungry."

"I can solve that case," Richard shot back. "Let's go."

Richard ever so gently placed his hand on the small of her back as she left the room in front of him. He estimated the elapsed time of that move was less than two seconds, just the right amount to send a signal. They took the elevator down to the lobby and stepped out on Eleventh Avenue to grab a quick bite to eat. The two were feeling increasingly comfortable with one another.

As the two sat opposite each other at a small street café, a composite picture of the Professor was being printed off the secure fax machine back at FBI headquarters, sent by an intelligence agency officer working for Captain Avi in Tel Aviv. It laid bare the general sentiment of everyone in the department.

From: *Shin Bet Headquarters, Tel Aviv*
To: *The FBI team that abducted the wrong man at Petra.*

***

"I need to get out of these clothes," Sarah confessed. *I wish I could help with that*, Richard thought, but he understood what she meant. The two were expected back by eleven for a teleconference with Shin Bet to discuss the incident at Petra.

"I'll walk you to your hotel," he replied. Richard summoned the waiter to bring their bill, and within a few minutes they were walking down Broadway.

"Would you like me to come up?" Richard asked hopefully as they approached the doors of the lobby.

"Not tonight," she said with a smile. "I'll meet you back at the agency."

Richard smiled in agreement. "Okay, see you in a bit."

He turned around and headed back toward the Javits Center. Something about being with Sarah and the exchange they just had persuaded him to forgo the taxi, and instead he walked back in the direction of the agency offices.

Not tonight, he mused, *not tonight*. If ever there were a signal that Richard had a chance with Sarah Goodman, this was it. He was going to have to play the long game, he thought, and he'd expect nothing less. He wanted to celebrate this small victory but did not have many options. Then he remembered he had the equivalent of a couple of lines of cocaine in a plastic bag he stored in the liner of his jacket. He turned toward a storefront to feign interest in late-night window shopping, transferred the contents of the bag to his index finger, and from there to his nostrils.

Richard was only about four blocks from the Javits Center, crossing the street at Eighth Avenue outside Penn Station when it happened. As he was halfway through the intersection, he heard a voice from behind, "Richard, wait up!" It was too dark to see who was approaching him, waving his hand. The man wore a headscarf and had a beard and mustache but did not resemble anyone in Richard's small network of acquaintances. As he waited for the man to catch up to him, a car swept behind him and stopped in the middle of the intersection. The rear passenger door flew open. The man who called to him reached him and used one hand to fire a taser into his side and used his other hand to push him into the back seat of the car. Another man emerged from the back seat to assist, covering Richard's mouth with a cloth loaded with a combination of chloroform and diazepam. The man outside slammed the car door shut once Richard was fully inside, and the car sped away in the night.

***

"Let's get this over with," Captain Avi told his team as they took their seats. It was just before eight in the morning in Tel Aviv. "The goal of this call is to find out what the Americans know about the Dubai bombing or Chad Kirin."

Avi aimed a hard expression at each face in the room. "Look," he continued, "I know many of you may be angry about the interference of the Americans, but there will be no airing of grievances on this call."

"Okay, let's get this over with," Special Agent Hunter told his team in the FBI command center in New York. It was 11:00 p.m. He stood in front of the large center screen in the room on which a Zoom call would soon be initiated. "The Israelis are angry about the way things went down in Petra, and with good reason. Be respectful if you have a question. Stay on topic. Let's see what they know about the target that got away." As Hunter spoke, his team's attention was distracted by the large image of Captain Avi looking down on them, a signal to Hunter to turn around and start the call.

"Captain Avi, thank you for taking the time for this call, we appreciate it. How is Agent Schalit?"

Hunter knew well enough to stay away from any discussion of Leosha Simakov.

"He is in hospital, in stable condition, thank you for asking." Avi wanted to pivot to his agenda. "As you know, we also lost an agent in the Dubai bombing. Do you have any intelligence on the perpetrators?"

"We've been able to intercept chats between perps that may be involved. From the specific exchanges, we believe that Iran may have funded the operation."

"Were you aware of the planned bombing before it happened?" The voice was not Avi's, but he could not blame his officer for asking from the back of the room.

"No. I can assure you, we had no warning. As I said, we've only just gained access to the cell. What can you tell us about the man you were pursuing in Petra?" It was time for Hunter to turn the conversation back to what interested him most.

"He operates under the cover of a university professor in Saudi Arabia. He likely has multiple aliases." Avi conveniently left out the fact that, until now, the Unicorn was a valued asset of Israeli intelligence. And it would be expected that the world's most intelligent intelligence agency would have an idea about his whereabouts.

"Agent Hunter," Avi continued, "we have reason to believe that he may be on his way to the United States."

23

Even though Muhammed never revealed that he was behind the plot, Jelani couldn't stop thinking about the bombing. He knew enough about his friend's beliefs, politics, and values to suspect that there was a connection. *No, it's not a suspicion*, he admitted to himself, *Muhammed did this.*

Jelani consumed as much of the news about the bombing as he could from the internet café in his village. He was looking for clues, searching for meaning, and trying to come to terms with his role in it all. There was still no claim of responsibility; no revelations that he could tie back to Muhammed.

"What are you looking at?" came a voice from behind him. as he sat in front of the computer at the internet cafe. It was his friend Kofi from school. Jelani turned away from the computer toward Kofi.

"Who are all those people?" Kofi asked.

Jelani was on a web page of the *Khaleej Times*, one of the major newspaper outlets in the UAE, the first to be offered in English across the region. The headline of the article on Jelani's screen read "Crown Prince Condemns Synagogue Attack." Below was a statement issued by the royal family, expressing outrage that a bombing occurred on their soil, irrespective of the faith targeted. Below this section, the paper published the names and photos of the deceased.

"Just a bunch of people that died in a bombing," Jelani replied, hoping Kofi would not take his inquiry any further.

"Why are you interested in that?"

"I was looking for the cricket scores, we played the UAE several years ago. Now be gone with you, I'll be using this computer for a while longer."

"We won by forty-two runs in the World 20 Qualifier," Kofi said with a smile as he walked away.

Jelani turned back to the computer. He promised himself that if nothing further was revealed by this article, he would put the experience behind him and abandon his work with Muhammed.

As he focused back on the computer screen, he saw the faces of the deceased. His eyes stopped, and nearly his heart as well, on the photo of Barbara Klein, the woman he had met at the Jumeriah Mosque, the day before the bombing that took her life. Jelani could barely breathe; his heart started to flutter, and tears filled his eyes.

***

"Ostaaza Erina," Basheer Aktar replied, employing the Arabic salutation to communicate respect. "I am sure your son will be released soon and that no harm will come to him. In any event, yes, I will check on him as soon as possible and let you know what I can learn from the authorities. Yes, I understand, I'll speak to you again soon, okay? Please do not worry. Goodbye, Erina."

Aktar stared across his expansive office. The call was from the mother of Hassan Al Saliba, the young man he dispatched several days ago to run "an errand" for the center. It seems Hassan had gotten himself into trouble and called his mother from the police station in Ann Arbor, about forty miles west of his home in Dearborn.

Basheer considered scenarios and how they might play out. *Did they believe Hassan's alibi? Did he hold up under the pressure of interrogation? Were the police or, worse, the FBI, coming for Aktar next?* He instructed his admin to cancel his remaining appointments for the week and booked a flight to New York.

***

Richard lifted his head slowly and surveyed the room. He was facing a door in the distance, a large white card attached to it, below a peephole. To his left was a small coffee table with two cups that held the remnants of tea. A window behind the table showed the lights of an adjoining skyscraper; wherever he was, it was a high floor. To the right was a short hallway, a faint light giving away the restroom that was there. He was in a hotel room, he concluded. He could hear voices behind him and thought to get up to find them. Then he realized he was strapped into the chair, his hands tied behind his back.

He was still dizzy from the chloroform, and he felt certain this was a case of mistaken identity. He vaguely remembered being with Sarah before being assaulted on the street, then carried by two men through a hotel lobby. "Best man at the bachelor party," one of them yelled at the hotel clerk who watched as they dragged him into the elevator. "He gave a great toast but didn't stop there."

Richard's fuzzy concentration was broken by voices behind him. A man spoke nervously in Arabic about someone detained by the police.

"What are we going to do now? What if he talks; he's just a boy." The man complained, no doubt to another person who remained out of view.

"He does not know anything," came the response.

Richard felt the presence of the men approaching him from behind, so he closed his eyes and slowly lowered his head, pretending to be unconscious. By now, the two men were standing in front of him. As he cracked his eyes ever so slightly, he recognized the voice of Basheer Aktar from the Islamic Center in Dearborn.

"I worry this will only raise suspicions of our community and our intentions," Aktar continued complaining, "you don't live here, you won't have to suffer the consequences."

"My brother," the man replied in a serious tone signaling the end of the discussion. "I would caution you not to compare the comfort with which you surround yourself with the lives of your brethren that have sacrificed themselves to the centuries-old struggle for recognition and equality."

The Professor's disdain with Aktar was obvious. Of all the assets he had recruited, Aktar was the most problematic and least reliable. The Professor could forgive him for the fact that he could only recruit from within the community of disaffected youth that associated with the Islamic center, but to have trusted Hassan Al Saliba with the delicate task of silencing Kristen Edwards was a mistake. Aktar's men were amateurs and represented the weak link in the entire operation.

The Professor turned to Richard and lowered himself so that his face was a few inches away from Richard's. Richard could feel the Professor's breath on his chin. He spoke softly, in English.

"My son, I fear you have swum so far from shore, how will you ever get back?"

He tilted his head upward to signal someone behind Richard. A third man, up to now quietly observing the situation, came forward. Through the small slit his eyelids made, Richard could only see the bottom of his trousers and shoes but suspected this could be one of the men who assaulted him. The man drew a tourniquet just above Richard's elbow, causing Richard instinctively to resist and open his eyes, allowing him a full view of the Professor, but within a few seconds he had been injected with heroin and felt it rushing through his veins. The man dropped the syringe on the coffee table and stood by the other two men, watching Richard's head fall even farther toward his chest. Richard's reaction to the drug was partially an act and partially an expression of "no mas," so that they might finally leave him alone. The men turned their backs to Richard and left the room.

Richard vowed to count down from one hundred before lifting his head, simply to verify that the room was now empty. He made it to seventy-eight. As he looked about, the room appeared as it did before. He did not know when the men would return, but this was his opportunity to escape. He rocked the chair back and forth, eventually landing hard on his left side. To his surprise, the men did not tie his hands to the chair but merely bound them with zip ties behind it. He was able to wriggle free from the chair and, after assuming the fetal position, he pulled his arms under his legs, so they were now in front of him. Looking around the room, he could not find a blade sharp enough to cut himself free, so he grabbed a towel from the bathroom, draped it over his arms.

Before leaving the room, he had the presence of mind to look around one last time in case there was anything of value he could extract from the incident. The room looked like it was clean, and there was no sign of any personal belongings or luggage. However, the guest chair against the wall had a copy of the Quran on top of a prayer mat, and on top of this, a book of matches from the Homa Hotel in Tehran. He was too manic to recognize the scene was staged.

In the hallway, he saw a couple waiting by the elevator in one direction, the stairwell in the other. If he took the elevator, he risked being discovered in the lobby, so he walked briskly toward the stairs, opened the door, and began launching himself downward. His prior experience as a user gave him a reasonable understanding of what to expect next.

Even had he not been doped up, he was sweating and panting more with each flight of stairs. The monotony of the steps began to play tricks on his sedated mind, and the view ahead started to blur. As he turned to tackle another flight, he became dizzy, tripping on steps he did not know were there.

Eventually, he brought himself gently down to the ground on the landing outside the ninth floor. He had the presence of mind to enter the hallway and, as he did so, he was discovered by a couple waiting for the elevator. That was the last thing he remembered before passing out.

24

Misha carefully placed the ten jars about a half meter apart around the ten-meter diameter of the circle painted on the floor of the room. The room itself was a perfect circle, with a door that was flush with the walls – there were no exposed doorknobs or hinges. In the center of the room was a round metal disc, the size and shape of a dinner plate. The radioactive cobalt sat below the disc; the disc was the top of a cage containing the lethal material. This would rise from below ground once Misha left the room and threw the switch. Each ray from deteriorating cobalt could bounce off the curved walls without any corners or metal hardware to influence its path. It would bathe the room with gamma radiation.

Every jar, about the size of a container of preserves, contained a fragment of human bone suspended in a liquid. Where the bones came from was never clear to Misha, but the purpose of having them exposed to cobalt 60 was to sterilize them via radiation for use in humans who required a bone graft. The radiation effectively degraded the collagen in the bone marrow, ensuring any grafts were not rejected by their new host. Misha presumed the cadavers were from Iranian soldiers or prisoners because Iranians themselves were not generally keen to donate their body parts after death.

The Bushehr Nuclear Plant where Misha worked was about twelve hundred kilometers south of Tehran. It performed multiple functions involving radioactive isotopes, some for medical purposes, and partly to keep the rest of the world guessing about its more nefarious activities.

After about twenty minutes, an alarm indicated to Misha that it was safe to re-enter the room and collect the specimens. The jars were originally clear glass, but they were now dark blue, taking on the color that gives cobalt its name. That meant the specimens were adequately sterilized by the radioactive material, and Misha placed each jar on a rolling cart. Then, he felt the cell phone in his lab coat pocket begin to vibrate.

"It's time." It was a text from the Professor, using a prepaid cellphone that he would be disposing of later that day. Misha deleted the text and returned the phone to his pocket. He would continue with his task. It was time to prepare the jars for distribution to hospitals across Iran.

Control of radioactive materials, even in a country as provocative as Iran, is subject to strict protocols. Inventories would be closely monitored. Staff accountable for handling nuclear material would be subject to stringent background checks. When the Professor met a nuclear laboratory technician while attending a science symposium in Tehran, he cultivated the relationship with as much care as if he were handling a uranium core with his bare hands.

Misha Amani was uniquely suited to the operation conceived by the Professor. Born in Mosul to an orthodox Jewish family, he fled Iraq in 2014 after the ISIS invasion put an end to virtually all Jewish communities in Iraq, and ended up in Iran, where Jews are still an integral part of society. Partly because he changed his name from Abramowitz to avoid persecution, and perhaps because the Bush administration insisted that his homeland possessed "weapons of mass destruction," Misha easily gained employment at the Iranian plant working near one of the largest caches of enriched uranium in the world.

But it was not Iranian radioactive material that the Professor was after. It was Russian nuclear weapons Iran acquired in 1997 as the Soviet Union was collapsing and simultaneously attempting to comply with its obligations under the nuclear arms reduction treaty. The treaty required the U.S. and Soviet Union to destroy all but six thousand warheads that were sitting atop missiles, which meant the Soviets had to collect and destroy thirty-two hundred warheads from Ukraine, Belarus, and Kazakhstan. Additionally, twenty-two thousand tactical nuclear weapons with smaller yields and shorter ranges were to be collected from these countries and destroyed. These weapons were designed primarily for battlefield use, some small enough to fit in a ski bag or suitcase. While Western democracies were skeptical that such an ambitious undertaking across fourteen newly liberated states could be accomplished with no weapons unaccounted for, they were too busy setting up a monitoring program to notice several go missing.

The Russian inventories of weapons were kept underground on the campus of the power plant to shield plant employees from radiation and hide them from satellites that might be looking for them. Access to the underground bunkers was not tightly controlled because who would expect an employee to walk off with a nuclear weapon? Misha would be returning late that evening, when security was barely present, to do exactly that.

***

Richard woke up in a hospital bed in New York-Presbyterian Hospital. Sarah Goodman, who was looking at him, forced herself to smile.

"Sarah, where am I? How did I get here?"

Sarah decided to answer the second question as the first was obvious. "You were found on the floor in a hotel, the Viking, I think, and you were unconscious."

"Sarah, I was abducted! How did you find me?"

"The paramedics held your phone to your face to unlock it, and I was the last number you dialed. I guess I am your 'ICE' for tonight."

"I need to get back to the agency. They need to know about this."

"Don't worry about that. The hospital has already alerted them, and I'll update them." Getting anyone to believe it didn't seem likely. It did not help that the paramedics cut off the zip ties that would have corroborated his story.

With that, Sarah reached down to kiss Richard on his forehead. Instinctively, he tilted his head back so that his lips met hers, and for at least three seconds, they were no longer merely colleagues. When Sarah pulled back, she offered a tentative smile, then left. Richard brought his head back to a resting position and briefly closed his eyes to relive the moment and imagine where it might have led had he not been in a hospital bed.

"Richard, my baby, are they treating you all right?" To Jill, her grown sons were still her little babies. Jill and Jerry O'Brien were at the side of the bed, interrupting his fantasy. The fog in his brain was clearing, and he wondered how it was that his parents were here and not in Michigan.

"Richard, why didn't you tell us?" his father interrupted before Richard could speak. "You're not an agent?" It was evident from the comment that his parents were briefed about his limited role in the FBI, and how the FBI believed he ended up face down on the floor of a hotel. While his mother cared only for his welfare, his father felt betrayed by a son who did not share the truth with his parents about his career. "Son, we would not have cared either way," he added.

The fact that Richard had a drug abuse problem was not unknown to his parents, but from the time he settled in Brooklyn the narrative he fed them was that of a stable, rising star within the FBI. He was ashamed to be in a hospital bed, the victim of a drug overdose, but he felt obliged by the code he followed within the FBI to refrain from discussing anything that might be sensitive and related to an active investigation.

"Look, I can't talk about the details of this but it's not what you think, and it's definitely not how it appears."

Alternating expressions of compassion, sympathy, and denial appeared on his parents' faces. Richard didn't need their words to understand.

"Dear, we are going to be in New York for a few days, at least until you get out of here. Get some rest. The doctor said you will be discharged today or tomorrow. We will be at the Marriott Hotel by Grand Central. Call us when you are ready to go home, and we will come by and get you, okay?"

Richard nodded in agreement, not really understanding what "home" his mother was referring to but not believing for a moment that his parents intended to bring him back to Michigan. Besides, he was in the thick of this case now, and on the trail of Basheer Aktar, his accomplice, and Sarah Goodman.

***

By the time Richard arrived at the FBI command center, it was mid-afternoon. He was discharged a few hours after his parents had visited but thought only about bringing his report to the FBI task force as soon as possible. When he entered the main conference room, a couple of agents were already there, arriving early for the next scheduled briefing. Richard immediately launched into a regurgitation of the previous twenty-four hours.

"and then I started to rock the chair back and forth and . . . "

As he spoke, Richard's attention shifted to the nearest side of the room where a series of suspect photos and sketches were taped to the wall, creating a tapestry of clandestine relationships. In FBI vernacular, this was often referred to as "the food chain." Lines connected each photo in a web form, but the general shape was that of a pyramid. From the bottom, he recognized Kristen, Myles's girlfriend. Next to her was a photo of Hassan Isa Saliba, and above them, Basheer Aktar. There were a couple of additional sketches that Richard did not recognize, but he most definitely recognized the sketch at the top of the pyramid: It was the man known to Israeli intelligence as the Unicorn.

"That's him! That's the guy that abducted me!"

As Richard looked at the sketch of the Professor, connecting the dots to his encounter the day before, Special Agent Hunter entered the room.

"O'Brien, you are expected in Director Pritchard's office immediately."

"But that suspect—"

"That's enough, O'Brien. Pritchard's office, immediately. Understand?"

"Yes, sir."

Richard presumed his meeting with Pritchard was merely a formality. Perhaps there were forms required by human resources, perhaps Pritchard simply wanted to see how he was feeling after the assault. He didn't expect Pritchard to buzz into his office his counterpart in the internal affairs department as soon as Richard appeared in his doorway.

"Richard, sit down. I assume you know why I've asked IA to participate in this meeting. It'll be quick."

Richard replied while taking a seat, "Well sir, actually—"

"Richard, the toxicology report from the hospital showed you had both cocaine and heroin in your system. This is a serious offense, particularly for an employee of the agency."

Richard realized that as an employee of the FBI, "private health information" was an oxymoron.

"But sir, the assault, they put those substances in me. I was drugged and tied to a chair—"

"Yes, that's all very interesting, Richard, and I'll allow the internal investigation to determine the veracity of your story. All I know is you were found passed out on the floor of a hotel. The toxicology report revealed the cocaine had almost fully metabolized in your system hours before you injected the heroin. Really, Richard."

Richard was not prepared for the ambush.

"Effective immediately, you are on administrative leave from the FBI. Clean out your locker and return your laptop to IT. Internal affairs will be in touch with you regarding next steps. That will be all, Richard."

As Richard left the office, he looked forward down the hallway but didn't see anything. Various agents passed him by, but he paid them no attention. As he returned to pass the conference room where the briefing had already started, he paused to see Sarah Goodman in the room, taking notes. He quickly left the building before anyone else might notice him and took the subway back to his flat in Brooklyn.

Richard entered the lobby of his apartment and collected several days' worth of mail from the lockboxes. As he entered his dark flat, he dropped the mail on a table by the front door and dropped his door key on top. He continued to the counter that separated the tiny kitchen from the even smaller dining area, threw his backpack on one of the barstools, and threw his body on the other. Then, he rested his elbows on the counter and his head in his hands.

How did I allow this to happen? I've become a "PNG" in the agency. He considered his options for the next several minutes, the most attractive being drugs and alcohol in generous amounts. Then he realized he could pair this with amazing sex with Courtney, who was eager to see him last night and always willing to do a few lines with him. Maybe he would have her come over in a raincoat with nothing underneath; a night of BDSM, femdom, and wild sex was just what he needed. He reached for the cellphone in his front pocket and dialed her up.

"*The voice mailbox you have reached is full. Please try your call again later.*"

Richard had dated Courtney on and off for several years but had never heard her phone reply with a recorded message. If anything, Courtney was a master of all things related to the cellphone and would never allow her voice mail to fill up. As much as he detested her roommate, Richard decided to call her up to see how best to connect with Courtney. He found Sandy's phone number in his contacts and dialed.

"You fucking asshole," Sandy shouted into the phone. "How dare you call me? You are such a jerk, I hope you go to hell."

"Whoa, Sandy, step back. I just wanted to get in touch with Courtney, her voice mail is full." Sandy's reply took more than a few seconds to come across. Her voice trembled.

"She's . . . dead, you idiot," Sandy replied, sobbing. "She slit her wrists in the bathtub last night. You're such a fucking asshole."

"What? She's . . . What? WHAT?"

"You don't string along a bipolar woman, make her pregnant, and then ghost her. You disgust me, you really disgust me. Fuck off and never call me again." The line went dead.

Richard stared ahead, effectively hypnotized.

Bipolar? Slit wrists? Pregnant? Richard realized he had made a promise to see Courtney last night. "*I really need to talk to you,*" she had said. Richard went to the kitchen sink. He felt an uncontrollable urge to vomit.

***

"Are we talking about state-sponsored activity or an extremist cell?"

Special Agent Hunter feared that question most because he could not answer it. And the question was coming from the chairman of the Select Committee on Intelligence during a briefing that was called to examine the findings from the Dubai bombing.

"Sir, we are not sure," he replied, quickly pivoting to what he *did* know. "But we have reason to believe the perpetrator recently arrived in the U.S., and he has potential support from here and abroad."

"What makes you think the Iranians are involved? Are we looking at a case of confirmation bias here?"

"Sir, the Iranians have their fingerprints all over this," Hunter replied. "We followed the money to an Iranian bank, the main suspect has ties to Iran, and the Israelis have found evidence of Iranian involvement in the Dubai bombing."

The last part was not something Hunter had confirmed, but verification from another intelligence agency would give significant weight to his report. If there was one thing that Hunter had learned from his years at the agency, you were simply pissing in the wind unless you have multiple verifications of any theory you put forward, so it was common practice to ad-lib to get traction for your story. "We can't have another 9/11" was used so often as an excuse to precipitate action that you could almost see it coming in any conversation within the agency.

"What does a bombing in Dubai have to do with statehood for the Palestinians?" came another question from the freshman senator from Ohio, a decorated army officer turned politician.

"Sir, sympathy for the Palestinians within the Arab world is a cyclical phenomenon. It rears its head every few years. By inflicting pain within the Arab region, it's likely an attempt to force the neutral parties, like the UAE, into the debate. Also, and perhaps more importantly, it's an indication they are willing to take this fight wherever they believe they can reach a larger audience. You know, Western democracies are nearly numb to the violence within Israel's borders. Any news about the Mideast conflict is replaced by the latest domestic issue in the media within a couple days. A threat beyond those borders is sure to grab headlines and to keep them there. Especially if those headlines included the phrase 'dirty bomb.'"

"What else can we expect?" The members of the committee leaned forward to hear what Hunter would say next.

"Sir, we are constructing most-likely engagement scenarios at this moment; it's a very fluid situation. But we have one operating theory that we believe is plausible. In 2021, the Iranians sent the *Makran*, an oil tanker converted to a military vessel, around the Cape of Good Hope in South Africa, into the Atlantic, and up the coast. At one point it appeared it would enter the Mediterranean, but at the last minute it changed course and headed to Venezuela.

"Our drones followed the vessel into port and verified they offloaded a cache of weapons, fast boats, and artillery there. We weren't surprised, the two countries have been trading partners. But had the vessel made its way into the Mediterranean, those weapons could have found their way into Gaza, and into the hands of Hamas."

This was just the opening John Hayden was looking for.

Hayden was not your typical guest at an intelligence briefing. While not a committee member, he was the current homeland security secretary and a retired four-star Army general. In 2010 he had been instrumental in denying the proposed Islamic Community Center & Mosque, known as the Cordoba House, near the original twin towers site in Lower Manhattan. The project planned to include community and cultural spaces to foster interfaith dialogue and promote peace and understanding while mourning those that perished in 9/11. Hayden would not have it.

"Agent Hunter," his voice projected across the room as if he were commanding a regiment, "are you suggesting that the Iranians are potentially about to arm Hamas with a dirty bomb or bona fide nuclear weapon?"

The proverbial eight-hundred-pound gorilla in the room was now awake. Iran's nuclear capability was an ongoing concern at the committee, and the administration's abandonment of the arms treaty in 2018 made Iran's nuclear program even more opaque.

"General," Hunter replied, "given the activity and level of coordination we are observing, I don't think we can rule that out."

Robert Gates, secretary of defense under George W. Bush, reportedly said on learning about Syria's secret nuclear reactor in 2006 that "every administration gets one pre-emptive war against a Muslim country." Hayden was tempted to quote Gates in the meeting but decided to keep that justification to himself for now.

***

Richard lay on his sofa in the fetal position with no sense of time other than recognizing that the sun had set. His head hurt, and he was dehydrated. As he pulled himself up, reality intruded. He was on administrative leave from the FBI. He made a woman pregnant, ignored her, and she committed suicide. His parents discovered he was a fraud. And the woman he felt the most comfortable with in all his life was slipping away.

Fuck, he thought. *I've lost a friend. And . . . a child? And I am still thinking about another woman. What the fuck is wrong with me?*"

He looked at his phone and saw a missed call from Myles. Myles was probably in touch with his parents and learned about his trip to the hospital. *By now he knows that I'm not an agent*, he mused. *I am such a jerk. What else can I pile on top of this*?"

His phone started to vibrate again. It was from a 202 number he did not recognize. He accepted the call.

"Richard?" It was Sarah.

"Yeah. Sarah?"

"Richard, we don't have much time. Do you still have it?"

"Have what?"

"The laptop. From the agency. Do you still have it?"

He looked across the room at the backpack sitting on the barstool at his kitchen counter. He had left the agency before returning the laptop.

"Yeah. Wait, where are you?"

"I am calling from a phone booth outside the agency, you know, to be safe. Look, Richard, you must log on right away. I'm taking a big risk here, and you have to do this before the latest intercept is downloaded and assigned to someone else."

Richard looked at his phone. It was Friday. Muhammed had promised to connect with Hassan, and an encrypted broadcast was expected from whoever was planning the next attack.

"Oh shit, yeah, I hope my credentials still work. How do I reach you?"

"I'll call you later," she replied.

"Sarah, wait, I need to—" The line was already dead.

Richard sprang up with energy he did not know he had and reached for his backpack. He dug the laptop out and slapped it on the kitchen counter. He prayed to himself that he would still be able to log on to the agency's network, Sentinel, and the Onion Router that allowed him to access the backchannel used by Muhammed to communicate with Hassan. The computer seemed to take forever to start up. He clicked the FBI icon that would send a code to his cell phone, a code he would have to type back into a dialogue box that would allow him access to the platform. Could he get back into the game, even though he was technically in the penalty box and potentially about to be let go? None of that mattered now.

25

Eli Cohen was recruited into the Mossad in 1960, trained as an Israeli agent, then sent to Buenos Aires a year later to establish a cover as a Syrian businessman before moving to Damascus in 1961. From there he would spy for the Israeli government while building relationships with high-ranking Syrian politicians, military officials, influential public figures, and the diplomatic community. He rose in power to become the chief adviser to Syria's defense minister before being outed as a spy and publicly executed in 1965. Cohen remains one of the most admired national heroes in Israeli history, a tiny country with no small number of national heroes.

The success of Eli Cohen's mission would inevitably cause the Mossad to consider running agents within other foreign adversaries, under the right circumstances. When a Jewish educator from Somalia contacted the Israeli embassy seeking refugee status, the Mossad intervened and re-opened the Eli Cohen playbook.

Isaac Shulman appeared a perfect candidate for the Mossad from the outset: a young man with no family ties in a country where he had little to no community connection. He was home schooled by his father, who was killed in a skirmish between U.S Marines and Somali rebels. His mother died when he was very young. He knew as much or more about the Arabic language and Muslim customs as he did his own Jewish faith. The Mossad felt Shulman could be groomed to take a position in Saudi Arabia, a country with an ambiguous attitude toward Israel, but one that still harbored extremists, including some of the 9/11 terrorists. After bringing him to Israel for evaluation, he was offered citizenship in exchange for a minimum five-year commitment to operate out of Saudi Arabia, working as a university professor.

The Mossad drew up Shulman's credentials and assisted him with establishing himself in Dammam. Based on forged credentials, he was able to secure a role in academia while feeding intelligence to the Israeli security forces about Saudi attitudes toward Israel in general and the activities of extremist groups in particular.

Shulman's world view was shaped by his environment: living in a country intensely hostile to non-Muslims, sympathetic to Palestinians, and devoted to the destruction of Israel. Even though he was stationed in Dammam, he believed the Mossad to be his extended family, and given that they rescued him from the horrors of living in Somalia, he considered himself indebted.

All this changed in 2021 when Benjamin Netanyahu, the longest reigning prime minister in Israel's history, was defeated by a coalition of eight political parties, including left-leaning, progressive, and even Islamist factions within Israel's dynamic electorate. Isaac watched these developments from afar and, with the right-wing government agreeing to pass on power to these other groups within two years, he understood that Palestinians had their best opportunity ever to secure statehood. While the Republican and Democratic candidates for U.S. president rarely were on the same side of an issue, they generally agreed it was time for the Palestinians to achieve statehood. Isaac could not tolerate such a scenario, recognizing the Palestinian's infinite appetite to seek the destruction of Israel.

But of all global developments, none had quite the impact on Isaac as the U.S. withdrawal from Afghanistan in 2021. During its coverage of the story, CNN interviewed a Taliban leader who claimed the group's goal was not only to convert that country back to strict practice of Islamic law, but to convert the entire world. "We are in no particular hurry," he said.

It was then, in the fall of the same year, that the Professor renewed an acquaintance he made years before, during the Gulf War, with General John Hayden from the United States. Isaac had already felt that cuts in the Mossad's counter-espionage resources rendered him less relevant and less supported. He reasoned the United States would be interested in his services, and he offered them up to Hayden when he was traveling through the region on a diplomatic mission.

"This is the worst of all bad ideas," Hayden said when Shulman explained his plan to have the Palestinians caught red-handed with a nuclear weapon, bringing the wrath of all Western democracies down on them. "You would need to build a robust network of operatives for the plot to be taken seriously. This is a ruse of epic proportions."

But Shulman, known to his Israeli handlers as Unicorn and to his Arab followers as the Professor, had already made great strides toward making his plan operational.

***

Richard's hands were shaking as he fired up the FBI laptop.

"Please, please, please…" he muttered under his breath as he entered credentials to patch into the secure portal where he could retrieve intercepts that Sentinel would have captured, specifically the chat he chose to "follow" from a few days prior.

"I'm in," he said aloud, as if Sarah Goodman was sitting next to him, cheering him on. "Now if I can just . . ." Richard grabbed his phone to authenticate his security clearance. An alert popped on his phone. He positioned the phone so the facial recognition would send the authentication to the server. That was the last step to accessing the latest message in his inbox.

Intercepted script, 0830 hrs. 18 March. Origination: New York.

Keywords: destroy, Hamas, Gaza, Iran, Palestine.

"The package has left Chabahar and will be transported to Gaza via My Angel in two days' time. This will afford Hamas the leverage to demand statehood, or to destroy Tel Aviv, or both. It will be a

glorious day for Iran and their brothers in Palestine."

Richard stared in horror at the translated intercept. The package? It would have to be a weapon; that was a weak attempt at deception for sure, he thought. But a single weapon big enough to destroy an entire city would have to be a nuclear weapon. And how is it that the origin of the message was from New York regarding a shipment from Iran's main seaside port? Could it have something to do with the people who abducted him? What was it about all these intercepts that didn't feel right? And finally, who is My Angel?

The scenarios dizzied Richard. "I have to get this information to Sarah," he muttered. He tried to think back to the abduction where, in the hotel, the bad guys must have been planning something nefarious. Still, something did not make sense. The words from his abductor kept returning: You have swum so far from shore . . . "

What am I missing, he demanded of himself.

The answer hit Richard like a brick against the head. Iranians speak Farsi, but the people that captured him spoke Arabic! The intercepts were also in Arabic, not Farsi; Richard was not fluent in Farsi, but he knew enough to recognize it when he saw it. Much of written Arabic and Farsi are similar. But not only did the man in the hotel room speak Arabic, but he did it with an accent that was unlike any Arabic speaker he had heard before. *If the Iranians are involved, wouldn't the intercepts be in their native language?*

***

It had been two days since Jelani had looked upon the pictures of the temple worshippers killed in the Dubai bombing, including that of Barbara Klein. Guilt on a level he never felt before followed him throughout his day, and he had difficulty concentrating on his job at the lodge or at home with his family. He wanted to confront Muhammed, whom he had known since childhood, but he was unsure how to broach the subject. The fact they could only communicate over a secure channel, and only through text, made that prospect even more difficult.

That made a new WhatsApp message feel even more like destiny.

"*My brother*," came the message to him from Muhammed. "*I need you to send fresh dates to our brothers in Palestine*." Jelani understood "dates" to be the codeword for "funds," the same term they used since the beginning when discussing the movement of money to and from banks that held the proceeds from his internet scam. Jelani was used to depositing funds but less familiar with how to send them.

"*Where am I to ship the dates?*" he asked.

"*My uncle is a fisherman there,*" Muhammed wrote. *"His name is Farouk El-Sayed. He lives near the port of Gaza. He is from Somalia, like us. You can reach him through the port authority in Rimal. He has ordered 300 dates."*

Muhammed looked back at the thread, confirming that he had not used any keywords that might trigger surveillance of his communications. The intelligence he received from Al-Qaeda had revealed the possibility of an American technology platform that would intercept messages referring to money, drugs, or weapons.

As the currency collected by Jelani was laundered through the trading company based in Dubai, it was common for the two to speak in terms of dirham, the currency of UAE, abbreviated as AED, and to drop off the trailing zeros to deflect any attention to their conversations that might be monitored based on the size of the transaction. What was not common was for Jelani to be sending three hundred thousand dirhams, over eighty thousand U.S. dollars, to a fisherman in Gaza.

"*How soon is this needed*?" inquired Jelani.

"*Do it immediately. Thank you, my brother. We will speak soon. May Allah be with you.*"

Jelani stared at the thread of the message. Muhammed was up to no good again. Jelani, on the other hand, thought about an opportunity for redemption.

26

The Professor walked out of Union Station in Washington at 2:04 p.m., then walked for several blocks to ensure he was not followed. After turning back toward the station, he hailed a taxi and headed to Southwest Waterfront Park along the Washington Channel. He stopped briefly along a boardwalk so he could casually drop his latest prepaid cellphone into the water. He then approached the designated park bench where he would meet his appointment.

General John Hayden was not a man to be kept waiting. He had recently turned fifty-eight but had the frame of a bodyguard or bouncer. Before serving as homeland security secretary, he was chairman of the Joint Chiefs of Staff, serving under President Baldwin, and before that he commanded NATO forces in Eastern Europe, the only impediment to Russian aspirations to expand beyond the Crimean Peninsula.

Hayden had presidential aspirations of his own, and he was convinced that keeping the status quo in the Middle East was the key to long-term stability in the region. A strong Israel would protect democracy and American interests, Hayden always said, and the Palestinians, having put Hamas in power, could not be trusted as serious partners in search of a lasting peace.

The Baldwin administration, on the other hand, intended to support the goal of a Palestinian state, and the U.S. ambassador, operating under the authority of the White House, was about to introduce a resolution outlining the process for Palestinian statehood at the United Nations Assembly. Hayden was vehemently opposed to the measure.

"You're late," Hayden complained as the Professor came around from behind the bench.

"General," the Professor replied while taking a seat next to him, "in my line of work it doesn't pay to be on time. It is far safer to be late."

"I've heard from the FBI. They know you are here. That was not part of the plan."

"Are they cooperating with the Israelis?"

"It appears so," the general replied. "And the intel they've collected still points to Iran. You've succeeded with the deception."

The Professor looked out on the river, silently contemplating. The general sensed that he had something on his mind.

"The synagogue bombing—" Hayden continued to speak, but the Professor interrupted him.

"With the synagogue bombing I have murdered my own people," he interjected. "I shall never be forgiven for that, no matter how great our victory, no matter how strong Israel becomes as a result. I will have to live with it."

The general could see that the subject of the Dubai bombing was too sensitive to discuss further, and he didn't need to. The job was done, and the

Professor succeeded in that mission. There was only one operation left for him to lead.

"What about the translator?" The general decided to change the subject. "Do we have any exposure there?"

"Mr. O'Brien has been a very cooperative asset, even if he doesn't realize it," the Professor replied. "He's supported the deception from the beginning and has everyone believing that Hamas are planning to acquire a nuclear weapon from Iran."

"And the device?"

"It will be transported via the most common route, initially to Yemen, then north through Sudan to Egypt. Entry to Gaza will be through a newly constructed tunnel unknown to the Israelis. Your navy will need to intercept the shipment before it arrives in Yemen, or you lose control of the device's specific whereabouts."

As Hayden had considered many times before, it was a daring plan. The most effective way to permanently end Palestinian hopes for statehood would be to catch them with a nuclear device, compliments of Iran. And to have a rogue Israeli agent handle the logistics, well, that just made plausible deniability more convenient.

For the Professor, it was critical that the threat of nuclear arms acquired by Hamas be deemed credible but tying the ruse back to Israel was not an option, or the homeland would lose significant standing among Western democracies. The discovery of the plot he had engineered would have to come about by the efforts of the intelligence agencies, it would have to appear well-coordinated and credible, and the weapon would have to be neutralized moments before it could be detonated so the world never entertains the idea of Palestinian freedom ever again. He imagined the headlines when it was all over: Israel Keeps the World Safe for Democracy.

Hayden stood up first. "Let me know when it has left Iran. I'll handle the rest. Have a nice trip home." Hayden was not entirely sure where "home" would be, but he did not particularly care. He left the Professor on the bench and headed back to his office in central DC.

The Professor, for his part, had just told the last lie in his ambitious campaign.

***

Misha Amani nervously lit a cigarette as he leaned against the back of his black Peugeot sedan parked on the side of a petrol station in Halileh, approximately twelve kilometers east of the Bushehr nuclear power plant. It was one fifteen in the morning, and the contact that the Professor arranged for him to meet was twenty minutes late. Misha would give him another ten minutes. On the other hand, he did not want the contents of his trunk to be in his possession one minute more. A look of vulnerability was on his face.

Finally, a pair of headlights from the highway appeared, growing in intensity as they approached the petrol station. At this hour, Misha presumed it would be either his contact, or the police. If it was the police, his story would be that he left the plant late but hesitated to return home because his wife did not permit him to smoke in the house and smoking anywhere near the plant was strictly forbidden. He would offer his remaining cigarettes to them, and then leave the scene as quickly as possible.

The approaching vehicle was a white minivan. The driver flashed his lights as he pulled into the petrol station to confirm his identity as the person that would transport the nuclear weapons across the southern coast of Iran, to the port of Chabahar in the southwest corner of the country. The van slowly rolled up next to the Peugeot, and parked. Only a couple meters separated the vehicles. A young, bearded man in overalls stepped down from the driver's side and walked to the back of the van, opening its two doors wide to reveal a long, waterproof container that ran the length of the truck.

He came to the back of the Peugeot, where Misha was waiting. Misha opened the trunk to reveal three crates, each the size of a rollaboard suitcase, and each containing a Russian nuclear bomb. Without speaking, the young man picked up one crate at a time and placed it in the container in the back of his truck. The container was fabricated for the purpose of transporting the crates, and all three fit snugly inside. The man closed the doors of the van and handed Misha an envelope containing more cash than he would earn in a year.

The man then drove through the night to the port of Chabahar, and loaded the container on a privately owned yacht that would head the following morning to the Mediterranean Sea via the Suez Canal.

27

The fishing boat made its way out of the Port of Gaza around nine. Farouk El-Sayed was at the helm, his eighteen-year-old son, Malek, by his side. The stars were making their presence known, much to the delight of Imram, a Hamas soldier based in the Rimal district of Gaza City who was crouching near the stern. He checked his dive equipment thoroughly as the vessel proceeded west to Egyptian territorial waters, along with Kashif, his favorite dive buddy, also a member of Hamas. Their specially outfitted boat contained a wire cage running under the hull, large enough to carry the cargo they were en route to collect. The two barely spoke as they focused on their mission and silently prayed for Allah to provide for their safety and success.

The ride out lasted about forty minutes. As the boat's GPS confirmed they were approaching the drop point, the boat's captain slowly brought the engine to idle and signaled his first mate to throw the anchor overboard. The boat backed up several yards to ensure the anchor was set. Fishing poles were erected on each side of the boat to support their alibi if they received an unwelcome visit from the Israeli navy.

The next step was one these soldiers had conducted a hundred times before. They cracked open the scuba cylinder and listened as the air hissed through the limp air hose, which became immediately very stiff. Next, they put on their masks, looked over their shoulders to ensure no obstructions were below them, and did a backflip off the boat into the black water. Any diver with experience would know to turn on their lights first, but this was not like any other dive. This was a mission to collect a nuclear weapon.

In 1995, Israel and the PLO signed the Oslo II Accords, which created a zone reaching six nautical miles from the shores of Gaza within which the Palestinians could move freely offshore to sustain their fishing industry. By 2018, Israel cut this zone in half, to three nautical miles, claiming that the fishing boats were smuggling in supplies to construct weapons. In the lead-up to that new restriction, over 1,200 incidents were recorded that led to the death of 8 fishermen, injury of 134 more, and confiscation of 209 boats. Israel continued to monitor this area carefully, conducting patrols and surprise inspections. To carry out their mission, Imram and Kashif would have to swim from within the safe zone into international waters, where the weapon was waiting for them.

Once in the water, the divers turned on their lights, pointing them down to prevent any broadcasting of their activity. They met at the anchor line and proceeded down. Imram checked his depth gauge while equalizing the pressure in his ears, five meters, ten, fifteen . . . he looked down to see if he would reach the bottom soon, but all he could see was black where his light failed to reach. Finally, after what felt like a very long journey into the depths, the sandy bottom came upon him quickly. He checked his gauge as he landed on his knees. He was in eighteen meters of water, about sixty feet deep, the anchor's long chain sitting next to him.

Imram looked up to see Kashif landing a few meters away from him. The two moved closer together, enough to see each other's eyes but careful not to shine their light directly into them. They each checked their air supply: about 172 bar or 2,500 psi, enough for a 56-minute dive without requiring a stop for decompression.

Although Imram and Kashif were experienced divers and understood how to calculate and conduct a dive involving a decompression stop, they didn't even want to consider such a scenario. No, they would need every one of those fifty-six minutes to locate the device and to haul it back to the cage situated under the hull of the boat. Imram checked his compass: the cargo was to the left on a heading 275 degrees northwest of where the anchor lay. Imram signaled the planned direction to Kashif, and the two brought themselves to about two meters off the bottom so they would not disturb the sand and hinder their visibility. The area they had to search could be large, and they had precious little time.

As the two divers proceeded along the sea's bottom, the nightlife could have easily distracted them from their mission. Tiny crabs, shrimp, and pipefish popped out of homemade shelters in the sand only long enough to recognize the divers as a threat and were instantly gone; small schools of mullet gave way and disappeared quickly into the blackness of the water. These waters produced some of the best tuna in the region, along with many other species that made up the diet of the Palestinian people.

Kashif stopped to check his air supply, landing in the sand. He knew he was not as conservative in his breathing as Imram, and that at seventy-five bar, they would have to turn around in order to have enough air to return to the anchor and to allow for a two-minute safety stop on their way back to the surface, standard practice even for a dive where a longer decompression stop was not necessary. Of course, they could always decide to come up short of the anchor and swim the rest of the way, but the risk of being struck by another boat or, worse, captured by an Israeli patrol made that option far less appealing. He was at one hundred bar, about 60 percent of what he had when he entered the water.

As he looked up from his gauge, he could see Imram waving his light excitedly. Once Imram got Kashif's attention, he turned his light off. Kashif knew to do the same. Suddenly the world around them turned pitch black, save for tiny flickers of light from the bioluminescence of the microfauna that absorb light during the day and emit it at night. But there in the distance, two strobe lights flashed in an alternate pattern, suspended about two meters from the seafloor. It was the signal they needed to confirm that they discovered the location of the weapon within its watertight container.

The two divers came upon the container from either side. It was about three meters long, three-quarters of a meter tall, and a half meter wide. It was made of industrial-grade plastic and designed for use underwater to protect the contents. Lights were suspended from each end; the divers turned them off. Then, they unrolled the lift bags they had attached to their buoyancy compensators, the vests that all divers wear to control their buoyancy underwater and to serve as a form of life preserver on the surface. Imram attached his unrolled bag to one end of the container with a carabiner, and Kashif attached his bag to the other. They glanced at each other from time to time as they worked through the drill they had practiced countless times. As they exhaled, showers of bubbles flowed upward, each bubble growing larger as it absorbed oxygen from the water on its way to the surface.

Next, each removed the regulator—the device that flows air from a diver's tank— from his mouth and shoved it into a bag. When they pressed the button in the center of the regulators, the bags filled quickly with air and began to lift off the seafloor. The container attached to the bags was now "airborne" and could be easily transported. Imram and Kashif swam at the sides of the container, pulling it by the lines attached to the lift bags. The container held three nuclear bombs, enough to kill half the population of Tel Aviv if positioned appropriately.

Imram calculated the return journey at eighty-five degrees southeast. Before long, the container would be secured under the boat, and the divers and crew would head back to Gaza, now a bona fide nuclear threat.

When the boat approached the channel markers designating the entrance to the marina, the captain slowed the engine so it would crawl toward the cleats on the dock that it had left earlier. The marina was shaped like a large, semi-square "C" with the top portion facing the water and bottom attached to dry land; boats entered the C from the right side and then, as if navigating an obstacle course, captains looked for any place they could either anchor or attach a line to the dock. Streetlights lined the top of the channel where a handful of locals sat along the steep sides on large boulders that led down to the water, some holding fishing poles, others simply smoking, enjoying the peaceful evening, and gazing out to sea. As the boat crept forward, the streetlight slowly revealed its name, painted on the stern: *Malaki*, which is Arabic for "My Angel."

***

The American Embassy in Nairobi was less than ten kilometers from Jamai Mosque, and the bus ran up A104 to Nairobi from Jelani's village, stopping midway between both at Kenyatta Avenue. It would be easy to persuade his parents to believe he was making a pilgrimage to the mosque and use this as cover for his visit to the embassy.

Jelani had misgivings about his new mission, not so much because of the fact he was potentially betraying his childhood friend but because of the prospect of meeting strangers and having to be the center of attention. No, he would not seek an audience in the embassy, he would simply drop off a couple of artifacts that would point them in the right direction. He carried with him an envelope containing a printout of the story of the synagogue bombing from the *Khaleej Times,* a receipt for the transfer of funds to Farouk El-Sayed, and assorted other documentation that would enable the authorities to connect the dots. He would walk up to the reception area and hand the envelope to anyone who would accept it. He would then go directly to the mosque to pray for his family, Muhammed, and the people Muhammed was planning to target.

He didn't think about the possibility of closed-circuit cameras.

***

Getting the details on Courtney's funeral would not be easy considering her roommate's attitude toward him, but Richard was determined to attend, if not for Courtney, then for himself. He scrolled through his phone to look for any texts to people they both knew, ultimately deciding to contact the yoga studio where she worked and to describe himself as "a friend."

The funeral was to be held at The New York Marble Cemetery in the East Village. It was nearly impossible to be interred anywhere in New York these days, and the fact that the funeral was held at the oldest nondenominational cemetery in New York City suggested Courtney's family had deep pockets and deep roots in the city.

As Richard walked through the gates of the cemetery, the tension he had felt in his shoulders the past several days gave way to helplessness and grief. The cemetery's lush garden enveloped him, along with the small crowd of Courtney's friends and family, all dressed in black. A few attendants in white coats wandered around the crowd carrying flutes of champagne.

The New York Marble Cemetery contains no headstones; it is an underground grid of marble rooms sitting below a large garden where funerals, weddings, and special events are held. A series of 78 tight shafts afford access to 156 total vaults. One of those vaults belonged to the Dubois family, of which Courtney was a descendant.

Large buildings bordered the cemetery on three sides, giving it a sense of isolation from the city's distractions. Green grass covered the entire area. Farthest from the entry gate were ten rows of white chairs organized close together; beyond them was a white pop-up tent and a podium underneath. It was there that Courtney's friends and family would come up, one at a time, to reflect on the love they lost, to tell a funny story about Courtney, or to read a poem. Richard had no intention of speaking and could not even bring himself to sit down. When it was time to begin the ceremony, he followed the crowd but stood off to one side.

As the proceedings began, Richard could see a couple in the front row overcome with grief, the woman sobbing on the man's shoulder, who did his best to console her. Next to them was a young teenager with blue hair, looking away from the podium, probably because she did not understand what was going on or she simply couldn't cope with the pain. Richard had never met Courtney's family, and at this moment, he realized how much he took advantage of the relationship.

He was too numb to pay attention to what was being said at the podium, and too tired to realize he was being followed. He never thought to look behind him at the man standing near the gate, about twenty yards away. But when he did, he saw Basheer Aktar, looking straight at him, wearing the same baggy pinstriped suit he wore during their meeting in Dearborn. Aktar had the photos showing the location of Richard's apartment; he thought to wait for his return outside his flat but decided a meeting in public might be in his best interest.

Richard's first instinct was to charge at him, but he resisted. Aktar was clearly there to see him, and at the same time, he was very likely unaware that Richard knew he was part of the team that abducted him. The tension in his shoulders returned as he walked toward the gate.

"What are you doing here?" he demanded of Aktar as he approached him, his fist clenched.

"I am very sorry for your loss," Aktar replied, ignoring the question. Aktar expected that Richard would be distraught but had no reason to suspect Richard was aware of his involvement with the Professor.

"What do you want?"

"Can we go somewhere to speak privately?" Aktar pleaded.

"Whatever you have to say, you can say it right here."

Aktar looked around the gate area where there was a steady stream of pedestrians crossing in front of the cemetery. He motioned to a corner just inside the gates, away from anyone else. Richard followed, his rage building.

"Mr. O'Brien," Aktar started, "there's been a terrible misunderstanding. Hassan is just a troubled young man, and he only wanted to scare the girl, not hurt her."

Richard was completely lost for a moment, as his mind was on the fact that Aktar was an accomplice to a kidnapping, *his* kidnapping. He had forgotten about Hassan and the fact that he was a member of the Muslim community in Dearborn. The look of confusion on his face persuaded Aktar to provide more context.

"Mr. O'Brien, I've found myself involved in a group that aims to harm many innocent people. Hassan was also involved, along with a few other young men from my congregation. I regret what I've done, and I don't know what to do."

Richard was not prepared for any of this. He was, after all, merely a linguist for the agency, and in quite a bit over his head for some time now. But as far as Aktar was concerned, he represented a way out. But what came next gave Richard no choice.

"Mr. O'Brien," Aktar said, "this attack on innocent people, it will be in the next forty-eight hours."

Richard did not need to hear anything else.

"Let's go," he said, and he flagged down a taxi.

28

Richard decided that the quickest way to restore his credibility with the agency was through Sarah. He did not want to compromise her position, so he thought carefully about his next move as he and Basheer Aktar rode in the cab to the Javits Center.

"*I have Basheer Aktar with me and he wants to share some intel. Will be there in 10 mins*" he texted to Sarah's phone. Within thirty seconds, he had her reply. "*Will meet you in the lobby.*"

Richard felt like he was reunited with a long-lost love on seeing Sarah again. The last time he saw her, he was leaving the agency in shame. Now, he felt he could crack the case wide open, or at least enough to allow him a narrow space to climb back into the game. His grief over Courtney was something he would put aside for now, he told himself, in the interest of national security.

He held Basheer's arm as the two entered the lobby, with enough force to make it clear that he did not intend Aktar any escape but not so tight as to make him feel uncomfortable. Because Aktar did not have any FBI credentials, Richard went no farther than to the metal detectors and security checkpoint within the lobby.

"Dr. Aktar, nice to see you again," Sarah smiled as she approached them from the other side of security. "Agent, please allow these two guests to pass."

The security guard motioned the men through the metal detector, and Sarah greeted them again with handshakes. She resisted a sudden urge to hug Richard.

"Sarah, we need to get Dr. Aktar to a comfortable place to sit while we speak privately," Richard said. "We have a waiting room on the sixteenth floor, which would work perfectly."

Richard knew the layout of the center better than she did, so Sarah nodded.

The three stood awkwardly on the way up in the elevator. Richard gazed into Sarah's eyes for a sign; Aktar gazed at the elevator buttons and LCD panel indicating the floors as they passed. Sarah simply looked forward at the doors, not wanting to start a conversation until she understood the terms of engagement. The conference room was sparse, no wall art, just a metal table and four chairs, two on each side. It was clear to Aktar that this was an interrogation room, evident from the large mirror installed on one side, and metal hooks present on the table and floor for those suspects that might be restrained. He rubbed his arms and started to shiver, although the room would probably be warm enough for anybody with nothing to hide.

"Dr. Aktar," Richard said, "you are not in any danger, and we just want to talk, you'll be out of here shortly. Allow my colleague and I a moment to look for someone working on this case. We'll be right back." Aktar nodded and sat down at the metal table in the center of the room, doing his best to remain calm.

In the next room, with a view of Aktar sitting, Sarah and Richard stood face to face for the first time since the evening at the hotel just before his abduction.

"Sarah," Richard spoke first, not knowing exactly where to start. Most of all, he wanted to apologize for anything he did that may have caused her to lose confidence in him. And right behind that confession he wanted to share everything he learned about the imminent nuclear threat.

"Can we talk about everything later?" she interrupted. "I think we need to get everything out of this guy now, you know, the information we wanted to get out of him in Dearborn. We don't have much time."

"Sure," he replied. "Do you want to bring in Hunter?"

"I think if we want to restore you on the case, you should speak to him. What do you think?"

Richard pondered that because he had hoped Sarah would simply advocate for him with the higher-ups. But if he asked her to do it, it would make him look weak. If he approached Hunter, he risked being escorted from the premises or arrested for illegal entry into a federal building.

"Sure, I'll be right back."

Richard immediately began practicing his lines for the potential confrontation with Hunter, who was far above his pay grade. Rather than take the elevator to the seventeenth floor and risk being discovered, he slid into the stairwell and walked up. He risked running into someone using the stairs for some exercise, but it was a better choice than walking into an elevator packed with federal agents. The rumor mill in the FBI was very efficient, and chances were quite good that his dismissal was already well-known. On the other hand, as a relatively low-level employee, maybe not.

David Hunter was a no-nonsense tactician, the kind of agent who took a pragmatic view to a mission. Unlike Swanson with his machismo and win-or-lose approach, Hunter was forgiving and open to improvisation. When Richard approached him in his office, he didn't overreact.

"O'Brien, what are you doing here?"

"Sir, I've brought in a suspect for questioning. He's on the food chain. It's Basheer Aktar."

"What are you doing working this case? You're on leave. You shouldn't even be in the building."

"Yes, I know, sir, but Aktar approached me earlier today. I met him originally when I was sent out to Dearborn with Agent Goodman. Sir, he trusts me. And he's in the interrogation room on sixteen."

Hunter looked at Richard from behind his desk, unimpressed. Richard continued making his case.

"Sir, Aktar was involved with Hassan Isa Saliba, who is in our custody, another Islamic Center guy on the food chain. You know, the man whose identity we used to access intelligence off the Onion Router. We believe Aktar has information regarding the nuclear threat."

Hunter looked at Richard, then he looked down at the files and papers gathered there, a menagerie of leads that led nowhere. This was not yet a "black swan," but it certainly had potential. "Okay, let's go, we have the next team briefing in thirty."

"Sir, I told Aktar I was bringing in someone working on the case, so that would be you. I think it best we try to avoid spooking him. He's already looking rattled."

"No problem, but I'll need to have a guard posted outside who can escort him out of the building afterward, and you as well, if this does not move us in the right direction."

Back on the sixteenth floor, Richard felt the need to manage introductions.

"Dr. Aktar, this is Special Agent Hunter who has been leading the investigation into Islamic extremism here and abroad. He'd like to ask you a few questions." Aktar looked up at the two men and did his best to manage a smile. He stood and shook Hunter's hand.

"Dr. Aktar, we appreciate you coming in," Hunter said, sitting as he spoke. "Sir, can you tell me your occupation?"

"I am the director of community affairs at the Islamic Center in Dearborn, Michigan."

"And how are you involved with Hassan Isa Saliba?"

Aktar hesitated. If he answered this question truthfully, there was no turning back. A few seconds passed before he found the courage to answer.

"Hassan is a young man in our community who got himself involved with a bad crowd. I did my best to guide him down a righteous path, but I'm not sure my efforts succeeded."

Richard could see that Aktar was dodging the question, perhaps having second thoughts or simply hard-wired to deflect questions that could expose the youth in his community. Hunter did not know enough to realize Aktar was spouting politically correct claptrap, and Richard was not about to lose the opportunity to redeem himself.

"Dr. Aktar, were you in the hotel room at the Viking the evening I was abducted?"

Aktar did not see the ambush coming. He looked directly at Richard, then down at the table. He was trapped.

He simply nodded his head. Richard looked at Hunter, then at Sarah.

"Dr. Aktar, why was I abducted?"

Aktar was still looking down at the table, shrouded in the shame of how deep he let himself get involved.

"The Professor wanted you to persuade the Americans that Iran was behind the Dubai bombing."

Richard suspected there was much more to this than Aktar was telling.

"Is that all?"

More time passed as Aktar weighed his options.

"May I ask," he said, "what consideration will I be provided by cooperating in your investigation?"

Hunter fielded this one.

"You'll have your freedom. For now."

Aktar realized that he couldn't negotiate.

"He wanted to detain you as you were making progress on his next attack."

"And where is this attack to take place?" It was Hunter this time.

"I swear to you, I don't know," Aktar pleaded, speaking rapidly and louder than before. "His organization is based in Saudi Arabia, and I am purposely kept in the dark about their activities. They support my work at the center with funding so long as I assist them by making available manpower, you know, like Hassan. You *must* believe me."

By now, Aktar was shaken, and it was apparent that any additional intelligence would be hard to come by.

"Dr. Aktar," Hunter said, "I'd like a list of all the organizations that are supported by the funding you receive. Some of these so-called charities may be covers for groups that are prone to extremism or violent acts."

"Yes, of course," he replied. "I'll have my secretary fax the list to you immediately."

"Thank you," Hunter said, as he did, he stood up and handed Aktar his card. "We may need to speak to you again soon. Please don't make any plans to leave the country."

"No, no, of course not," Aktar replied.

"Please follow security out of the building."

With that, the meeting was over.

"Nice work, O'Brien," Hunter whispered as Aktar was escorted to the elevators by the guard. "I'll speak to your supervisor about reinstating you on the case."

Richard turned his attention from Hunter to Sarah, who smiled.

"Thank you, sir."

"I've got to get ready for our next briefing," Hunter continued. "I'd like you to join us in the command center and be prepared to update us on anything else you know."

Hunter headed back to his office, leaving Richard and Sarah in the conference room. Many rivers had been crossed since the last time they were alone together, and she may have been the only one in the agency to believe his story.

For his part, Richard was done with pretending; he was determined to close the deal. He moved to within inches of her in the back corner of the room and leaned into her just enough to show his feelings, staring intently at her. She reached over with her right hand and grabbed his wrist.

"Not here," she whispered, smiling affectionately. "Not yet." Richard leaned back, standing erect, and showing he got the message. But the look on his face made clear his concern: *then when?*

Sarah wasn't a stranger to pursuit, but she had always wanted to control the rules of engagement when it came to intimate relationships, at least until Swanson came along. If Richard was interested, she was on board as well. But outside the agency. She was not about to risk her career for a casual fling.

"Okay," he replied. "Can I come by your hotel later?"

Sarah leaned down into her purse that was resting on the chair next to them, fumbled around briefly, and pulled out a hotel key. She slipped the key card into Richard's hand. "Room 1411," she said, looking into his eyes, "I'll get a replacement from the front desk." With that, she turned back, picked up her purse, smiled at him one last time, and left the room.

Richard's heart was beating as if he had just run a marathon and took first. He had to sit down. He looked down at the key card that Sarah provided him, and scenarios of what was to come ran through his mind. He imagined holding Sarah close, ravaging her body, and beginning a new chapter in his life with Sarah as the main character.

As stream of consciousness took control of his thoughts, his daydream was interrupted by thoughts of Courtney. He reckoned with the fact that he treated her poorly. This was unfinished business. He would honor her memory and become a better person. He was not exactly sure how.

Within twenty-four hours of having read the briefing of the interview with Basheer Aktar, General Hayden contacted the Department of Justice and persuaded the Attorney General to have the offices of the Islamic Center raided, evidence gathered, and doors shuttered.

29

There was a buzz in the command center. Just a few hours before, the American Embassy in Nairobi sent via scan a trove of documents that they suggested could assist with the investigation. Hunter projected one of the documents on the screen, the clipping from *Khaleej Times* concerning the bombing in Dubai.

"All right, team, let's get settled," Hunter yelled, trying to get above the fray. "We have a lot to cover."

"This is one of the documents we just got that draws attention to the Dubai bombing while offering us fresh intelligence that could help us identify the perpetrators. More importantly, we believe whoever dropped this off is trying to help us avert the next attack."

"Do we know who made the drop?" came a question from the crowd.

"No," Hunter replied, "but we have video surveillance of the Embassy lobby and are looking at every visitor on the day of the drop. We *will* find him.

"I know you all remember Richard O'Brien from Linguistics. I've asked Richard to rejoin the team. He's produced some additional intelligence for us, and I'd like him to give us an update."

Richard was not quite prepared for stepping up to the front of the room, but the adrenaline and subsequent endorphin flow in his veins propped him up. After all, he thought to himself as we walked to the front of the room, *I only have to be perfectly articulate for the next five minutes.*

"I haven't seen the embassy material," Richard began, "but I did translate a message implying the weapon left Iran's port of Chabahar and is on its way to Gaza. So, it's probably Israel, and not the U.S., that is the target."

More buzz in the room, And maybe some relief.

"The message was unclear on the mode of transport for the weapon but based on my analysis of all messages I translated, I've come to the conclusion that these perpetrators are not Iranian. Nobody in the food chain speaks in Farsi, they only speak in English and Arabic." He decided to leave out the experience of being kidnapped as the key development that led to his epiphany.

"Today, I assisted agents Hunter and Goodman in an interrogation of an operative within the Islamic community that essentially confirmed the existence of an active cell that is organizing the attack, and he's providing us a list of organizations that might be harboring them."

Richard paused for a moment, closed his eyes, and tilted his head downward, one last effort to make sure he did not miss anything relevant.

"Oh," he popped up his head, eyes wide open, "the weapon is being transported by what the perps are calling 'my angel.' If we can find 'my angel,' we can find the bomb."

The room fell silent. There was a lot to absorb in Richard's report, and some of it, particularly the assumptions about Iranian state-sponsored terrorism, suggested that the team had wasted considerable effort.

Hunter spoke next. "Thank you, O'Brien. Look everyone, we will have Richard's intercept, the notes from our interrogation, and all documents from the embassy uploaded to the shared drive in the next fifteen minutes. Some of it is already there. We need to redouble our efforts to find these people, and I'll be conferencing with the Israelis now that we've confirmed they are the target. Let's go people, I want some suspects currently operating in the field to be ID'd by tomorrow morning."

***

The nimbostratus clouds started to block out the daylight by five in the afternoon, and shortly after sunset, they began releasing their accumulated moisture in a torrential downpour. The streets were abandoned, tourists returned to their hotels, and rainfall became the soundtrack for the evening. About one thirty, Richard rolled slowly off the mattress, confident that the rain produced enough white noise that he would not disturb her.

Crouching down as if this would make him even more stealthy, he stepped gingerly over to the desk where his backpack lay against one of the legs. He sat down and reached into the pack, pulling out the folder containing all the documents related to the case. He turned on the small desk lamp to illuminate the files and started going through them.

Richard first reviewed all the intercepts he had translated since the first to arrive when he was staying at the Tropicana. Some were arrogant and threatening; others were technical and objective. Clearly, there were multiple players involved. Was one of them 'My Angel'? Was 'Angel' one of Aktar's associates? Was it the man whose photo was posted at the top of the food chain, the same man who spoke to him in the hotel?

The document that interested him most was the chart of accounts that Aktar had emailed after their interrogation earlier in the day. It arrived just after the meeting in the command center, so it was truly fresh intelligence that was being looked at closely by several agents working the case. Most of the organizations listed were in Arabic so, while Richard was not a trained investigator, it offered him another opportunity to contribute.

The chart of accounts was a list of organizations, charities, and people that had either received money from or provided funding to the Islamic Center. Richard was specifically interested to see any organizations based in Gaza, but it was reasonable to expect some of the funding recipients were intermediaries based somewhere else. Within Gaza borders was a children's hospital, a mosque, and the Fishermen's Syndicate, a union whose income was significantly impacted when the Oslo Accords drastically reduced the free fishing zone off the coast.

He was so focused on studying the list that he did not hear Sarah come up behind him, gently placing her hand on his bare shoulder.

"What are you doing?" she whispered, leaning over him from behind.

"Oh, hey, I hope I didn't wake you."

"I wished you would," she cooed, wrapping her arms around his neck and leaning down to put her cheek next to his. Richard tilted his head to the right, maximizing the surface area contact between them.

"I feel the black swan is in here somewhere," Richard said, feeling he earned the right to use the agent's slang for a breakthrough in the case. "I feel we are close."

"Close to finding My Angel?" Sarah mused.

"*My* angel is right here," he replied, "but yeah, otherwise, yeah."

"See you later then," she replied, "when you return to bed, you had better *wake me up.*"

Sarah kissed Richard's neck, then turned to the bed. As she did, Richard looked back. Her red silk teddy fell to the small of her back and just above her behind; she wore no panties. *I am being tested,* he thought as he turned his attention back to the documents.

Richard pulled more papers from the folder, including a receipt for funds transferred to a Farouk El-Sayed. *Who was this? Could this be My Angel?* He looked across the most common sites first: Facebook, Google, and LinkedIn. This turned out to be a common name shared by a surgeon, an IT professor, and a professional soccer player.

He checked the leadership of the organizations based in Gaza, starting with the children's hospital and charities. As these organizations depended on contributions from abroad, they all had an online presence, so it only took a few minutes to conclude that none of them made mention of a Farouk El-Sayed. If this person was important enough to be identified by the person providing the tip, he must be found.

He looked more closely at the bank identified in the transfer, Al Intaj Bank, well-known as the bank of Hamas. Then he looked at bank names in the Islamic Center's chart of accounts, finding that the Fishermen's Syndicate also named Al Intaj as the bank to which contributions would be made by bank wire. *What if,* Richard thought . . . he went back online to find the Fishermen's Syndicate and the register of boats permitted to dock in the Gaza port. Only boats over nineteen feet in length overall were required to register, which amounted to eighteen boats. There, in the middle of the list that was organized in alphabetical order, was a boat registered as *Malaki.* Richard's heart skipped a beat. He found "My Angel."

***

The Professor had a few hours before his flight abroad. As he had done in the past, he would fly first to Toronto, then to Abu Dhabi, and from there to Dammam. He realized that it would theoretically not matter what route he was taking if he were on a watch list. But flying to Canada first would naturally be less stressful as the first step, for reasons he could understand but not explain.

He sat in the conference room of the WeWork center just outside the DC Beltway, positioned in front of a laptop computer equipped with a camera. He reserved the room under a false name, as he did most things, and paid cash. It was finally time to claim responsibility for the bombing in Dubai and make further demands that would compel Western democracies to recognize the full threat of Islamic extremism.

"Professor, we are ready here," said the young digital arts student back at Bin Faisal University. "Remember, you just need to look into the camera; we will take care of the rest. Speak slowly and with little expression, just like we've done in rehearsals."

The "rehearsals" were a series of recordings made previously so that the computer's AI (artificial intelligence) application could "map" the Professor's face to establish a synthetic media profile, the first step in creating a deep-fake video. The publication of these videos had been distorting reality for several years, and the university had recently started a program within its School of Digital Arts to explore positive applications of the technique. Despite disrepute due to bogus videos that parodied celebrities like Tom Cruise and Donald Trump, some governments had used these video techniques for the public good, such as communicating with marginalized communities using spokespeople they would recognize and trust. This was particularly effective in increasing vaccination rates during the

COVID-19 outbreaks among indigenous populations in New Zealand, Australia, and Canada.

At Bin Faisal University, the students were still learning, but the technology was advanced enough that the Professor was confident it would suit his purposes. It was especially important that the students he approached for this project were already involved with Muhammed in a pro-Palestinian activist group on campus.

"All right," he replied. "Give me a moment to collect my thoughts."

"Go ahead and start speaking whenever you are comfortable. We can edit out anything before we finish up the project."

The Professor knew this day would come, and while all other elements of his plan were thoughtful and nearly error-proof, he had many moments of doubt. *Is this all worth it?* he thought. When he mocked Richard O'Brien about "swimming so far from shore," did he realize he swam even farther? The moral dilemma of having murdered his own brothers and sisters to secure the future of his homeland was something that would haunt him, but he could not turn back now, as he was so close to achieving his goal. He focused his eyes on the little green dot at the top of his laptop and began to speak in English.

"With the blessings of God, we have made our statement that the Arab nations will not be marginalized any more. That statement resulted in the destruction of the synagogue in Dubai and the worshippers within it. On behalf of the Palestinian people, we claim responsibility for this act."

There, he thought, *I said it.* He took a deep breath and continued.

"Now be aware and listen well, for the future of peace in the Middle East will depend on how Western nations handle our demands. We demand that the Palestinian people achieve statehood in Gaza and the West Bank. A homeland for the Palestinian people is the only way you can avoid a catastrophe of epic proportions."

"We have demonstrated our ability to deploy radioactive weapons, your so-called dirty bombs. Our next attack will be more than ten times as deadly as the last attack. Do your research and you will find that nuclear weapons from Russia went missing in 1992. We have them." With this, the Professor held up a picture showing three explosive devices, the markings clearly showing Russian characters and three consecutive serial numbers. The Professor knew that the intelligence agencies would waste no time in verifying the existence of the bombs.

"In the name of God, the most merciful, we shall have statehood for our brothers, or thousands more will die."

The Professor intentionally did not go into any further detail about the planned attack. The intelligence agencies were already making progress toward figuring this out on their own.

"I am finished," he said, exhausted from the stress of the moment.

"It looks good from here," the student replied. "We will need a few minutes to scrub the images, then we'll run a GAN on it. Do you want us to send it to the contacts you provided, or do you want to see it first?"

A generative adversarial network, or GAN, represented the latest advance in synthetic media and leverages artificial intelligence. A computer "trains" an image generator, in this case the face of the target identity, and it also trains a "discriminator" in an adversarial relationship. The generator creates new images from the latent representation of the source material, while the discriminator attempts to determine whether the image is real or generated. This causes the generator to create images that mimic reality extremely well because the discriminator catches any defects. Once complete it can be superimposed on the "model," in this case, the Professor. The power of GAN in creating deep fakes was only recently being appreciated in the U.S. intelligence community. Israel, on the other hand, had been actively developing technologies to combat this new form of digital warfare.

"Go ahead and send the file to Al Jazeera and CNN," he replied. "I'll be catching a flight soon to return to Dammam."

"Okay, Prof. Hey, will you put a good word in for us when it comes to finalizing our grade for the semester?"

"Of course," he replied. "You've done well and have supported an important cause. The world will have an opportunity to appreciate your work in the coming days."

***

"In the name of God, the most merciful, we shall have statehood for our brothers, or thousands more will die."

The name Ayman al-Zawahiri, general emir of Al-Qaeda, ran across the bottom of the video, but anyone working within the intelligence community anywhere in the world wouldn't need that to recognize the man making the threat. Ayman Mohammed Rabie al-Zawahiri was the face of Al-Qaeda, its most prolific leader, replacing Osama bin Laden following his death in 2011. He had published over fifty videos since 2003 and was one of the most studied personalities within the sphere of Islamic extremism.

CNN's director of programming contacted the FBI on receiving a link to the video. The station agreed not to share access to the video on its online platforms or show it on television. However, it indicated it would publish broad details of the threat as it was in the public's interest.

"Jesus Fucking Christ," came John Swanson's response to the video after he saw it in the New York FBI office. "I did not see that coming." U.S. intelligence agencies celebrated the drone attack that was to have killed al-Zawahiri on July 31, 2022, only to learn later that it was his body double under the rubble.

"Well, this corroborates one thing," Hunter said. "O'Brien was right. This is not an Iranian-funded operation. Al-Zawahiri is no friend of Iran."

"It also confirms another thing," Swanson replied. "He's still alive."

The choice of al-Zawahiri as spokesman for the ruse was a natural one for Isaac Shulman. As a teenager in Somalia, he knew of al-Zawahiri due to his vocal support of al-Shabab, an Islamist insurgent group based there. Shulman lived in fear of al-Shabab; the radicalized youth in Somalia bullied him and would have potentially killed him if they found he was a Jew. Later, on being sent on assignment to Saudi Arabia, he found al-Zawahiri was a local hero, a legend who had studied medicine there. To be sure, there was ample material to source when it came to understanding how best to create a digital copy of him.

Still, the Professor recognized the possibility that the video could be quickly deemed a fake and that he may even be exposed by new technology. He recognized this tit-for-tat in the evolution of cybercrime and criminal justice interdiction would not end anytime soon. However, by making the video he would earn "the liar's dividend." That is, creating something fake, even if it is discovered as fake, would cause people to question what was real. "If you didn't believe that Joe Biden won the U.S. election," he once said, "then as far as you are concerned, he didn't." Even if the Mossad eventually identified him as the face behind the video, what could they conclude from that? Nothing that would change the outcome of what he was about to do.

The papers carried the vague threat from al-Zawahiri on their front pages, and outside the intelligence community, it was anybody's guess where the next attack would take place. This served the Professor's plan well; the more world attention and fear his video generated, the better.

In Washington, General Hayden watched the video from the Situation Room in the basement of the West Wing. He was sitting with the National Security Council members, including the secretary of defense, secretary of state, attorney general, and the president.

"How credible a threat is this?" President Baldwin asked.

"Sir, first off our intelligence suggests this threat is directed toward Israel, not the U.S.," Hayden said. "This is based on a considerable amount of chatter the FBI has been following this past week."

"Well, that's a relief, but I'll repeat the question, how credible is it?"

"Sir, the Russian foreign minister won't confirm nor deny that the bombs were lost," the secretary of state said. "The intelligence we inherited from prior administrations are of the consensus that these bombs are probably out there, somewhere."

"So let's say they have them. What does Al-Qaeda have to do with the Palestinians? And why now?"

"Sir, the destruction of Israel is indeed part of the Al-Qaeda manifesto, even though we've not seen them devoted to this lately. We've kept them busy in Iraq, then Afghanistan, but all the while they have been consistent in their demands. They may see this as a way of showing up Hamas for not being able to get the job done on their own. It's tribal warfare, sir. And a struggle to remain relevant."

"How much time do we have?"

"That is the part we are most concerned about," the defense secretary said. "We believe the weapon is already in Gaza."

"What the hell?" the president said. "How did we let that happen? Okay, never mind, we need to reach out to the Israelis immediately and share what we know."

"Yes, sir, we are on it."

Hayden excused himself to make a call to the Professor, who was waiting for his flight to Toronto from Dulles. Hayden didn't bother considering the need for a secure line.

"Well, that was a fucking academy award performance," he said, not bothering to introduce himself.

"I am not interested in that, as you know. What matters is the world sees Hamas and the Palestinians as the true threat they are."

"Well, that's just great," the general continued. "The only problem is that the weapon did not come through Yemen as you told me, we boarded the only Iranian ship in the region over the past week and there were no radioactive materials in it. But our intelligence is saying the weapon is probably already there."

"Well, general," the Professor replied, "then we had both better get busy finding it. Because Hamas will waste no time using it. Goodbye, general."

The Professor hung up and left the general staring at his phone in disbelief. *Was he just played?* Whose side is Shulman on anyway?

***

The conference room in Tel Aviv was standing room only, and the crowd included staff from all counterterrorism agencies: Shin Bet, Mossad, and Mista'arvim. The blinds were drawn. The screen at one end of the dark room had just finished showing the video of Ayman al-Zawahiri threatening to detonate a nuclear weapon unless the Palestinian people were guaranteed statehood. Israel's cybercrime prevention was unparalleled, however.

"The video is really a primitive attempt at creating a deep fake; it's a pretty amateurish work product," said Yossef Daar from Cyabra, a team made up of veteran cybersecurity experts who had served in the Israeli Defense Forces' Special Operations Department. Daar was the first person Avi thought to call on seeing the video for the first time. He and Daar came up through the army ranks together. While Avi sought advancement within the IDF, Daar demonstrated a more entrepreneurial spirit and started his own company.

Daar introduced an analyst who described how Cyabra had broken down the video and revealed its true character, but the audience was only interested in the outcome of his efforts.

"First, we took the file you saw here and broke it down into separate audio and visual channels. The audio was syncopated, which was a dead giveaway that the voice you are hearing is not that of al-Zawahiri."

"Yes, and so?" Avi asked.

"This is what al-Zawahiri sounds like in comparison to the video we just received."

The analyst started to play another audio file when he was interrupted again by Avi.

"We are not interested in that. We only want to see who made the video, if not al-Zawahiri, then who. Address this please."

A bit disappointed but no less enthusiastic about his work, the analyst moved on.

"Next we took the video file and separated the superimposed digital images from the original source material," he said.

"Let me show you how it looked when it was originally recorded." The next image was of the Professor.

"What the fuck," came a voice from the back of the room. "That's Shulman."

Anyone who had been with Mossad for any length of time remembered Shulman. He was a highly regarded and capable agent, sent into Saudi Arabia under a false identity. The Mossad lost contact with him about five years ago. *Had he gone rogue?*

Avi scoffed.

"Shulman?" he said. "No, that is an informant we recruited from Saudi Arabia, his handle is 'Chad Kirin.'"

Moshe Peretz, director of the Mossad, spoke next. "Avi, he was one of ours. Isaac Shulman."

This was not the sort of revelation to spring on a top intelligence official during a crisis. Especially one with a volcanic temper.

Avi turned red with anger, and it took all his strength to remain composed at this juncture. This was exactly the type of problem that happened when two of the most capable intelligence agencies in the world were incapable of cooperating and sharing what they had found. It was a topic that caused him to butt heads with Mossad ever since he made captain in Shin Bet. But now? With an existential threat at the doorstep?

"Look, Avi," Peretz continued, "we can examine how we could have managed this better once we deal with the immediate threat. Right now, we need your help finding Shulman and recovering these weapons. We don't have much time. The Americans want to talk to us."

***

The U.S. secretary of state, Mark Reagan, was anxious for the opportunity to conference with his counterpart, Eli Rosoff, the Israeli foreign minister. Reagan was the first to see Israel's deconstruction of the video, sent in advance of the call. Both men were speaking from their respective offices on speakerphone. Reagan got straight to the point.

"I want you to know that I've been instructed by the president to share sensitive information with you and to cooperate with you in any way to defuse the threat and bring the perpetrators to justice."

"I appreciate that very much and will convey that message to the Prime Minister, thank you, Mark."

"Eli, we believe the bombs may be on their way or are already in Gaza," said Reagan, "they will be smuggled into the Gaza port on a boat by the name of *Malaki*.'"

"How do we know this is not a hoax?" Rosoff replied. Having discovered that the video was produced by a former Israeli intelligence agent, and thanks to the liar's dividend, Rosoff was not sure what to believe.

"We've reached out to the Russian foreign minister to confirm these bombs were never destroyed, but as you may know, they've denied their existence for over twenty-five years," Reagan replied. "I can tell you from our earlier assessments during the START treaty inspections that we believe the weapons are real. And they are capable of mass casualties if detonated in an urban environment."

"I appreciate this information," Rosoff replied. "We will take necessary countermeasures immediately. Mark, were you able to identify the man in the video and to ascertain why he traveled to the United States?"

"We are working on that," Reagan replied. "We've identified a terrorist cell that he was working with here and believe he is from an Arab country, not Iran. We are working up a psychiatric profile on him in hopes of predicting his next move."

Rosoff was relieved that there was no recognition that the Professor was an Israeli asset.

For now, that knowledge rested with General Hayden alone on the U.S. side.

***

Hunter called an impromptu meeting of whoever was available to view the video just received from the Israelis. Richard and Sarah, both pretty much living at the Javits Center, were sitting side by side near the back of the command center. Most people in the room didn't understand what the fuss was about. After all, they had seen the "al-Zawahiri video," as it was called by now, several times over.

"Okay, listen up," Hunter proclaimed, "the Mossad had some Israeli cyber experts come in, and they believe the video is fake. Our team is on the same page with that assessment. What I mean is, it's not al-Zawahiri—it's this guy."

He tapped the computer in front of him, and the Professor appeared on the big screen, giving the same speech that everyone had heard before.

"It's him!" came a response from the audience. Many others turned to the food chain on the far wall to reconcile the man in the video with the image at the top of the pyramid.

"Yeah," Hunter replied, "we are back to focusing on finding *this* guy. Look, we believe the bomb is already in Gaza and have given the Israelis all the intelligence we have on where it might be, but this guy may actually still be in the U.S."

Richard stared at the image of the Professor, a higher quality image than the photo on the wall, fomenting more anger that this man was still at large after having abducted him and nearly destroying his career.

"We've had an hour before this meeting to look closely at the video to see if it would betray his whereabouts," Hunter continued. "As you can see, he's done a good job of creating a sterile space around him. We blew up and examined literally every pixel. Just as we were about to give up, we found this—check it out."

Hunter pushed a button on the computer to zoom into the Professor's face with one hundred percent magnification. His glasses reflected something at the other end of the room from where he was recording the video. It wasn't very clear but appeared to be letters on the glass door to the conference room. It read

Ɔᗡ ʞɹoWəW

which was obviously "WeWork DC."

"So, he's in DC?" came another question from the crowd.

"That's likely." Hunter replied. "If he doesn't believe we are on to him, maybe he's not in a particular hurry."

"How many WeWork offices are in the DC area anyway?"

"Look," Hunter interrupted the group. "We don't have the luxury of time to get photos of this guy out to all the precincts in DC and to the federal agents we have working in Reagan and Dulles. On top of that, we must assume he's got the fake identities needed to avoid being stopped at airport security. We don't even know the name or alias he is using today. If we want to grab this guy, we need to be smarter. I am looking for ideas. Richard, you are the only one that has laid eyes on this guy, what are your thoughts?"

The room went silent.

"Richard?"

Richard had left the building. While everyone was transfixed on the video, Richard had decided that because he alone had seen the Professor, he would head to DC to find him.

When Sarah saw that Richard was gone, she reached into her purse for her phone to call him. She noticed that her FBI badge was missing.

Richard had gone to the nearest train station that would take him to Dulles airport. He reasoned, correctly, that the Professor would try to leave the country and that Dulles had more international flights than Reagan Airport. He felt he could get through security and into the relatively small international terminal with the help of his ID and Sarah's gold badge. He knew that if he waited for photos to reach the people who could apprehend the Professor, it would be too late.

He had a four-hour train ride to Dulles. While that sounded like an eternity, the Professor would probably need at least that much time to get from the WeWork office to the airport, check in for an international flight, pass through security, and arrive at the gate. And if he did not decide to leave the U.S. today, well, at least Richard would be in position for when he did arrive at the airport, and at Dulles he could coordinate with the local agents that he would expect to arrive once alerted by New York. Richard never considered the possibility he would be in deep trouble for acting unilaterally and without permission.

He arrived at Dulles in the late afternoon. That left a handful of red-eye flights the Professor might take to London, Paris, Dublin, and Frankfurt, and a flight to Toronto that would be leaving earlier, at six fifteen. Flashing his ID and Sarah's badge whenever necessary, he walked onto Concourse C, which handled the bulk of international flights. Thirty gates and four restrooms. *I'll find him,* Richard thought. He had not spent much time thinking about what would happen if he did.

30

The problem with sending an agent from Israel into Gaza is that there would be a very good chance he would not return. While agents in Mista'arvim were selected because they had a physical appearance similar to Arabs, spoke like Arabs, and could pass for Arabs, they were in constant danger of being discovered operating in Gaza and, if alone or in a small group, they would be murdered by an angry Palestinian mob.

According to intercepts and threat assessment scenarios, the weapons were likely to be deployed via short-range rocket or taken directly into Tel Aviv by a suicide bomber or a perpetrator savvy enough to detonate one from a safe distance. They were small enough, about twenty-four by sixteen by eight inches, to be concealed within a piece of luggage, adding to the challenge of finding them. If not for the tip provided by the Americans, the Israelis would have had to turn Gaza upside down to find them.

For this mission, the IDF turned to Shayetet 13, an elite commando unit of the Israeli navy specializing in sea-to-land incursions. An Israeli operator would not enter Gaza through a traditional checkpoint but from a navy boat patrolling the port, a fixture off the coast that Palestinians saw so often they no longer saw it at all. Once the ship was at the closest rotation to the shore, it would slow to allow the agent to slip into the water.

Doron Shimon was a certified divemaster and had completed multiple missions with little backup. He was a perfect fit for this assignment; he had a practical, no-nonsense attitude toward completing a mission no matter the obstacles.

Shimon entered the water off the stern of the vessel at 0330 hours and submerged. He had enough air in his scuba tank to swim to the marina in the port of Gaza. He would stay as deep as possible to avoid detection and swim along the side of the channel to avoid boats traveling overhead. Sending a stream of air bubbles to the surface was an unfortunate necessity, but at that hour of the night, the likelihood of detection was small, and even if someone noticed the bubbles, they would not likely attribute them to an assassin.

Shimon knew he had reached the marina because of the barren sandscape littered with soda cans and other trash and the fact that light was penetrating the shallow waters, revealing the hulls of moored boats. He was briefed about where to find the *Malaki,* and the metal cage attached to her hull made the identification that much easier. What he did not know was what to expect upon boarding her.

He had to be as silent as any other creature moving in or on the water within the marina. On reaching the starboard side of the boat, he dropped his fins in the water. Next, he removed his scuba tank, cranked off the air, and dropped the entire rig as well.

He silently climbed up the swim ladder off the stern of the boat.

Malaki was a twenty-five-foot vessel, which was ample for fishermen who might need to spend a night on the boat, but not so big that you would not immediately realize that company had arrived. As soon as Shimon stepped aboard, he heard someone wake up in the cabin below. It was Malek, the captain's son, who had partied and drank bootlegged wine with friends that evening and decided to crash on the boat for the night. He was alone, still slightly inebriated, and once he climbed up the cabin to see what had rocked the boat, he was dead. Shimon came from behind him, slit his throat, and quietly lowered him to the floor of the boat. The agent could operate freely now after confirming that no other passengers would need to be dealt with.

He reached back over his shoulder to drag down the zipper of his wetsuit and let in some night air. It was a bit difficult to maneuver wearing a half-body wetsuit, or "shortie," and he was glad to be able to reduce its grip on him. He removed the waterproof pack attached to the suit's chest, a sack containing a few essentials: a Leatherman, phone, lock picks, and small, battery-operated Geiger counter. He ensured the Geiger counter volume was set to silent so that he needed only to consult the tiny monitor showing the level of radiation in a fifteen-foot radius around him. If nuclear weapons were on the *Malaki*, it wouldn't take long to find them.

Some residual radiation indicated the weapons were on the boat at one time, but not now. He made his way from the stern to the bow, where the signal popped, but it was still too weak to confirm the presence of the weapons on the boat. Maybe they were now on the dock?

Shimon stepped off the boat and onto the wood planks. By now, it was four in the morning, and ambitious fishermen would be up just before sunrise. He had to pick up the pace. He noticed a long locker near where the *Malaki* was berthed. As he approached it, the needle on the Geiger counter meter began to swing erratically.

He knelt to assess the lock on the container and then grabbed the pick that looked like it would work. He gently jiggled it inside the lock, feeling the pins release. He removed the lock, swung up the latch, and stood up as he held the top of the locker and lifted it open.

There they were.

The Geiger counter's needle was bouncing erratically, but Shimon was looking down on two suitcases, and his assignment was to recover three. He did not have time to search anymore and was already risking excess radiation exposure just standing above the suitcases. No, he would have to settle for recovering two bombs for tonight.

Shimon reached into the locker and removed one suitcase at a time. He closed the locker, put the lock back on, and returned to the *Malaki.* He put both cases below deck, next to the body of Malek that lay on the floor of the galley. He went to the helm of the ship and found the keys still in the ignition. Shimon started her up, and as she idled, he jumped on the dock to release the bow and stern lines. He hopped back on the boat and backed her up. As the sun was starting to rise, the horizon revealed an orange glow, announcing a new day was about to begin. Doron Shimon navigated the *Malaki* out of the marina and used the coordinates on his phone to guide him to the Israeli navy ship waiting for him to return.

***

The three men looked down at the casing that sat on a metal table in the basement of Shin Bet headquarters. Each wore a protective gown to guard against possible radiation exposure. The place looked like a morgue, except the men were not looking at a body. They stared down at a Russian nuclear bomb that was recovered the night before from the port of Gaza.

"Can you do it?" one man said to another. He directed the question to the man who had the stethoscope around his neck and was using a plastic wand to poke carefully at the loose leather straps at the corners of the device.

"Yes absolutely," said Benjamin Kay, a man whose self-confidence was legendary in Shin Bet. Kay, a U.S. educated expert in nuclear explosives, came to Israel to attend his nephew's bar mitzvah in 2013. He never left.

"These devices were specifically designed to be armed by one person; no authentication necessary," Kay said. "We simply need to adapt a remote detonator to be on the same frequency as the bomb's receiver. We can detonate it either remotely or on a timer. To detonate it remotely, however, we will need to be within line of sight to the device, you know, to be sure."

The third man looked at Kay, incredulously.

"Anyone here want to be within line of sight of this thing when it goes off?"

***

By four, Richard had walked the length of Concourse C several times, making note of the flights that would be boarding later that evening. He had used Sarah's badge to access the various airport lounges, taking the time to investigate each of the conference rooms in case the Professor was making another video. He also buzzed through the other terminals that had a handful of flights and, by five, he was getting tired.

The Professor arrived at the airport around five thirty. It was natural for him to always look at least 20 feet ahead of him for potential threats, far more than the typical person that would look no more than a few steps ahead while walking on a flat surface. So it was the Professor that first spotted Richard coming toward him, and not the other way around. He stepped into a souvenir shop before Richard looked up and waited for him to pass.

What is he doing here? the Professor thought. Richard was a linguist, not an agent that would typically be in pursuit of a suspect. Perhaps he was going out of town. The Professor could not take the risk, having come this far, that Richard was not alone, but part of a team coming after him.

Richard walked into the bathroom and sat in a stall. *What was he thinking anyway*? He was not a bona fide agent, and he was not looking to be a hero, but at the same time, he felt he needed to do something. *Is this all about revenge? Fuck yes.*

At the sinks, he looked into the mirror. There. Behind him. Richard spun around and locked eyes with the Professor, aka Unicorn, aka Isaac Shulman. If the Professor hadn't been sure whether Richard saw him in the hotel room, he was sure now.

Richard knew he was at least 15 years younger than the Professor, so he naturally thought he could take him down. What he did not realize was that the Professor was an assassin with training in hand-to-hand combat. Richard was no match for him.

As Richard reached out to try to grab him, the Professor looped his arm within Richard's and spun him around. Richard tried to punch the Professor in the face but being spun around caused him to lose his orientation. He swung his fist up at the Professor's face, missing on the way up but scratching his cheek and drawing some blood on the way down. As the Professor continued to spin him, he took his other arm and grabbed Richard's neck, slamming his head on the porcelain sink. Richard blacked out and fell to the floor.

The Professor dragged Richard into a stall and sat him upon it. He locked the door from the inside and crawled out below it. He checked his watch. By the time Richard might wake up, he'd be safely on his way out of the country. He looked in the mirror and cleaned the blood off his cheek. He straightened his tie and shook the wrinkles out of his brown suit. Then he left the restroom and prepared to board his flight.

***

Neither the Professor nor Hamas leadership expected Western powers or Israel to support Palestinian statehood based on a threat, and so the process of deploying the Russian weapons started immediately on their arrival.

Marwan Issa, the deputy commander of the Hamas Izz ad-Din Al-Qassam Brigade, wanted to launch the Russian nuclear bombs using a conventional rocket, but the supreme commander would not entertain the topic. For one thing, fitting the bomb into a rocket would be a huge and dangerous experiment, with no way to judge how the added weight would alter its trajectory once it was airborne. Add to this the fact that the Israeli's Iron Dome air defense system successfully intercepted about 90 percent of rockets fired, and the entire effort to secure the weapon could be squandered with no casualties, just fireworks.

No, he said, the bomb would be taken into the country through the Erez border checkpoint, concealed as a piece of luggage as its designers intended. As a conciliatory measure resulting from international pressure, the Israelis had begun allowing up to 600 Palestinians across the border every day, many of whom would travel on to the West Bank to work. The bomb would be hiding in plain sight in the trunk of a car driven to the border, disguised as produce. All that was needed was a car. And a martyr.

***

Samir Suleman was nineteen years old and learned to drive in Gaza when he was twelve. He was raised in a home intensely hostile to the Israeli occupation and joined Hamas as soon as he finished the sixth grade. He had the blessing of his father who could not find work because he was on the Israeli watch list and prohibited from entering the country. The youngest of three brothers and one sister, Samir was anxious to contribute to his family's struggle. He would have preferred not to die trying. His mother would only know about his plans until it was too late.

Issa sat behind his desk in a bombed-out building in a secret location in Rafah. Before him was the young revolutionary who was to carry out the most important mission on behalf of Hamas since they rose to power in 2006.

"My son, you have been chosen and will become a martyr for the Palestinian cause. With your sacrifice, we will finally achieve statehood for our people. I could not be more proud of you."

The deputy's aide, standing at attention to the right, would now take the young man through the planned operation.

"You will approach the checkpoint and cooperate with the Israelis, providing them with the documentation we've worked up for you."

"You are bringing olive oil to your uncle's market in the West Bank. The bottles of oil are in each crate, it will be clear from markings that this is oil we produced in our homeland. There will be several near-identical crates in your trunk, and the bomb will be pushed far up the trunk and jammed in, making it difficult for the guards to retrieve it, and after examining up to five other crates, they won't bother and will presume it contains the same oil."

He said they would send several cars behind him to increase some pressure on the guards, and a well-timed disturbance of protesting civilians would further distract them.

"Finally, we will have some of our own soldiers in disguise at the checkpoint in case the guards discover the bomb. They will fire upon the guards, and you will drive as fast as you can into the country."

The deputy instructed Samir to take the A4 highway into Tel Aviv. He showed him the detonator that he would trigger only when he was in the position to cause mass casualties. The detonator, he explained, would be in the car's glove compartment.

"You MUST detonate the bomb in the center of the city. We have highlighted your route on a map that you must memorize before your journey."

Issa stood to indicate the meeting was over.

"Allah will welcome you into his arms once this mission is completed. You will live forever in his kingdom and as a martyr here in Palestine."

Samir returned a tentative smile as he also stood. He was no longer in control of his future.

***

Richard regained consciousness in the airport lounge, having been discovered by another passenger, and he was now lying on his back in a private room with an airport security guard watching over him. He was still in pain from having hit his head on the bathroom sink. He correctly surmised that the Professor was on the flight to Toronto because it was the only flight near the restroom that was not a red-eye. He shared the information with agents who questioned him, and they confirmed that the Professor wasn't in the terminal. He didn't know what alias the Professor was using, but Richard knew what he looked like, what he was wearing, his approximate height and weight, and that he now had a fresh cut on his right cheek. That would hopefully be enough, he thought, as he tried to get up to call Sarah.

"Hey, what do you think you're doing?" the guard asked, reaching over to push Richard's shoulder back down on the couch.

"Look, I need to get out of here, I need to call the agency."

"Man, you're not going anywhere. You're in custody."

It took Richard only a moment to process what he heard. He left the agency acting as a lone ranger, and he could imagine that he probably violated several protocols in doing so, including impersonating an officer. Then, he was discovered as the losing contestant in a bathroom brawl. No amount of charm would likely get him out of the guard's grasp.

"Can I make a phone call?" he pleaded. The guard got up and stepped over to the table where Richard's wallet, phone, and keys were sitting. He passed the phone to Richard.

Richard called Sarah to convey the details that would be communicated to the Toronto airport security and the Royal Mounted Police. They were asked to detain a man coming in from Dulles to Toronto Pearson Airport, wearing a brown suit, and having a cut on his right cheek. Between the time of the call and the flight's arrival, there was ample time for the Ontario police to distribute pictures of the Professor to their team. Having the video sent over merely punctuated the urgency of the matter and gave them a good advance look at Isaac Shulman.

“Richard,” Sarah said, “you’re in no small amount of trouble for taking off like that.”

“I know,” he replied. “If it’s the last thing I do for the agency, it will have been worth it.”

With that, Richard lay down and closed his eyes. The sedatives provided earlier by the paramedic had finally kicked in.

31

"David, I need that drone," Avi said, talking through the speakerphone on his desk. "Don't make me go over your head by calling the PM."

Avi meant the experimental DroneRad UAV being tested by the Israeli air force in partnership with FlyCam, a drone and camera technology company based in the United States. So long as one or more bombs were still in Gaza, the threat to Israel remained unacceptably high. That was not lost on David Shepherd, the director of Israel's technology assessment unit within the IDF.

"I understand, Avi," he replied. "I just want you to understand the limits of what this thing can do. We've never deployed it into the theater of combat. If it gets shot down, that IP becomes accessible to the other side."

The IDF's interest in DroneRad was to detect and help destroy Iranian capability to enrich uranium, and since acquiring the prototypes a year ago, the focus was on perfecting the sensitivity of the onboard systems at heights that would render the drone undetectable to the naked eye. They had not even begun to tackle the fact the drone could not successfully make the trip all the way to Iran from Israeli bases.

The DroneRad's original purpose was to detect radiation levels within sites where a breach or meltdown had occurred; its goal would be to provide sufficient data to scientists to help identify whether radiation levels remained lethal and if they were decreasing. The Israeli's intended use went far beyond the original vision, but Israeli technicians were confident they could build on the drone's infrastructure and boost its capability.

"Can you equip the unit with an explosive that would detonate if it were shot down, you know, something sensitive to impact?"

"Yes, I suppose that would be easy enough to do, but you understand that we can at best pinpoint to within ten meters but only if we fly at the minimum recommended altitude of five thousand feet? On a clear day, it will be visible to anyone looking in its direction."

"I understand," Avi replied. "Please prep your new toy and bring it directly to Hatzor this afternoon, it's the closest base we have to Gaza."

The prospect of detonating the bomb in Gaza to prevent Israeli casualties was not acceptable to Avi or anyone else in the Israeli military. Success depended on acquiring and disposing of the weapon with minimal loss of life. The drone would not carry any firepower of its own and would be essentially defenseless. But if it could pinpoint the block in Gaza where the bomb might be hidden, it could give ground forces enough intel to capture the terrorists plotting to use it.

***

The 1972 Mercedes 280SE drove behind the warehouse across from Shifa Hospital in Gaza, not far from the marina. One of the bombs was already in the trunk, ready for transport into Israel. Three men in overalls came to meet the car. One of them popped the trunk while another carefully removed the crate containing the bomb. The third man opened the garage door to the warehouse and used a handcart to bring five identical crates to the side of the car. These crates were spray-painted with the words "Fragile: Olive Oil from Gaza" diagonally across each side. One of the men applied a stencil to the crate containing the bomb and painted identical labels on it. Once done, it was loaded first and pushed up as far as possible within the trunk, followed by three other crates. Loose bottles of oil were distributed on either side of the crates, making full use of the space. Two crates would not fit, so they were placed on the back seat of the car. The car was locked and covered with a large tarp. Then two of the men disappeared while the third pulled up a chair to guard the car, an assault rifle hanging from his shoulder.

***

A specially outfitted trailer arrived at Hatzor Air Base at 2200, ready to monitor the flight of the DroneRad UAV into Gaza. Inside, three Israeli air force officers sat with their backs to each other, each concentrating on a specific monitor. One, the flight officer, would control the aircraft with a joystick, while another would monitor radiation levels the drone detected. The third, the navigation officer, monitored the video transmission made available by the drone and was responsible for directing any evasive action.

Two drones had been outfitted with night vision cameras and self-destruct features. Although the officers had only piloted the DroneRad in controlled environments on Israeli soil, they had ample experience with similar drone technologies used for surveillance or combat purposes.

To avoid detection, the first drone was scheduled to leave Israel around 1:00 a.m. Its battery provided for six hours of flight, so the team would have only a couple of hours for surveillance of the Gaza target area before having to return to base. The second drone had been prepped to head back to Gaza when the first drone returned. A second crew was set to relieve the first set of drone operators later in the morning.

"Approaching target zone," the navigation officer shouted out.

The drone leveled off at 7,500 feet just west of the Gaza port. There would have been no reason to store the weapon far from the port unless it was already on its way to Israel, so the target zone used these coordinates as a starting point. Gaza City was about seventeen square miles, so it would not take much time to cover the entire area. About twenty minutes into the drone's surveillance activity, the officer in charge of monitoring radiation levels leaned into his monitor.

"Can we descend below the ceiling? I think I may have something here."

"Descending to four thousand feet." The officers recognized they were breaking with protocol to descend below five thousand feet, but it's not like the drone would risk hitting a skyscraper in Gaza, and it was just as unlikely that the drone would be spotted in the dead of night.

"Signal acquired!" the officer yelled.

"Are you sure it's not coming from that hospital?"

"Negative. It's not detecting X-ray or gamma rays. The isotope is either uranium or plutonium. Besides, the hospital is probably not running any equipment this time of night."

"I've got the coordinates," said the officer in charge of navigation. "Sending these back to base. And by the way, we need to abort. It's time to bring baby home."

Within thirty minutes of receiving the coordinates, the commanding officer of the base had communicated with the director of Mista'arvim, and an agent living and working undercover in Gaza was at the designated corner within the coordinates that were provided. Captain Avi was tagged to lead the operation going forward, and he was set up in front of his own video monitor showing the agent's GPS-guided location.

"I'm here," said Joshua Bronstein, a Mista'arvim agent who had been living in Gaza for the past two months. He was outfitted with an earpiece and wireless mic inside a traditional Palestinian robe. Bronstein looked out on an intersection that included a hospital on one side and a large, aluminum-sided building on the other. As he approached, he noticed a man sleeping on a chair outside the building, a rifle hanging to the ground from his shoulder. A car in front of him was covered with a tarp, but the wheels were visible underneath. Bronstein walked past the intersection in case the guard was watching him. He stopped just as far as necessary to have eyes on the guard and the car.

"I'm in position," he radioed. Bronstein communicated the details of everything he could see from his concealed location. A warehouse, car, armed Palestinian, a dumpster, and an abandoned street vendor's storefront. If the bomb were here, he suspected, it was either in the warehouse or in the car.

"Settle in, Joshua," Avi suggested. "If someone comes for the car, we may need you to take them down, as well as the guard, and run the car to the border." Bronstein did not like the sound of that, not so much that he would have difficulty neutralizing two enemy combatants, but he'd probably be shot by others trying to steal the vehicle.

Samir woke early that morning and was determined to leave the house before his mother might see him and wonder about his plans for the day. He said his prayers in his bedroom, grabbed a piece of bread from the kitchen, and started driving his beat-up Toyota Corolla toward the hospital.

His instructions were to drive the Mercedes throughout the city on a random route to ensure he was not followed as he approached the Erez crossing. The guard posted outside the warehouse would drive the Toyota behind him and offer a cushion between the Mercedes and any other cars trying to reach him. He was to check the glove compartment where there was a map and forged papers allowing him to enter Israel.

"Target approaching," Bronstein whispered into the hem of his robe as Samir parked the car behind the Mercedes and approached the guard.

"Do you believe the weapon is in the car?" came the voice through his earpiece.

"No way to be sure, but all signals point to it," came the response from Bronstein. The drone could not pinpoint the exact location of the bomb, and without confirmation, it made little sense to confront the guard now.

"See if you can ID the vehicle," Avi said.

Samir and the guard prepared to pull the tarp from the front to the back, but Bronstein's view of the car was blocked by a street sign, and the tarp was covering the license plates. He could only tell it was an old Mercedes. They were common in Gaza, and Hamas operatives used them often.

As the tarp was coming off the car, the sound of men yelling followed by gunfire was heard about a block away.

Samir looked over his shoulder at the commotion, then back at the car.

A cheer was heard, and seconds later, an explosion swept debris and dust in a giant cloud down the street, in the direction of the intersection that Bronstein was monitoring. A group of Palestinians had seen the incoming drone flying at 4000 feet and shot it down with a Russian-made "Strela-2" shoulder-fired surface-to-air missile.

"What was that?" came a voice into Bronstein's ear.

"Not sure," he said, looking to his left at a crowd of militants standing around a heap of metal, “it appears that something was shot out of the sky. Maybe our drone.”

At that moment, Avi received separate confirmation that the DroneRad had gone off-line.

As Bronstein turned his attention back to the intersection, the Mercedes eased out of the parking lot and into the street, with the Toyota so close behind that it concealed most of the car’s identifying marks. Bronstein was helpless to do anything other than to report back.

“Blood red Mercedes, classic model, sedan, leaving the site. Toyota Corolla follows. Assume package is inside one of the vehicles.”

32

Probably no other country in the world could mobilize its people as quickly as Israel, where in the vicinity of Tel Aviv you could find bombs showering down throughout the year. When the plan was hatched to detonate the nuclear weapon on Israeli soil, the government evacuated communities in the Negev desert region along Route 34 in under twenty-four hours. A few *kibbutzim* communal farms in between were also approached and evacuated. With the evacuations and a guarded perimeter around the planned blast zone, Israeli citizens were expected to be safe.

The Israeli army knew the threat that was coming their way, but they were told to stand down and, at the checkpoint, appear oblivious to the terrorist plot. But they were not sure what car would be carrying the explosives, so they had concealed Geiger counters on each side of the roadblock where the cars would be inspected. When Samir eventually pulled up in the blood-red Mercedes, guards walked around its perimeter with a mirror at the bottom of a stick that would reveal anything under the car. They skimmed the driver's documents. They opened a suitcase in the back of the car. They opened the trunk and looked inside. While behind the vehicle, one of the guards pulled from his pocket a timed, back-up detonator and placed it on the inside of the trunk, magnetized so it would stay in place on the underside of the trunk lid. Then, they let the car pass.

It all happened so quickly that Samir did not have time to get nervous. As he drove the Mercedes into Israel, the border patrol radioed the commander at the Israeli air force to transfer responsibility for the operation. The air force ordered all commercial and military air traffic out of an area within two hundred miles of the Negev desert. Then they scrambled four Israeli F-15 fighter jets and an unmanned drone.

***

Samir left the Israeli checkpoint at Erez convinced that the most dangerous part of the mission was behind him. However, shortly after crossing into Israel, he approached another checkpoint. This was not covered in his briefing, probably because the road was under construction and the area straight ahead was blocked by cement trucks. There was far less formality that he could see as he slowed down behind a couple vehicles in front of him.

"Where are you headed?" the soldier asked, peeking into the car. He was wearing a bright orange vest as if part of the construction crew. He had one hand on a rifle hanging from his shoulder, and the other hand on the windowsill.

"Nablus," Samir replied nervously. "Delivering olive oil to my uncle." Samir pointed with his thumb extended to the back seat to lend veracity to his claim.

Samir was about to reach for his identity papers on the seat next to him when the soldier replied.

"You'll have to turn here onto Route 34 due to the construction," the soldier replied. "Follow the signs toward Hebron." With that, the soldier waved him through.

There would not be much traffic on A34 on account of the evacuation. The IDF was determined to minimize casualties while ensuring they would have control over the bomb's eventual disposal. Otherwise, it would have been a far simpler mission to fire upon the car carrying the weapon as soon as it reached the Erez border crossing.

Samir did not recognize that the highway was deserted because this was the first time that he drove beyond the borders of Gaza. He assumed all of Israel claimed the wide-open spaces for themselves while forcing his brothers to live in crowded, unhealthy conditions. He remained focused on driving responsibly, and just below the speed limit. But now that he was on a detour from Tel Aviv, he grew nervous that his mission was at risk. He reached for the glove compartment where the detonator rested on top of an Israeli road map. While he knew his original instructions were to drive up the A4, he now needed to determine how to reach Tel Aviv through another route, as he was currently traveling in the wrong direction, toward Be'er Sheva. He pulled off the road to consult the map and noticed he was not far from route A6 which would take him back up to Tel Aviv. He tried to relax and continued driving.

The drone floated over Samir at twenty thousand feet, monitoring his vehicle and transmitting a video feed back to the Shin Bet headquarters. This was an American-made MQ-9 Reaper capable of carrying an eight-hundred-pound air-to-ground missile. Just in case.

Samir did not spot the drone, but he did notice the four jets flying in formation in circles above him at high altitude, and he gripped the steering wheel with enough force to practically bend it. Driving faster would not solve anything, he realized, so he continued driving, looking above at the jets from time to time.

Samir became familiar with the jets' repeated pattern, so it surprised him when two broke off and flew to the east and two went west at the same moment, as if they were called away to something more important. He let out a sigh of relief just as he saw the signpost indicating he was approaching Be'er Sheva. As he approached the intersection leading to A6, he saw this road was also closed, so he would have to drive further on, past the city, and figure out how to turn back north.

Samir was accustomed to roadblocks in Gaza, as well as construction to build back structures that were destroyed by the Israelis, so he would never have considered that he was merely traveling in a maze constructed on his behalf to keep the population centers safe.

He was traveling at ninety kilometers per hour when he hit the caltrop strip laid across the road. His front tires exploded first, then one of the rear tires, and he began to skid across the freeway, the car turning at a forty-five-degree angle for about five meters before it slid to a stop on the edge of the freeway. Samir did not have the time to realize that the jets circling above him earlier did not have something more important to do; they were flying away from the blast area that would follow detonation of the bomb he was carrying in the trunk of the car. A few seconds after the drone's video feed confirmed that the car had come to a full stop within the blast zone, the Israeli's activated the remote detonator that was being carried by the drone. The failure of the drone to record anything further indicated what was expected – the explosion destroyed it.

The blast shook the ground for miles. An intense fireball, appearing as quick as lightning but a thousand times brighter, appeared and then compressed itself into a massive column of fire. The heat from the blast incinerated whatever life remained at ground zero, and the ultraviolet radiation changed the color of all surfaces within ten miles. Hurricane strength winds knocked over trees, whipped up groundcover, and blew out the windows of abandoned homes and buildings. A column of fire and smoke the width of a football field rose far above the horizon.

The mushroom cloud was visible across the west coast of Israel, but the lead fighter jet still radioed back to base the computer-generated codeword, "Colorado," to indicate the mission was a success, lest anyone fear that the bomb detonated anywhere close to Tel Aviv. Families that were evacuated a couple of days earlier could witness the reason for their urgent relocation. On top of the evident devastation, the invisible radiation would prevent anyone from entering the perimeter for at least a year. No families or farmers would hold the government responsible for being hastily ejected from their homes.

The images captured by Israeli jets were horrific. The explosion turned the world's attention to the reality that terrorists can access nuclear weapons. A nuclear bomb had not been detonated in years outside of North Korea's periodic shows of strength, and never on Israeli soil. Israeli media and political establishment played the event up for all it was worth, identifying Hamas and Iran as culpable for the attack. They hailed the effectiveness of their intelligence agencies in revealing the threat and avoiding significant loss of life, and their military for executing the operation to mitigate collateral damage. Still, the blast created a zone where significant radiation would persist for years, requiring constant monitoring. Israel was profoundly harmed, but it could have been much, much worse.

The bomb exploding on Israeli soil did more to persuade the world that Israel has a right to defend itself than any scenario the plot's architects could have anticipated. The Israeli government announced a return to the strict measures prohibiting passage into Israel from Gaza, allowing Palestinians to cross into the country only after extensive background checks and only for humanitarian assistance.

The fallout of the explosion had implications for Hamas leadership, as well. While they predictably hailed the attack as a success within their own news reporting, Palestinians saw the return to draconian Israeli policy, just as progress was being made toward a two-state solution, as a huge step backward. In the next series of elections, Hamas leaders were soundly defeated.

In a final insult and testament to the impact of the failed attack, the United Nations formally revoked the State of Palestine's standing as a "non-member observer," essentially relegating it to the status of a pariah state.

The Professor's plan worked perfectly.

EPILOGUE

Isaac Shulman stepped off the plane at Toronto Pearson Airport and into the Plaza Premium Lounge within the international departures terminal. He paid for a private conference room where he could use one of the lounge computers to send a private message. The message was sent to the email he had for the director of Mossad. It read:

My dear Moshe,

The last time we were together, I was a senior foreign agent for Mossad and you were an aspiring young officer. We have overcome many obstacles since that time. Let me assure you that the clues I provided to Israel and the Americans were always designed to guarantee discovery and to avoid mass casualties. The needs of the many outweigh the needs of the few, and with this behind us, the need for our homeland to enjoy a secure future has been guaranteed for generations to come. You won't hear from me again, my friend, my work is done. Don't try to find me. I will live out my days in another land, but I will always, always be an Israeli.

Shalom Aleichem, Isaac

Shulman stood up and took the remaining plane tickets to Dubai and Dammam from the liner in his suit jacket. He tore each up in small pieces, putting half in one trash bin and the other half in his pocket, which he would discard in a separate bin on leaving the lounge.

As he stood and prepared to leave the lounge, he was besieged by a half-dozen officers from the Royal Canadian Mounted Police, who took him into custody without incident. Shulman had intended to live out his life in obscurity somewhere in Canada but never considered the possibility that he could be arrested there. And as he had to dispose of weapons to enter the airport, he was defenseless when the police approached him. He was extradited to Israel shortly afterward, where he would stand trial.

The prosecutor within the Israeli Judicial Authority was not entirely sure what charges to bring against him at first, but after having prosecuted civilians for building settlements on occupied lands, he was confident they could find ample cause to try one of the most brazen rogue agents in the history of Mossad.

***

Sarah and the rest of the team in the FBI command center were patched into the conference room in Shin Bet headquarters to watch the culmination of the nuclear bomb case in real time, compliments of Captain Avi. A collective sigh of relief traveled like a wave over the room when the meaning of "Colorado" was announced.

The next day, Captain Avi visited the gravesite of Tamara Rosen. He put a bouquet at the base of the tombstone, and with his left hand placed a pebble on the top of the marker. He would visit her often in the months ahead.

***

Information provided by Jelani to the U.S. Embassy had been shared with the Mossad in the days leading up to the explosion, and within a few hours they were able to cross-reference the photo of Muhammed with their own developing profile on him and establish his location using spyware previously installed on his phone. Two agents posing as husband and wife were dispatched to Saudi Arabia; they traveled first across the border to Jordan with fake Jordanian passports, then flew to Dubai, and on to Dammam.

When Muhammed sat down at the café as he typically did after prayers each morning, a scooter came from around the corner with a woman driving and a man riding as a passenger. As the scooter passed the café, the man in back pulled a gun equipped with a suppressor and shot Muhammed in the back of his head. As the scooter sped away, Muhammed slumped in his chair and died.

Leosha Simakov was grateful to the Mossad for allowing him the opportunity to pull the trigger.

***

Richard spent three days in the hospital as they ran tests and treated him for a severe concussion.

He had lost consciousness shortly after making the call to Sarah Goodman and was taken by ambulance to Reston Hospital Center near Dulles. When he woke from a nap, Sarah was looking down on him, smiling.

"We have to stop meeting like . . . you know," she said.

"Hey, I heard we did some good together," he replied, smiling back, even though it hurt to do so.

"We sure did. And under any other circumstances you would be getting one hundred percent of credit for the collar."

They locked eyes, just smiling at each other.

"Hey," Sarah said, "do you think I can have my badge back now?"

"Oh, yeah, sorry. The hospital staff put my personals in a bag over there. Hey, have they told you when I can get out of here?"

Sarah walked over to the bag lying on a chair and shuffled around, looking for the badge. She found it, pulled it out, and placed it in her purse that was at the foot of Richard's bed. As she withdrew her hand, she pulled out an arrest warrant.

"Unfortunately," she said, "we have to deal with this first. Impersonating an officer can result in serious jail time."

"Oh yeah, that," Richard replied quietly.

"Look," Sarah replied, "Hunter wouldn't even let me discuss this with you if he wasn't grateful for the risks you took. Otherwise, you'd have a guard outside this room. If you do serve any time, it will be short and to send a message that we cannot have linguists calling the shots and, you know, running the agency."

Richard looked stunned by the possibility of jail time; his face took on a deer-in-the-headlights stare that Sarah could not ignore.

"Don't worry," she added. "We will figure this out, together. And after we do, I'm taking you out for XLB, and you-know-what."

***

Kenya's Jewish community dates to 1903, when the British colonial secretary, Joseph Chamberlain, offered the Zionists a part of the territory in Kenya and Uganda to establish a homeland of their own. The proposal generated much controversy, but Jews from around the world began to settle there, and today one can visit synagogues established across the country from Nairobi to Nakuru. Their congregations include many black Jews, originally of Messianic origin, who had concluded their beliefs to be incompatible with Christianity and converted to Judaism. Still others who practiced Judaism for generations claim to be descendants of the ancient "lost tribes" of Israel. Taken together, Black Kenyans who identify with Judaism number in the thousands.

After dropping off the parcel at the U.S. Embassy, Jelani walked to the Nairobi Synagogue a short distance away. It was by now four in the afternoon, and he would have to head back to the bus station in the next hour to return home that evening. As he approached, a huge Star of David greeted him, constructed in stained glass and positioned at the entrance of the grounds. Jelani recognized pagan symbols and knew of their association with witchcraft, so he was startled to see one outside a place of worship. But then he noted the six points of the Star of David. He took comfort in its symmetry; the pagan symbol, he recalled, had five points. He was about to turn around and head back to the bus station when he saw a Black couple with two children emerge from the synagogue entrance. The man wore a small round cap on his head, his son had a beautiful white shawl around his shoulders. The boy's sister was dancing as she walked. The family had a glow about them. The boy, Jelani finds out later, had just celebrated his bar mitzvah.

Jelani turned back toward the synagogue. Calling upon all the courage he could muster, he went inside to the lobby. From there he heard the most beautiful harmony. He went forward to find a large congregation hall, many worshippers were still standing and praying, chanting the mourner's Kaddish, the Hebrew prayer for acknowledging the loss of loved ones, the last prayer before the end of services. Being moved by the harmony and remembering why he made the trip there, he stood at the back of the congregation, against a wall where he might not be seen, and began to recite to himself the *taratibu ya kuzika maiti*, the Swahili prayer for the dead, not realizing that this prayer, and that of the congregation, were essentially the same.

***

As time passed, the news cycle moved on from the nuclear explosion to the next crisis worthy of the day's headlines. The specific whereabouts of Isaac Shulman, who was presumably sitting in an

Israeli prison cell, or maybe not, was never made clear to U.S. diplomats. Although the status of his trial was on the agenda for many phone calls and visits between the U.S. and Israel, finally, in the interest of diplomacy, the United States stopped asking. In Israel, for those who knew the real story, Shulman was regarded as a national hero. General Hayden destroyed what limited evidence he had that would tie him to Shulman. He continued to argue on Capitol Hill that Hamas represented an ongoing threat to democracy in the Middle East.

***

The return of families to ground zero years after the explosion renewed interest in "the real story" behind the incident. By that time, an urban legend had developed that Israeli intelligence staged the whole thing. Under pressure from the media, the government formed a "Truth and Reconciliation Trial," and the truth about the Mossad's involvement finally came out. The Mossad director and several in his orbit were forced to resign. In an act of reconciliation, The Knesset, now dominated by the liberal leaning Yesh Atid party, passed a measure providing a path for self-determination and ultimate recognition of statehood that would be presented jointly at the United Nations by the Israeli ambassador and the Palestinian president.

Israelis began planting trees at ground zero as soon as radiation levels in the soil were nominal, much as they did in other parts of the country whenever a boy or girl celebrated a bar or bat mitzvah. Eventually, the young trees came to surround the perimeter of a grassy field. A soccer field was created, and, before long, scores of Arab and Israeli children began enjoying the rejuvenated space. Although never officially sanctioned by the government, the area came to be known as "Shulman Park."

About the Author

Ian Rodney Lazarus has been publishing technical articles and opinion pieces in various magazines since 1989. "The Con" is his first novel, drawing from his international business travels across five continents. A native of Detroit and graduate from the University of Michigan, he now lives in San Diego with his wife, three children, and occasionally a cat. He is a certified sailor, advanced scuba diver, and "Six Sigma" blackbelt.

Coming Soon by Ian Rodney Lazarus

CEASE TO EXIST

Made in the USA
Las Vegas, NV
20 January 2024

84667331R10187